DAUGHTER'S DRAWINGS

A NOVEL

NICK BOTIC

First Edition: May 2023

Daughter's Drawings
Copyright © 2023 Nick Botic
NickBotic.com

ISBN: 979-8-8693-2462-7

For Kimmy, for my family,

and for the NoSleep community

Praise for Daughter's Drawings

"Daughter's Drawings is an eight-cylinder, 450 hp, high-octane thriller whose engine is already rumbling on page 1. From there, it's full scream ahead, as Nick Botic lays on the gas and roars into a story of steadily escalating tension and terror. A strong debut, *Daughter's Drawings* is one lean, mean machine. Strap in." — John Langan, author of *Corpsemouth and Other Autobiographies*

"*Daughter's Drawings* is a harrowing Hero's Journey through nightmare realms of profound grimness. The fact that Botic tells such a story in clean, measured prose while also knowing when to press the rocket fuel pedal is a testament to his skill, which is considerable. This novel is both a confident debut and a promise of more good things to come." — Matt Cardin, author of *To Rouse Leviathan*

"When I close my eyes at night I no longer see soft memories, morning anxieties, or chronological sheep. No - my nights are now terrorized by the unspeakable things I saw in Nick Botic's debut novel, *Daughter's Drawings*. At first, I enjoyed the easy reading, the seamless way the prose relaxed me into a manageable and familiar universe. However, it wasn't long before the creeping, sinister nature of Botic's world was revealed - and the horrible things inside of it. Be wary, those who harken dire warnings, for this book made me feel something few other horror novels have managed: *afraid."* — C.K. Walker, co-writer, Netflix's *The Haunting of Hill House*

"Surreal, methodical, and tormenting, *Daughter's Drawings* is the worst nightmare of parents everywhere and a relentless juggernaut of a thriller. Botic deftly weaves the horrors of stolen innocence and psychotic obsession across his debut novel, and the result is an onslaught of anxiety for all who have ever taught their children the phrase 'Stranger Danger.'" — Felix Blackwell, author of *Stolen Tongues*

"A terrifying journey of paranoia. Nick Botic's *Daughter's Drawings* kept me up late into the night, dreading what I would find when I turned the page." — C.B. Jones, author of *The Rules of the Road*

DAUGHTER'S DRAWINGS

Prologue

My wife Kimmy and I spent a weekend at her parent's house before they retired and moved out of state. We'd been together for five years at that point, married for just over one of them. Kimmy was seven months pregnant, fully ensnared in all the pain and discomfort accompanying such a state. The five-foot-two love of my life had foregone her usual routine of makeup and hair maintenance, temporarily accepting a more natural look alongside keeping her hair in a perpetual bun. Also on hold were the mornings of pairing this top with these pants, that top with those shorts, the never-ending battle of fashion and function; for those last months, she found no better comfort than sweatpants and hoodies. What remained was the shine in her ochre eyes, the sharp wit always at the tip of her tongue, and the inspiring optimism of what tomorrow might bring.

Shawn and Dana Hill's home was nestled in a cul-de-sac of an affluent neighborhood. Five large bedrooms were scattered throughout the two-and-a-half-story single-family house, but Kimmy and I found ourselves in none of them that Saturday night. Instead, we had both fallen asleep on the absurdly large couch in the living room, bathed in the dull glow of an episode of Family Guy that, at some point, had reverted to a black screen and left the room with a dark, staticky illumination.

Kimmy noticed it first. While I was still asleep, she was awakened by the gentle tapping and scraping of thin branches against the large windows that lined the face of the house. I recall that I could hear them in my sleep, in the way noises creep into your subconscious and implant themselves in your dreams. Accompanying the intrusive foliage was a soft humming, an unfamiliar, barely audible tune, as if whoever was out there was providing their own soundtrack to their misdeeds. I actually awoke when Kimmy nudged me, and when I came to, I followed the fearful arch in her brow and her hyper-focused gaze to the window, where a dark shape was milling about along the front of the house.

Initially, we were both stuck in the state of shock that overcomes a person when faced with a situation wholly unexpected and never before experienced. We watched as this ill-defined mass of inky black shambled through the dead bushes, making its way from left to right - from the side of the house toward the front door.

It stopped at the rightmost window, making movements we couldn't discern.

I turned to my wife and took in a look I had never seen in her eyes: a familiarity, a torture, a fear that enveloped her and, for a moment, rendered her totally incapable of movement, of thought. I took her hand and whispered that it would be okay, that she needed to be quiet and go to her parent's room. She sat paralyzed for a moment, her pained eyes staring straight ahead, but, I think, not actually seeing anything.

The figure outside stilled for an instant, and then two thin strips of skin pressed against the glass.

The face followed.

It was the vague shape of a man's visage, the subtle suggestion of eyes, a nose, a mouth. It peered into the living room where Kimmy and I sat perfectly still, our bodies rigid and anxious. The man outside appeared to survey the room, though I can't imagine he saw much; his gaze passed right over Kimmy and me, either not seeing or not reacting to us one way or the other. The face receded an inch or two, and, for some reason unbeknownst to us, he stuck his tongue out. He opened his mouth wide, tongue hanging out, still humming. The man outside contorted his face for the next several seconds, seemingly playing a game with his reflection. The display didn't seem to be for our benefit, but for his own. Again he pressed his face against the window, looked around with his nose scrunched up to the left, then to the right, to the left again. Finally, unable to see inside, the man moved away from the window and began heading for the front door.

I gently but urgently encouraged Kimmy to move, at which point she snapped out of her daze, muttered "please no" to herself in a horrified tone, and climbed off the couch, staying as low as her pregnant body would let her. As she shuffled off to her parent's room, I quickly strode to the kitchen and withdrew the butcher knife from its marble holder, all the while on my phone after having dialed 9-1-1.

A habit that Kimmy's family exhibited, one that I always questioned and swore never to adopt, was leaving their front door unlocked. I supposed that their wealth had afforded them the luxury of living in all but crime-free areas their entire lives, but my middle-class upbringing had instilled in me a cautious optimism regarding my fellow man. As such, before we'd laid down that night, I'd locked the front and back doors and checked all the windows on the ground floor, which I was pleased to find were locked.

The 9-1-1 operator had picked up after the second ring. I informed the woman who answered of the current situation we found ourselves in and noted that the prowler was now skulking around the front entrance to my in-law's home. After being instructed to hide, I was transferred to the responding officer, who kept me on the line as he hurried from wherever he was when the call came through.

My initial reaction had been to confront the person who apparently felt that the things my wife's family had worked hard for their entire lives would be better in their possession. Still, six years of having that impulsive side of me tempered by Kimmy meant I was stuck anxiously waiting for the police to arrive.

As I listened to the responding officer communicate with the dispatcher, the prowler tried to open the windows on either side of the front door, to no avail. Every bone in my body yearned to exit through the back door, make my way around the house, and flank the criminal myself, to end this situation before it could go any further, but the quiet scrape of the opening screen door told me that there would be no time for that.

The doorknob turned slowly to the right.

Slowly to the left.

The prowler continued humming whatever tune he thought appropriate for the occasion, and all other sounds seemed to mute.

I gripped the knife, turned on the speakerphone, and set my cell down on the small table next to me.

A gentle thud against the door.

The humming, slightly louder.

A quicker turn of the knob.

I extended my fingers, bolstered my grip on the steel handle of the knife.

Another thud.

A frantic wiggle of the doorknob.

The humming interrupted by a frustrated grunt.

A louder thud.

And then the roar of the police SUV's engine and the blue and red lights illuminating the night sent the prowler sprinting away. The vehicle's spotlight illuminated the intruder for half a second. Gleaned more from the afterimage left by the bright flash of light, I saw that they were wearing a once-white wife beater with gray basketball shorts, blonde hair bushy and wild and unkempt. He leaped down the steps, up the driveway, and through the neighbor's backyard. I pushed aside a blind and watched as the officer sped past the house and screeched to a halt at the end of the circular block.

Two more police vehicles arrived within the next few minutes. The officer from one hurried off to assist the first responding officer while the other made his slow but steady ascent up the long stairs to the house's front door, at which point I opened it and welcomed him in.

Officer Nebel was a portly man of maybe fifty years, his face weathered by a few years too many on the force. He radioed to the others that he was in the house, then asked me if I was the only one there, to which I told him I was not.

He waited in the large foyer while I made my way down the hall to retrieve Kimmy and her parents. As I approached the door, I heard talking from within the primary bedroom, voices interspersed with the sniffles of stifled crying. I gently rapped my knuckles against the wooden door. The lock clicked after a moment, and I found myself face-to-face with Dana Hill, my Filipino mother-in-law.

Dana immediately turned around and began walking back into the room, which she shared with her husband on any typical night, but on this night, she shared with him and their daughter. I looked to the bed and saw my father-in-law comforting Kimmy, with her face buried in his shoulder.

"Shh, shh, shh, it's gonna be okay." he comforted her, looking up at me.

"It's all okay," I replied as I crossed the threshold into the room. "Um...the cops are here; they want to talk to everyone."

"Come on, honey," Shawn said to his frightened daughter.

Together the two stood, the Hill patriarch with his arm around my pregnant wife. I met them in the middle of the room, where Kimmy transferred herself to me.

"It's okay," I whispered before I planted a light kiss on her wavy brown hair. "The guy's gone, the cops are here, I'm here. We're all good. You're okay."

Kimmy didn't seem to take solace in my consolation, as evidenced by her trying and failing to take a deep breath, only to then bury her face in my chest and resume her battle to hold in the emotions that clearly wanted to come out. Shawn and Dana brushed past us and headed out of the room, turning down the hall to meet the officer in the foyer at my direction.

When Kimmy and I first got together all those years ago, there was an avalanche of qualities she possessed that I desired in a partner. Every time we met, I seemed to learn something new that checked off another box and even more that I hadn't had on my list but found that I wanted all the same. Chief among those attributes was my future wife's aversion to theatrics.

As any person does, Kimmy reacted to things out of her control, but the way she approached every situation from a logical standpoint was indescribably appealing. She was undoubtedly intelligent and inspiringly passionate, her entire demeanor different from the other women I'd spent time with during college. She had a confidence about her, a surefootedness that I found intoxicating. But more than anything, her rationality put her on another level compared to her fellow freshman coeds.

That historic sensibility stood in such stark contrast to the state she was in that night. The police were there, everyone was safe, the situation was contained, and no one had anything to worry about, at least so far as I could tell. But despite that, Kimmy was reacting as though the situation had unfolded entirely differently. From someone on the outside looking in, they couldn't be blamed for presuming that someone had entered Shawn and Dana Hill's home that night and committed a murder.

Kimmy trembled in my arms as we stood in her parent's bedroom, and it was all I could do to walk her down the hallway to the foyer. I walked Kimmy on her shaky legs down the few steps into the front room of the house.

"Hey now, young lady," Officer Nebel's gruff voice took a softer, more comforting form as he took notice of my wife's state. "There's nothing to be afraid of. We have some units out there, got two coming in from this side, another two on the other side of those little woods there behind your neighborhood. We'll get him. No need to worry, you and that little one are gonna be just fine."

Kimmy nodded as she looked up at the stout peace officer and cleared her throat.

"Do...do you know who it was?" she asked meekly.

"Well, there's been a few break-ins in the area lately. I personally think on account of so many folks going on vacation, it's vacation season. I can't say why they'd try to get into your house, you know, you got the cars in the driveway, TV on. Coulda been on drugs—no, please excuse me, I don't mean to speculate. I just think the most likely scenario is that whoever it is that's been breaking into folks' houses around here lately came by yours tonight. And we'll get him. He won't be coming back."

Kimmy looked at him with tear-filled eyes and asked him a question in the most vulnerable voice I've ever heard her speak with.

"...are you sure?"

"Hey, sweetie," Shawn cut in before the officer had a chance to respond. "why don't you and Nick go up to the living room and let us talk to Officer Nebel, yeah? Is that okay, sir?"

I saw my father-in-law flash a glance at the police officer.

"Uh, ah, yes! No problem, you two go on up there, grab a glass of water, maybe. Young man, I'll need to speak with you in just a minute, seeing as you're the one who placed the call, yeah?"

"...yeah. Sure." I said in a dry tone. I looked at Shawn and Dana, the former offering me an altogether unconvincing smile, the latter nervously chewing at her thumbnail while looking out the window.

Kimmy and I went back up to the living room while a hushed conversation began behind us. We sat on the couch that had been our bed less than ten minutes ago, and I looked at my wife.

"Is there something else going on?" I abruptly asked.

Kimmy sniffled and looked at me with her bright, brown eyes. I could tell that her mind was fighting with itself, engaged in an internal debate over whether to divulge whatever she was holding inside.

Due to the circumstances in which Kimmy and I met, we began our relationship from a place where we knew most, in not all, of one another's deepest shames and regrets; our forthcoming union was unique in that it began from a place of unadulterated honesty and openness. Since then, we've shared a relationship in which those very same features have been seamlessly woven.

Each of us has our own things we keep to ourselves, as any healthy relationship does, but they are essentially things of little consequence. We are as aware of one another's past relationships as any couple needs to be; it's accepted that we are indeed not the first partner the other has had, as any mature person would understand, but we know that those people are no longer involved in our lives, and thus are rarely, if ever, brought up.

Kimmy's lip trembled as though the words were raging waters about to burst through a dam. Instead, she let out a sigh and nestled her head into the crook of my arm. I ran my fingers over her hair a few times while unsuccessfully doing my best to hear the conversation in the foyer. Before long, I heard Shawn's heavy footsteps ascending the stairs, followed by Dana's light ones.

"He's ready for you," Shawn said to me from behind.

Kimmy loosened her grip around me and I slid off the couch, nodding my head to Shawn as I passed him by. As I stepped down to the foyer, I saw Officer Nebel on the opposite side of the screen door, his cell phone pressed to his ear. He held up a finger, signifying for me to wait, and I did my best to listen again, assuming that whatever call he was on was connected to the conversation he and my in-laws had done their best to keep quiet just moments before.

"Yeah, sure. Yeah, let me know. Thank you, Bill," was all I heard the policeman say before he hung up and walked back through the door into the front room.

"What's going on?" I didn't skirt the question. I wanted to know. Too many aspects of the situation told me I didn't have the entire story. It was an odd feeling; I was the one who had been most present for the entire ordeal, but at this moment, I was the only one who didn't have all the information.

"Ah, yes, I just need to get your statement."

"...my statement, yeah. I know you know something else is going on. I want to know."

"Let's uh...let's get your statement down, take care of this bit of business, and then you can go ahead and talk with your family. That sound okay?"

It didn't sound okay in the least, but what could I do? I stood there with Officer Nebel for the next fifteen minutes, providing him with my information and recounting the night from when I woke up to when he arrived. All the while, his fellow officers kept coming through on his radio, offering updates on their search for the person who had started all this commotion. Just as I finished my ultimately boring tale, the front pocket on his uniform began buzzing.

"Oh, excuse me, just a sec, here," he said as he fished his phone out. He stepped back through the screen door, and I made no attempt to hide that I was trying to hear whatever he was saying.

"Hey, Bill...yeahp...you're sure? Okay, yeah, I figured. Just thought I'd give these folks some peace of mind...I appreciate it...give my best to Jackie and the kids. Yup, we'll talk to you soon...thanks, Bill."

He ended his call and stepped back inside, and just as he opened his mouth to say something, his radio went off yet again, this time with an officer number and the declaration that they'd caught the person they were looking for.

"Excuse me, son, I'll be right back with you. Why don't you go up and be with your family? I'll be back in just a second, just have to run out to my vehicle quick," Officer Nebel said.

I trudged back up the stairs to the living room, where I found the Hill family all sitting on the mess of blankets Kimmy and I had been under earlier in the night. Kimmy looked back at me with bloodshot eyes, eyes that I could tell were still hiding behind some information that she was equal parts trying to keep inside and get out.

"You okay?" I asked, doing my best to mask my irritation with being kept on the outside regarding something that was apparently important enough to hide.

Kimmy sniffled and nodded her head, wiping away the residual dampness from her eyes.

"Once the police leave, we'll talk, okay?" Dana said, and I gladly accepted.

I leaned against the wall for the next minute or so until Officer Nebel tapped his knuckles against the screen door and let himself back in. Instead of having us return to the foyer, he met us in the living room.

"Okay, good news, folks. They caught the guy who was skulking around your house. From what I gather, one of our units on the other side there, he saw him hop into a dumpster behind the plaza. We don't really have any way of knowing if he's the same one responsible for the other incidents around here lately, but you'll be kept apprised of things."

"Wonderful, thank you, officer," Shawn said in his booming voice.

"I, uh…" Officer Nebel stole a glance at me that I could tell he tried and failed to hide.

"It's fine. We're all gonna have a talk as soon as we're done here," Shawn announced.

"Right. Probably a good idea. So anyway, I got a call back, and he's there."

"Thank god," Kimmy said in a sort of loud whisper.

"Yes, ma'am. He's been in his cell all night, far as they can tell."

"Thank you, officer," Dana chimed in.

"My pleasure, folks. I'll get out of your hair. Mr. Botic, I'm sure we've got everything we need, but you might get a call from us sometime in the near future in case there's something we missed."

"Sounds good."

"You all have a good rest of your night, now."

And with that, Officer Nebel walked back down the stairs to the foyer and left the house. I walked down and locked the door behind him, then went back upstairs to learn what I hadn't been privy to this entire time.

"Take my seat, Nick." Shawn took his arm from around Kimmy and pushed himself to his feet, then walked over to his recliner and sank into it.

I sat in the now-empty space on the couch and expected Kimmy to curl up into me, but that didn't happen. Instead, she nervously picked at her fingernails and wouldn't look at me.

"Kim?" Shawn said, urging his daughter to begin the conversation.

She sniffled and took a deep breath, not moving from her position or looking at me. "I didn't not tell you, there just was never, like, a good time. It's not a big deal."

Shawn scoffed under his breath, which I took note of.

"Tell me what?" I dug.

Kimmy hesitated, and her dad saw the conflict being waged within her. I tried to decipher my wife's expression and demeanor, something I'd always been adept at, but I couldn't pinpoint it. She seemed to me to be exhibiting aspects of shame and fear, each enveloped in severe, crippling anxiety.

"When Kim was...what...sixteen? She got involved with a guy, a real...fuckin'..." Shawn began. I could see his anger instantly rise at the expression of these apparently long-buried memories. "She mentioned that she was seeing somebody, but, you know, it was high school. We figured if she wanted us to meet him, we would."

"He told me he was nineteen," Kimmy took over the story. "And...we were together for, like, six months or something, but then I found out he was twenty-eight. He just looked young."

"Jesus," I said, almost involuntarily.

"When I told him we were done, he..."

"He didn't accept it," Dana finished her daughter's sentence, her native Filipino accent dripping off each word.

"The crazy son of a bitch fucking stalked her," Shawn corrected his wife, his grip on the armrests of his chair tightening. "He would call our house all day and night, he would drive past our house, thirty, forty, fifty times a day. He caused problems for Kim at school, at work. He slashed the tires on all of our cars. We called the cops, obviously, but he was smart about it, I hate to say. He'd borrow cars from people and use them to drive by, borrow their phones and call and hang up all the time. We're pretty sure he used one of those apps that can give you a new number. And the cops said that if he didn't do anything illegal at her job, there wasn't anything they could do about it.

"We pressed charges for statutory rape, but he posted bail. And when we got a restraining order, he started harassing Kim's friends and coworkers, eventually got Kim fired. Even showed up at Dana's job a few times."

"What the f--?" I caught myself before I finished my thought. I reached my hand over to my wife's and gave it a gentle squeeze. She finally looked at me with red eyes, and I could practically see the effort she was exerting to keep tears from streaming down her face.

"I'm sorry. I should have told you," she said, her voice barely above a whisper. She turned her attention back to her lap.

"Hey...look at me," I replied in as soft a tone as I could. Her eyes met mine. "Don't apologize. I know we've been more open with each other than most people are, but that doesn't mean you need to tell me everything. This is obviously a...difficult subject for you. I'm here to make your life easier, not make you relive horrible shit from your past."

A stale silence hung in the air. Shawn and Dana sat with concerned looks on their faces, all of us trying to figure out the easiest way to proceed. I felt the urge to squirm in my seat, the palpable tension weighing down on me and pushing the words up from my stomach and out of my mouth.

"So what happened?"

Kimmy and her parents all turned their heads toward me and then toward each other, silently debating over who would regale me with the rest of this painful recollection. Eventually, Shawn took a deep, audible breath in.

"After Kim got fired, we decided to take a vacation, just to, you know, get away from everything. She wasn't doing too well. This had all been going on for a year or so, and we took a trip. It was, what, a few months before your eighteenth birthday?"

Kimmy didn't acknowledge the question.

"Anyway, I woke up one of the mornings while we were away and I had a ton of voicemails and missed calls. This detective we'd talked to a few times had been trying to get a hold of us because that...little...fucking weasel Chris had broken into our house.

"They got him as he was leaving; we'd told a neighbor we were taking off for a bit for exactly that reason, and she'd called the police. But the shit that psycho had done..."

Shawn's brow furrowed and his jaw clenched as he tapped his thumb against the armrest. There was a clear and present anger that had overtaken him, one that displayed the fact that the Hill family hadn't talked about these frightening times since they were done living in the midst of them.

"He'd written this...this proclamation all over our living room wall, right over there," he continued, pointing to the largest open wall in the room. "all about how he...loved Kim and how she was going to be with him, blah blah blah. Carved a heart deep into the hardwood floor, stuck a knife in the center of it, and left it there. It was all a bunch of really...cliché stuff, but Christ..."

"...wow." I immediately felt the weightlessness behind my response, but at that moment, I deemed it more appropriate to say less.

"Yeah...they arrested him, and he had...something on him. Cocaine, I think. So the drug charge coupled with the burglary charge and then adding in everything he put Kim through, plus the statutory rape, they gave him twelve years, eight inside and four on probation, but he still didn't stop."

I raised an eyebrow as if to silently urge him to continue.

"As soon as he got sent to prison, the letters started coming in. Multiple, every day. All about how she was going to wait for him. Not asking her, telling her that she would be. And he did it through his friends, like he'd mail them the letters and have them mail them to us, you know? Eventually, the prison took our complaints seriously, and they revoked his mail privileges. And it finally stopped."

I looked at my wife and found an inexplicable guise of shame across her face. We all sat in a silence that wasn't so much awkward as it was one of understanding. I squeezed Kimmy's hand again and got a gentle squeeze in return. I slid closer and wrapped my arm around her, pulling her close and resting her head on my shoulder.

"I know you said you had a crazy ex, but that might be the understatement of the century," I said, and my comment elicited stifled laughs from my family, effectively breaking the tension in the room.

Kimmy sniffled and rubbed her nose before looking up at me.

"I'm sorry I never told you," she said.

"Stop it. There's nothing to be sorry about." I planted a kiss on the top of my wife's head, then moved my hand to her pregnant stomach.

"He's up for parole in a few years, but we're going to be writing to the parole board to tell them we don't feel safe with him out," Dana said, her accented voice charred from crying.

"I won't let anything happen to you," I said to Kimmy, who seemed to be calming down.

"We know you won't," Shawn said. "We're glad to have you around, Nick. We know you won't let anything happen to our girl."

With a grunt, my stocky father-in-law pushed himself off his recliner and stepped over to the couch.

"Where's my hug, Kimmy Cat?"

I helped my exhausted wife up from the center cushion of the couch and stepped aside to give her a moment with her dad. Shawn and Kimmy embraced one another in a hug that was much needed.

"It's okay, honey," Shawn whispered, just loud enough that I could hear him. "It wasn't him. He's still gone, and he's going to stay gone. You never have to worry about him again. I would say you have Nick to protect you, but I know it's the other way around."

Kimmy laughed, nodded her head, and squeezed her dad tighter. Shawn then kissed his daughter on the top of her head and passed her off to Dana, who rose from the couch. The Hill women hugged, with Dana offering similar comforting words. Shawn turned to me and thanked me for being there for Kimmy, to which I said no thanks were necessary. He then announced that he was returning to bed, a sentiment Dana echoed.

Kimmy's mother and father retired to their bedroom, shutting off the hall lights behind them.

"I know you, and I'm gonna say right now, don't you dare apologize again," I said, trying to look serious behind the smile that was begging to come out.

My wife feigned pouting and stepped forward into me, and I held her close to me, resting my chin on her head.

"You're okay, yeah?" I asked her.

She nodded in affirmation. "I just hadn't thought about that in a long time."

"And you don't have to think about it ever again, alright?"

She looked up at me, her eyes finally back to their shining brown instead of red and finally free of the withheld tears. She kissed me, and then I helped her lay back down on the couch and covered her in blankets.

I turned on a new episode of Family Guy and sank into Shawn's recliner with my laptop.

As Kimmy fell back into a restless sleep, I checked the prison inmate website and confirmed for myself that her ex was still in the same place he'd been for the last five years.

If nothing else, this night reaffirmed a vow I'd made long ago.

I would always protect my family.

One

|

The clock read 8:58 as the sun dropped below the trees to the west. I sat behind the wheel of our Hyundai, guiding it down a long, empty road through northern Kansas while Kimmy slept in the passenger's seat, headphones on while her phone played the news on YouTube. Behind her sat our four-year-old son, Alex, similarly positioned as he slept with an iPad on his lap, the bright colors of whichever cartoon he fell asleep to casting his face, an almost perfect recreation of his mother's Asian-European countenance but topped by a mop of brown hair, in a frantically shifting glow.

And next to Alex was Katie, our six-year-old daughter, who alternately heard from people that she was the spitting image of her mother or me but never us both. She possessed my wide, brown eyes and slightly concave nose, her mother's flowing brunette hair and effortless charming smile. The section of the car where she sat was littered with capped markers and colored pencils and half-finished works of art. A large sketchbook rested open on her lap with a purple pencil laying vertically between the pages, the very same place it had dropped when it fell from her hand as she drifted off along with her mom and brother.

My eyelids had been sinking in unison with the sun, and at the same moment I noticed that, I also noticed the growling in my stomach. It had been almost ten hours since we'd had what I still consider the best breakfast we'd ever had at a mom-and-pop restaurant that morning. Because of the generous portions of eggs and pancakes and sausage patties and hash browns, none of us had felt the need to stop for lunch at any point.

As my mouth watered again at the mere thought of that day's first meal, my eyes landed on a billboard quickly approaching on the right side of the road. The billboard consisted of a white background with four tall words in red letters:

DAISY'S DINER

NEXT EXIT

I placed a hand on my wife's leg and gently nudged her awake. She rubbed the sleep from her eyes and surveyed our surroundings.

"Morning," I said.

"Mm...where are we?"

"I believe we're in Cannibal County, Kansas."

Kimmy scoffed out a laugh and rolled her eyes.

"Speaking of which, I'm starving. You wanna stop somewhere? We just passed a sign for some diner, exit should be coming up soon," I said.

"Only if the food is as good as this morning," she replied; clearly, our breakfast had had the same impact on her as it had on me.

"If you aren't gonna eat unless the food is that good, then we might as well tell the kids we live in Oklahoma now."

Kimmy and I laughed, and she agreed that we should stop.

The exit presented itself another mile and a half down the road, and I veered off the main highway. At the intersection at the end of the long exit stood another sign, this one no larger than a stop sign, that read, **Daisy's Diner - Left - 3 Miles**.

We made the left at the intersection and traveled those three miles past acres upon acres of what appeared to be meticulously maintained farmland and the dwellings that housed those responsible for the maintenance. Before long, we rounded a bend, and the diner appeared on our left. I turned our car into the parking lot as Kimmy unbuckled her seatbelt and turned in her seat to wake up the kids.

II

Daisy's Diner looked to me to have once housed some other business that wasn't food related. There was no distinct theme to be gleaned from the outside decor; it was simply a square white building, the face of which had windows that stretched from floor to ceiling and from a few feet from the corner of the structure to the entrance. On top of the building was a neon sign that identified the eatery in large, red cursive letters.

The parking spaces were perpendicular to the face of the building, and the three spaces immediately in front of the door were cordoned off by thin orange cones and masking tape, and the white handicap logo on two of them looked to have been painted very recently. Next to those spaces were three vehicles in the following two spaces, an empty space, and a car in the space next to it.

I pulled into the space next to the lone car that didn't leave us sandwiched between two vehicles, and my family and I piled out of our car. As soon as I opened my door, a gust of wind brought an inviting aroma that seemed to bode well for the meals waiting within Daisy's Diner.

"Dad?" I heard a small, tired voice call out to me from behind me, turning around to find my daughter looking up at me with an attaché case clutched against her torso.

"Yeah, sweetie?" I replied as I shut my door.

"Can I bring my portfolio in?"

"Well, we don't want to get any food on it, so why don't you leave it here for now? And I bet this place will have a kid's menu, and you can create a brand new work of art on it. That sound okay?"

Katie cautiously nodded her head and put the folder back on her seat in the car. The collection of finished and unfinished art projects that Katie proudly referred to as her portfolio was, without parallel, her most prized possession. She was accompanied by her portfolio as surely as her arms and legs accompanied her everywhere she went. I saw the look of apprehension on my daughter's face.

"Tell you what, why don't you grab your favorite colored pencils?" I tried finding a happy medium between what Katie wanted and what was feasible.

The look of agitation was replaced with a smile as she reached back into the backseat and, after some fumbling, returned with the unopened pack of twelve colored pencils that we'd gotten her the day before we left on our trip.

"Those are your favorites?" I asked with a smile.

"Maybe. I don't know yet. I have to find out!" the joy in her voice was contagious and made my wide smile wider.

On the other side of the car, Kimmy had gotten Alex out and was waiting for Katie and me to come around to go inside Daisy's. We walked on the sidewalk along the front of the restaurant and the door opened with a welcoming *ding* as we pushed it open and entered the home of the appetizing smells wafting around outside.

The walls were decorated with various road signs and pictures that seemed to portray life around the small town that Daisy's Diner called home. Framed photos of people posing outside the restaurant as we knew it rested on the wall next to pictures of it from long before the current renovations had been made. In those pictures, the white paint was less chipped and marred by time and the elements, and the sign was more like a billboard on top of the building without a neon letter in sight.

Inside the entrance sat the front counter with the cash register and a cup full of pens, and to the left was the rest of Daisy's. Two of the four booths we'd walked in line with on the sidewalk outside were occupied, one by a young couple and the other by a single man. Along the connecting wall were five more booths, all empty. Opposite those booths was the counter where two men sat next to each other and another lone man a few seats down.

"Hey folks, take a seat wherever ya like. I'll be right with ya," a voice rang out from the kitchen. A portly server with a face that screamed she'd been working there for far too long flashed us a warm smile as we walked down the aisle through the booths and counter and piled into a booth. Like the rest of the establishment where she worked, the waitress had a very small-town-USA vibe to her, with a uniform that looked plucked out of the nineteen-eighties.

The kids sat next to the wall, and while Alex quietly but excitedly scanned the array of pictures that adorned it, the thin paper placemat immediately consumed Katie's attention resting on the table in front of her.

"Perfect!" she exclaimed. A smile as bright as her light brown eyes crawled across her face as she started to open her newest pack of colored pencils.

"Hang on a second, missy," Kimmy said as she scooted in next to her. "Let's figure out what you're gonna eat."

Kimmy reached over and retrieved the two laminated menus that sat in a small metal holder against the wall and handed one to me. Without even a glance at the menu, Katie blurted out her food of choice.

"Mashed potatoes!"

"You want just a...a giant plate of mashed potatoes?" Kimmy asked with a smirk.

Katie raised her eyebrows and nodded her head enthusiastically.

"She's definitely your kid," Kimmy said with a laugh.

"That's my girl," I replied. "But, my little Kate Kane, cousin of Bruce Wayne, otherwise known as Batwoman, you should get something else too. They have like...chicken nuggets, cheeseburgers--"

"Cheeseburger!" both of our children exclaimed at the same time.

"You guys both want cheeseburgers?" I asked.

Both kids nodded in the affirmative.

"Looks like they have mashed potatoes. Alex, you want fries?" I asked, to which I got another nod.

"I'll get an extra big plate of mashed potatoes for us to split, too." I smiled at my daughter and got a smile back.

"You guys are so weird," Kimmy laughed.

The server walked behind the counter opposite us and called, "Some drinks for you folks?"

I quickly rounded up our drink orders and passed them on to the woman, who moments later was approaching our table with a Pepsi, a Diet Pepsi, and two chocolate milks. As she set the drinks down, I took note of her name tag: Roberta.

"How're you folks doing tonight?" she asked.

"Not too bad. How about yourself?" I replied.

"Be a lot better at 6 A.M., that's for sure," Her tone was tired, but her professionalism lent it enough joviality that it was adequately masked.

"Oof, 6 A.M.? No, thank you," I replied.

"Six days a week. Gotta keep the lights on somehow!"

"Well, we're happy to contribute to you not living in the dark." Me, Kimmy, and Roberta shared a laugh.

"What can I getcha guys?" the waitress pulled a notepad from her apron and a pen from behind her ear.

I motioned to Kimmy, who reflexively looked at and pointed to the menu as she ordered.

"Okay…" she began. "He will have the kid's cheeseburger and fries. She'll have the kid's cheeseburger, and then can she have mashed potatoes instead of fries?"

"She sure can," Roberta replied, quickly scribbling down our orders in what I can only presume was the same shorthand I used during my tenure as a server years ago.

"Okay, thank you…and I'll have the…can I have the French dip, please?" Kimmy finished her order.

"Best thing on the menu if you ask me," Roberta offered. "Fries okay?"

"Oh, yes. And can I get a thing of mayo on the side?"

"Absolutely. And for you, sir?"

"I'll just have the cheeseburger, the one…not for kids. And can I get pickles?" I said.

"No problem. Fries good?"

"Fries are great."

"Alright, anything else I can get ya?" Roberta returned the pen to its resting place behind her ear.

"Can we please have a big plate of mashed potatoes, please?" Katie's voice rang out, equal parts meek and confident, the voice of a girl exercising the coveted independence of placing a part of her own order while still consumed by a child's innate shyness.

Roberta looked at me to confirm that she should add the side to the order.

"Ah, yes. Sorry, I almost forgot the most important part of the meal."

"Got it," Roberta confirmed. "I'll get that right in for you."

"Thank you!" Kimmy replied.

Roberta trudged away on pained feet and disappeared back into the kitchen. As we waited for our food, Alex hosted a climactic battle between his Spider-Man and Venom action figures while Katie drew her latest masterpiece on the back of her placemat. I eyed the work-in-progress, knowing better than to ask her what it was going to be; a quality that she inherited from her mother's own artistic process, she never told anyone what a particular piece was going to be upon its completion, as she herself often didn't know until later in the work's life.

Meanwhile, Kimmy and I discussed our trip. We'd left our home in Walnut Creek, California with the destination of Orlando, Florida, but with a very loose definition of an itinerary. Our expressed plan was to drive from California to Florida without a clarified route and make any stops along the way that anyone wanted.

As we traversed the country, we would present places to the kids - locations or events that might be going on that could interest them - let them decide, as well as a few places my wife and I wanted to visit. We weren't constrained by time; summer afforded us the opportunity to move at whatever pace we liked. We'd made a few stops up to this point, and Kimmy and I sat on our phones in Daisy's Diner, trying to decide where we would head next.

We pondered a stop in Des Moines, another in Chicago, and yet another in Kansas City. Before we could determine our next semi-spontaneous activity, Roberta returned to our table and set up a tray jack on the floor in front of it, and moments later returned with our food. She distributed our meals, making an especially big deal of the plate of mashed potatoes she laid in front of Katie.

"That is the biggest side of mashed potatoes I've ever seen at any restaurant in my life," I said, looking at it with wide eyes.

"Well, it sounded like she's a fan of em', and we've got the best mashed potatoes in the state, so I doubled em' up for you, on me," Roberta replied with a smile.

"Oh, you didn't have to do that," I offered, secretly happy she had.

"Thank you," Kimmy chimed in. "We should only need about six or seven more plates this size before they've had enough."

We all laughed. Roberta asked if we needed anything else and, upon our assurance that we were all set, tended to the other customers.

My family and I ate our meals, not knowing that it was the meal that would precede the most difficult time in any of our lives. The food was fantastic, certainly matching the inviting smells that had pulled us inside from the parking lot. It was a meal that was perfect at the moment but that, in retrospect, is marred by what followed it.

III

As we were nearly finished with our meals, the bell above the door that led in and out of Daisy's Diner chimed, as it had a few times while we'd been there. But then a voice called out through the restaurant.

"Whoever's got that blue car out there, looks like someone ransacked ya."

My ears perked up, and I turned around in my seat. It was only then that I noticed that all the patrons who had been in the restaurant when we'd arrived were now gone, replaced by two new men sitting at a booth together. The man at the door was in his sixties and wore the clothes that I imagined all the residents of this small town wore: a flannel shirt, weathered jeans, and work boots, with a NASCAR hat topping his head of thin gray hair.

At that same moment, I also realized that we couldn't see our car because of where I'd parked and where my family and I had sat inside the restaurant.

"What?" I said as I stood up. "Blue Hyundai?"

"Yep. Right down there." The man pointed down the wall of windows towards our car.

"Stay here with the kids. I'll be right back," I said to Kimmy. My blood was boiling. I balled my fists up as I stomped through the restaurant past Roberta, the men at the booth, and the man at the door.

As soon as I stepped outside, I could see the evidence of the break-in. Various papers were scattered on the ground around the car, and the light was on as a result of the driver's side door hanging wide open.

You gotta be fucking kidding me; I thought to myself.

I peered down the street, finding nothing but darkness in both directions; no tail lights shrinking in the distance with whatever its occupants had stolen. I rushed around the cars in the parking lot, my own included, and circled the diner, finding nothing once again. As I returned to the parking lot, I approached my car, picking up the papers that had been removed. I quickly realized that they were the contents of the glove compartment. I placed the registration and other documents back in their rightful place and quickly surveyed the rest of the car.

The navigation system looked to be untouched, and the ignition didn't appear to have been tampered with at all, so it seemed to me like stealing the car itself wasn't the intention of the person who'd broken into it. That fact only made the rest of the scene stranger.

There were things strewn about the floor of the car. Various pens that were in the cupholder were on the floor, a few chargers and other cords were out of their usual places, and the middle console was opened. It was strange that the large cup of change inside that central console that at that time was almost entirely quarters and amounted to at least $100 was left untouched. Two pairs of Kimmy's sunglasses, both designer brands, also rested on the driver's seat, their value either unknown to the man who moved them or ignored.

Each of our overnight bags, which we kept separate from our suitcases, had been opened, but as far as I could tell, everything was in them. My spare MacBook charger, a Kindle Fire, and an iPad were inside mine. Similar items were still inside Kimmy's bag as well. The trunk and computer bags containing several thousand dollars' worth of electronics had apparently been ignored.

I climbed out of the car, unable to think of anything that was there before that wasn't now. I didn't get it. Although confused, the fact that we apparently weren't robbed offered relief, but I was still seeing red. I locked the car doors, something I was sure I'd done when we'd first arrived, and huffed back into Daisy's Diner. This time, the bell above the door irritated me in a way it hadn't before.

"Didn't find em', huh?" asked the man who had informed us of the break-in.

I ignored the question and turned my attention to Roberta, who was standing at the cash register.

"You have a non-emergency number for the police?" I asked.

"I'll have to look it up, yeah. Give me just a sec."

As Roberta retreated into the kitchen, I walked down the aisle between the booths and the counter towards my family, who were now standing.

"You okay?" Kimmy asked me, a look of concern plastered across her face. Our kids inquisitively looked up at us from their seats, sensing the tension in the air.

"Yeah, I'm good," I replied, digging my phone from my pocket. "Whoever did it is gone. It's weird, there's nothing missing. They went--"

"You ready?" Roberta called out from the front of the restaurant.

"Yeah! Go ahead." I unlocked my phone and punched in the numbers she recited.

The line rang once, twice, three times before a muffled noise came from the other end.

"Hel--" the man on the other end of the call began answering casually, then stopped himself and cleared his throat. "Police, this is Dave."

"Hi, yeah, my car was broken into. We're at Daisy's Diner."

"Just a moment, please."

Dave didn't put me on hold proper, instead just set the receiver down on some surface. I listened as his footsteps receded, and after a moment, I heard those same footsteps return with the lawman speaking to someone whose replies I couldn't hear.

"...their car, yeah...no, I---yeah, they're up at Daisy's...yeah, okay. Yeah, probably was...should talk to her...I'll tell him...alright, thanks...yup, bye."

A shuffling sound emanated from the earpiece on my cell phone before Dave's voice resumed pouring through it.

"Hey, you there?" he asked, his previous air of professionalism seemingly needing a moment to recharge.

"Yeah, I'm here."

"Thank you for holding, sir. A unit has been sent out and will be with you shortly. Please wait inside Daisy's until our officer arrives. Is there anything else I can help you with?"

"How long until they get here, you think?" I asked, making no attempt to hide the irritation coursing through my body.

"Well, Joh—Officer Billings is just down the road, so he shouldn't be longer than a few minutes," Dave replied reassuringly.

I thanked Dave and ended the call before returning to our table. I stood at the end of the booth and surveyed my family. Alex was half asleep, his eyes heavy as he sat slumped against his mother. Kimmy sat back down and listened intently as our daughter showed her the nearly finished picture on her placemat.

IV

Katie had spent our time in Daisy's Diner crafting a picture of her own restaurant, aptly named "Katie's Diner." It included the building itself, the parking lot complete with three vehicles, and through the window, one could see a table being waited on, with a family similar to our own placing their order, and another at a different table eating steaming hot food.

It never ceased to amaze me how competent my daughter's artwork was at such a young age. She was a better artist at six than I was at thirty, having been passed down her keen sense for illustration and all the tenets therein from her mother. She took great pride in the pieces she made, and I already knew that the first thing she would do once we got back to the car would be to put the picture of Katie's Diner into her portfolio.

I turned around and saw Roberta wiping down the counter across the aisle.

"Ma'am?" I asked. She looked up. "Do you have cameras here?"

"Got two outside, but they ain't worked for a while. Just keep 'em there for show."

"Fuck," I muttered under my breath. "What about the people who left since we've been here? You know em'?"

"Well, I didn't know the kids. But I can tell ya, I saw em' get right in their car and go. Two boys at the counter, I know em', I can vouch for em'. One of em's the pastor in the next town up, comes in for the steak and eggs, other one is my nephew's godson. Other gentleman at the booth, he runs the hardware store, spends more time in church than the pastor."

I sighed. "Alright. Thank you."

I sat back down and not five minutes later, the familiar and now grating ding of the door rang out, and I turned around to see a thin, middle-aged police officer in a light brown uniform and a look on his face composed of more annoyance than concern. I told my family I was going to speak with the man and stood up from the booth.

As I approached the front of the diner, the officer and our waitress said something to each other, then both looked at me.

"This is Officer Billings. He'll take care of ya," Roberta said, turning back towards the kitchen.

"You the one called?" the cop asked, his voice gravelly with fatigue.

"Yup," I replied.

The cop sighed as though I was inconveniencing him. "Well, let's go." He made a condescending sweeping gesture with his arm to direct me outside.

I looked back at Kimmy, and we exchanged a nod, and I followed the officer back outside.

"What'd they take?" he asked, his brusqueness already starting to get under my skin.

"I mean, I looked, and they definitely went through all of our shit, but I can't really find anything missing."

The officer pulled a pack of cigarettes from a pocket on the front of his uniform's shirt. He retrieved a lighter and cigarette from the pack and lit it, sending thin tendrils followed by a plume of smoke wisping away in the light breeze.

"So what do you wanna do?" he asked, the annoyance in his tone of voice increasing with every syllable.

"I do something to offend you?" I bit back.

Officer Billings eyed me with cold regard and clenched his jaw, then lifted his cigarette to his lips and took a long drag.

"Not yet, but we just met," he said.

"Well, you're being kind of an asshole."

"Oh, is that right?" Officer Billings rested his hand on his holster, though it looked more out of habit than threat.

"Yeah, that's right. Would you disagree? Or is this just how you do things around here?"

The cop stared daggers into my eyes as smoke dripped from his nose as he exhaled. Before he could answer, another police vehicle pulled into the parking lot. I watched as another cop got out of his car. This one was younger, but he shared a likeness with Officer Billings. When he was close enough, the pale lights on the outside of Daisy's Diner revealed his name tag with a familiar identifier: Billings.

"How we doin' tonight?" the younger lawman asked.

"Hell you doin' here, boy?" the elder Billings replied, ignoring the question.

"I was passin' by, didn't hear anything on the radio, thought I'd see what was what. How are ya, sir?"

I looked up to the younger officer, then at the man I was all but certain was his father.

"Someone broke into my car," I said dryly.

"But they ain't take anything," the older Billings cut in. "So I'm supposin' he wants us to take fingerprints, pull security footage in every direction for miles, maybe get some DNA swabs, bring in the FBI."

"I don't know what you're fucki--" I started, my anger taking control of the muscles in my throat. Luckily, the younger officer cut me off.

"Don't listen to him. This old sonofabitch dun'nt have a cordial bone in his body. We're all just waitin' for those cigarettes to finish the job," he laughed.

I didn't reciprocate it.

"Someone broke into your car, huh? That's Old Ben's truck, this one yours here?" he continued, taking a few steps toward our vehicle and pointing to it.

"Yeah, that's ours," I replied, turning away from the rude Officer Billings as another cloud of smoke rushed from his lips.

"And they didn't take anything, that right?"

"Yeah, I mean, not that I can tell. Anything worth taking is still there, so…I just thought I should call you guys, anyway." I turned my head and saw the older Billings head back inside Daisy's.

"Nah, it's good that ya did. Better ta' get these things down on paper, you know. Just in case." He walked around the side of our car, inspecting it and the space around it. "You know, if I'm being honest with ya, we have some youngins around here who get up to no good. Ain't too much to do around here, sometimes they get a little stir-crazy. Doesn't make it right, but that's what I'd put my money on for what happened here."

I didn't know what to say.

"Tell you what, how about we get a report down, somethin' for the record? I'm not promisin' we'll ever nab the kids who did this, but…you know, just in case."

I agreed. The younger Billings walked back to his cruiser and returned with a notepad. I provided him with my information and our phone number, periodically looking back through the window into Daisy's to check on my family. They continued sitting at the booth where we'd eaten, and at one point, I made a funny face at Katie, who was staring out the window, surely wondering what was going on.

Once the younger Billings had all the necessary information and had written out the report, I signed it and was given a carbon copy.

"Real sorry about this, Mr. Botic. This ain't indicative of how things are around here, I promise you that. This is a real just kinda…wrong place, wrong time, opportunistic kinda thing," he said.

"Yeah, I get it," I replied, much calmer now, having dealt with a cop that wasn't harboring an inexplicable deep-rooted resentment toward me. "Uh...you know where the closest hotel is around here? We were gonna get some more miles in tonight, but after this..."

"Sure, sure, sure. Yeah, you uh...you take a left outta the parkin' lot here, head down about...three miles, on your right'll be the Whitmore Motel. It ain't five stars or anything, but you'll be able to get a few hours of shuteye."

"Alright, I appreciate the help." I shook the officer's hand, and he escorted me back into Daisy's. The older Billings flashed me a dirty look as I walked past him to my family, then started a conversation with his partner and possible son. Kimmy stood up as I approached the booth.

"Done?" she asked.

"Yeah, finally. Let's get out of here. There's a motel pretty close by." I looked at the check on the table, then took my wallet out of my back pocket and pulled out a few bills. I dropped them on the table, reached further into the booth, and gently shook my son awake.

Katie had finished her piece just as Kimmy slid out of the booth and was busy gathering her things. In a moment, we were all walking down the aisle towards the exit, and while the food was delicious, I was of the mind that if I never returned to Daisy's Diner again, it would be too soon.

"Money's on the table," I said to Roberta, who was standing at the register with the two police officers. "Thanks for everything."

"Thank you, folks. Sorry for the trouble."

"Tell em' John Jr. sent ya when ya get to the Whitmore," the younger officer said.

"I'll do that," I said with a half-laugh.

The elder cop silently eyed my family and me with unwarranted disdain, and I met his eyes with an identical fire.

"You have a great day, sir!" I said much too loudly. The younger cop laughed as the bell dinged, marking my and my family's exit.

"What was that about?" Kimmy asked.

"The older cop was a real piece of shit," I explained.

"Oooooh." Katie pulled at my hand, shocked at my usage of such a vile, despicable term.

"Oops. Sorry baby," I laughed.

As Kimmy got Alex back into the car, Katie and I walked around to our side, where I opened her door. I pulled her seatbelt over her, and once she was sufficiently strapped in, I shut her door, opened my own, and climbed into the driver's seat. Kimmy eyed the mess that the car had become at the hands of its mysterious intruder.

"We'll have to stop somewhere and pick everything up tomorrow," I said.

"Daddy?" Katie's voice called out.

"Yeah, Katie?"

"Where is my portfolio?"

"Ah, it probably got moved when I was messing around in here before," I looked at Kimmy, signaling for her to look in the front while I checked the back.

I got out of the car and went to the back, opening Katie's door. I checked the floor by her feet, leaned over, and checked the space between her and a now-sleeping Alex. I opened the trunk and checked on and between all of our luggage.

I checked everywhere inside the car and got down on my hands and knees and checked underneath it too. I checked everywhere that my daughter's portfolio of artwork could've been.

Someone had broken into our car and left a cup filled with over $100 in quarters.

Someone had broken into our car and left three iPads, two MacBook Pros, and several thousands of dollars' worth of various other electronics.

Someone had broken into our car, and the only thing they'd taken was a folder filled with my daughter's artwork.

Two

|

Katie had been an artist since the moment she had the dexterity to hold a marker. She would join Kimmy in her studio, working on her own pieces while her mother worked on commissions. She loved all aspects of the artistic process and method. Whatever the medium, she proved adept - drawing with graphite and charcoal pencils, coloring with crayons and markers, oil painting and watercolor; if it could be used to create, she utilized it.

Those creations generally reflected the things in her life. There were countless works of our family and home, of our two cats, her brother and mother and of me, of all her favorite activities and places to go.

My favorite piece of Katie's is a portrait of us all standing in front of our house - the quintessential refrigerator picture. But the reason I love it so much isn't that it simply exhibits our family, but rather the minor details and structure of the piece as a whole that reflect the various aspects of all of us.

On the left is me, wearing what my wife calls the "Nick Botic Uniform" - a plain white t-shirt and khaki shorts. Next to me is Katie, her hand in mine. Then there's a small space, and next is her little brother, holding Kimmy's hand as she stands on the right. The space between Katie and Alex was deliberate; it didn't indicate a distance between siblings, but rather it reflected the roles of each of the children in relation to their parents.

Katie, since birth, has always been "daddy's little girl," a quality she, somewhat ironically, got from her mom. Kimmy and Katie shared a wonderful relationship, but my wife said on the day that our first child was born, "She's gonna be a daddy's girl. She's gonna love you more than you can imagine." On the other hand, Alex was an unabashed mama's boy like myself. I similarly said to Kimmy on the day he was born, "You think Katie loves me? Just you wait. He's gonna be living with you until he's forty, guaranteed."

Despite her portfolio being meticulously organized by when each piece was finished, she made sure that one was always the first one you'd see if you opened it. It was the crowning achievement in a collection of examples of her greatest passion.

And her pain was heartbreaking when it all went missing.

Katie did her best to hide how crushed she was, but Kimmy and I knew that this was the single worst thing that could've been stolen from our car. It was tantamount to someone losing a limb; Katie's portfolio was all but physically attached to her.

"I'm sorry sweetie, it's...it's gone..." The words tasted sour as they passed my lips.

The tears welled in her milk chocolate eyes and her bottom lip quivered; it was clear that her entire world was crashing down around her. I was speechless. A million things to say ran through my head, and not a single one seemed adequate. I took her small hand in mine and gave it a gentle squeeze as I tried desperately to think of something, anything, to help soften this monumental blow. I looked at my wife, and she met my pained gaze with her own sorrowful eyes. I opened my mouth to say something, but Katie squeezed my hand twice and stopped me before I could form a word.

"It's okay…" she said, clearly holding in the utter despair she was undoubtedly feeling. But she sniffled hard and took a deep breath. Even in this painful moment, she looked at her younger brother, asleep in his seat, and whispered so as not to disturb him. "…I'll just have to make new pictures and…and start a new portfolio."

I didn't know how to respond. I looked at Kimmy, who was similarly floored by our daughter's display of patience, understanding, and maturity.

"It's okay to be upset, honey," my wife explained. "This is a bad thing that's happened, and you don't need to hide how you're feeling."

I nodded my head in agreement. Katie used her free arm to wipe the tears that had begun traveling down her cheeks.

"…it's okay. Maybe somebody just liked them so much that they wanted them. They could have asked, but if they like them that much, then at least someone will have them who likes them, and then it's good that they can have them."

Katie's inner battle was between her sadness at losing all of her artwork and her hope that whoever had taken it did so because they liked it so much, and she stumbled over her words as she tried to express them. I wondered if Kimmy had told the kids what was happening when I went outside to address the car break-in, but that didn't seem like something she'd do.

Instead, it reminded me of just how perceptive our daughter was. She had the uncanny ability to connect dots she hadn't yet been made aware of. As Kimmy would say with a laugh, Katie is too smart for her own good.

"Are you okay?" I looked my daughter in her glistening eyes.

She hesitated, then wiped her eyes again. A small smile crept across her face as she nodded and squeezed my hand again. "Yeah. I get to make new pictures now. I'm gonna make an even better portfolio!"

I matched her smile with my own and leaned forward, planting a kiss on her forehead.

"Sounds like you've got a lot of work ahead of you," I said as I stood up and prepared to close her door. "You're gonna need a lot more supplies."

Katie vigorously nodded with a big smile. I closed her door in awe at my daughter's ability to look on the bright side. I slid into the driver's seat and looked at Kimmy, who raised her eyebrows, similarly impressed with our firstborn's optimism. After turning our car on, I took her hand in mine.

"How far is this place?" she asked.

"Just a few miles down the road, apparently."

"Should we GPS it?"

"The cop said it was on this road, we should be good." I let go of her hand and reversed out of our parking spot, then left Daisy's Diner in our rearview mirror with no plans to ever see it again.

Just under three miles down the road, we rounded a bend that revealed a tall sign on the right that stood out against the dark rural background it rested upon. The sign read **The Wh tmo e Mot l** with a neon indicator remarking the establishment's vacancy underneath. As we turned into the parking lot, the various light poles bathed the asphalt and the garbage that littered it in a pale yellow glow. The parking lot was empty save for two cars, one on either end. The long structure containing the motel's rooms consisted of eight doors with a corresponding window next to each one. It was as foreboding a place as I'd laid eyes on, but that night, it felt like our only option.

II

"Whew...luxurious," Kimmy said.

"Eh...the cop said it wasn't the nicest place in the world."

"Did he mention it was the motel from every horror movie ever?"

Kimmy and I shared a laugh but agreed that the building looked well kept enough, that the parking lot was sufficiently illuminated, and that those two qualities were enough for us. I pulled into a spot next to the car in front of the small, disconnected building with a sign next to the door marked OFFICE.

"Alright, you guys wait here. I'll get us a room," I said as I slid out the driver's side door and shut it behind me.

The door to the office sounded the same ding that Daisy's Diner rang out when opened. The inside of the small structure was decorated similarly to the diner as well - various road signs and framed photographs of people posing at the Whitmore Motel adorned the walls in a disorganized array.

A small rack held assorted maps and travel guides and a small selection of dime store novels that, at a glance, were limited to the erotic thriller genre. Behind a small counter sat a thin man in his late sixties watching a tv show on a small flatscreen TV. As that bell *dinged*, it startled him to attention.

"Hi—hi," he said, seemingly confused. Thin white hairs crawled across the back of his head from ear to ear, and a thick pair of glasses rested on the bridge of his thin, delicate nose, magnifying his eyes considerably.

"How's it going?" I asked as I fished my wallet from my back pocket.

"...good. Do yeh...yeh need a room?"

"Yup, can we get a room with two beds?"

"We got, eh...one'a those." The man stood up from his seat and stepped over a tackboard behind the counter that had numbered keys hanging from it. He grabbed a keyring with two keys from the third hook from the left on the top row, then turned to the counter.

"Gonna need yer credit card and eh...ID. Yer ID," he said, his voice fairly deep but riddled with uncertainty in every word. "Room is, eh...sixty...five...dollars?"

"You sure?" I said with a half-hearted chuckle, almost positive he was assuming I had money and thus raising the price. I was too physically tired and mentally exhausted to argue the point.

I took out the requested cards from my wallet and handed them over to the man, who silently entered the information from my ID into a computer and slid my credit card through a terminal. After a few minutes of wishing I hadn't left my phone in the car and awkwardly pretending to look at the things that populated the walls, a grunt pulled my attention back to the man behind the counter.

"Here yeh go," he said, handing the two cards back to me. He grabbed the keyring from the counter and lumbered around me. "C'mon. I'll take yeh there."

As I followed the man out of the office, he advised me to park the car in front of the third door on the face of the motel. I got back in my car and followed his direction. Kimmy looked at me as if to ask, "everything good?"

"Everyone here is just...weird," I said to Kimmy. "I mean, he's nice enough, but he's just awkward."

"As long as he gave us a room, he can be as awkward as he wants. We'll be out of here in the morning," my wife replied.

In about ten seconds, I'd pulled out of the space in front of the office and moved to the spot in front of the third door of the motel, on which a small brass 3 hung by a single nail. As Kimmy and I stepped out of the car, the man from the office reached the door to our room and unlocked it. While Kimmy attended to our kids, I met the manager as he flipped the light switch in our room, blanketing it in a dull light from the ceiling fixture.

The room was exactly what I expected. Against the right wall and extending to the middle of the room were two queen-size beds that looked terribly uncomfortable and were topped by decades-old bedspreads, each with a different horrid floral pattern. A single dresser sat against the wall to the left, and on it sat a twenty-four inch tube TV and DVD player.

An alcove to the room's rear housed a closet hidden by double sliding doors on one side, a large mirror and counter in the middle, and a bathroom with a shower on the right. But there was one unexpected feature that I wasn't anticipating, a feature that gave me immediate pause.

To the left of the dresser was a door that connected to the next room over.

"You don't have any rooms that don't connect?" I asked.

"Not with two beds, I don't," he replied, taking a pained step toward the door. "But lookit."

The manager unclipped a keyring with more keys than I could count from his belt and cycled through a number of them before landing on one. He unlocked the connecting door and opened it, revealing a dark room on the other side.

"Ain't nobody else here. Probly won't get'nyone else tonight neither. 'Nif we do, I'll put em' down the way. Only one other lady stayin' here t'night, she won't bother yeh. Yeh'll be fine."

I apprehensively accepted his assurance, and he closed and locked the connecting door while Kimmy led our kids into the room. She gave me a concerned look as she put down our overnight bags, but I subtly shook my head to put her mind at ease.

"I'll...get outta yer hair," the manager said. "Eh...drop th'keys off in the morning. Check out's at eleven. Have a good night."

The man from the office shuffled out of our room, closing the door behind him. Our tired children didn't even take the opportunity to jump on the beds and instead followed their mom's direction to pick one of them to share. Katie and Alex climbed into the bed they were closest to, the one by the window and door.

I sat down on the end of the other bed and let out an exhausted sigh as I flopped down onto my back. Kimmy came and sat next to me, leaning down and giving me a comforting kiss.

"You look tired," she said.

"Ugh, I am. I can't tell if I'm tired-tired or just exhausted."

"Probably both."

I reached my arm around my wife and pulled her down, so we were both lying down, and she rested an arm on my chest.

"I can't believe Katie's portfolio was taken." Kimmy's voice dropped to a whisper. "Like, who the fuck would steal a little girl's artwork?"

"Who would leave the like...five grand in computers and iPads and shit? It's bizarre."

"Well..." Kimmy began as she sat up. "...we'll leave in the morning and never have to think about it again. Oh! Can you go get the computers and stuff?"

She leaned over, kissed me again, and then got up and went to the bathroom. I got up and covered up our already sleeping kids with the blanket that sat folded on the end of the bedspread, then went outside and retrieved all of our computer bags, not willing to leave them in the car overnight in a town where our car had already been broken into once; I didn't think we'd have good enough luck to find another burglar who would leave the most valuable things our car contained.

After going back inside, I locked the door behind me and checked the window next to the kid's bed, confirming that it was also locked. I then walked over to the connecting door and turned the brass knob and pulled, relieved to find that it didn't budge an inch. I plugged in mine and Kimmy's phone charger on either side of the bed we were going to sleep in and changed into a pair of shorts.

Kimmy soon returned from the bathroom, and we both lay down. We talked for a short while about the trip, about stopping somewhere to get Katie a new binder or folder to keep all of her work in and new art supplies, and I lamented this small town and the people in it.

Soon after that, we each drifted into a deep sleep, the last peaceful sleep I would ever truly have.

III

I had been asleep on my side, facing the wall, and when my eyes opened, they saw nothing but the dated yellow-brown wallpaper that coated the room. Sunlight spilled in through a gap in the curtains that hung over the window, providing the space with a single stream of light colliding with the wall I'd woken up looking at. It had only been seconds since I'd woken up and rolled over, and my bearings hadn't quite returned to me.

I rolled over, expecting to see my wife, but he wasn't there. Past her, I would've expected to see the kids, but they weren't in their bed either. I stood up a bit quicker than I meant to, subconsciously anxious that something terrible had happened. I wasn't sure what that something might be, but one of Kimmy's favorite things to make fun of me for was my propensity for waking up in an overly alert, unreasonably concerned, and almost violent confusion.

But as I stood, my children came into view. Alex sat on the floor near the door playing with toy cars, an iPad propped up with his favorite show on and headphones in his ears. Katie was on the floor between their bed and the window, propped up on her elbows, working on a new masterpiece with her newest colored pencils.

At that same moment, the noise of the shower swam through the air and finally entered my ears, and I was finally fully aware of my surroundings.

I stood up from our bed and looked over at Alex, ensuring he was content. I crawled onto the bed the kids had shared, and as I did, I noticed a once-folded piece of paper on the floor just inside the door. I assumed it was the receipt for our stay and ignored it for the time being as I checked on Katie.

"Hey, you. Kate Winslet, the esteemed 1998 Academy Award Nominee for Best Actress. Yeah, I'm talking to you," I said with faux aggression.

"You're talking to me?" she looked up from her drawing, trying to hide her smile.

"Well, I must be talking to you. I don't see anybody else on this side of the bed to talk to, do you?"

Silence lingered as Katie and I jokingly glared at each other, trying to get the other to laugh first, a battle I won. Her laugh filled my heart with a joy I knew I would never tire of, the smile in her eyes brighter than the sun illuminating our room.

"You doing okay?" I asked.

"I was sad, but it's okay. I'm still sad, but I can make new pictures. I'll miss my old ones, though. But I'll make better ones."

"You're handling this really well, Kate. I'm sorry this happened. Sometimes bad things happen to us. They shouldn't, but that's just the way life is. Bad things happen to everybody. It's about how you respond to the bad stuff, and you're responding really well. I don't know, I'm bad at motivational speeches. You're just awesome, alright? Deal with it. I love you."

Katie looked at me and smiled exaggeratingly wide.

"I love you too, daddy."

The words warmed me to my core. Katie returned her attention to her project, a multi-medium portrait of the motel in which it was being crafted. She set down the blue colored pencil she'd had when we began talking and picked up a gray marker, and I watched for a moment as her creativity poured out onto the page.

I sat up and turned towards my son, sliding down the end of the bed and sitting on the floor next to him and his collection of miniature cars and trucks. The folded piece of paper on the floor caught my eye again.

"What's up, dude?" I asked.

"Racing!" Alex replied enthusiastically, a tiny car in each hand, zooming back and forth across the radius of his four-year-old arms.

"I see that! Who's winning?"

"This one!" He held up a toy version of a red Ferrari. "But it's close. He's catching up."

He put the Ferrari back on the brown carpeting and mimicked a race, with the lime green Lamborghini in hot pursuit. Vroom Vrrrr Vrmmmm sounds emanated from deep in his stomach as the toy cars engaged in a heated competition, twisting around imaginary turns in the make-believe road.

"My money's on the Ferrari." I tussled my son's hair and stood to my feet.

The sounds of the shower ceased as I stepped towards the door, bent down, and picked up the once-folded piece of paper.

"Hey guys, your mom's outta the shower. You should start getting your stuff together. She'll be ready in about six hours," I said, loud enough for Kimmy to hear in the bathroom. Katie laughed, aware of her mom's habit of taking an obscenely long time to get ready.

I turned around to head back to our bed and unfolded the paper. I stopped in my tracks, and my heart instantly sank to the pit of my stomach as my vision narrowed. I got lightheaded and felt my legs nearly give out from under me.

I stared at the piece of paper for what felt like a lifetime, desperately wanting the image on it to twist into the receipt I had been expecting, but it didn't.

The folded piece of paper was the very first page of her portfolio. It depicted a crayon rendition of our home, and standing in front of it were me, Kimmy, Katie, and Alex.

Drawn similarly in black crayon behind Katie and me was a poorly rendered drawing of a man with a smile and a hand up as though he were waving. The addition also included a caption in an unrefined scribble - **Nice to see you**.

Because it was drawn in crayon and clearly not the work of a professional, I couldn't discern anything about the man. What I did know is that whoever had broken into our car at Daisy's Diner had followed us to the Whitmore Motel and slid the picture under the door.

"Dad, what's this thing on the door?" Alex asked, using his little green Lamborghini as a pointer to show me what he was talking about. He was referring to the piece of rubber that ran along the bottom of the door.

"That's...I don't know the name for it, but it's there to keep in heat or air conditioning, and to—to keep out leaves and snow and shi—

stuff like that." My thoughts were scrambled in my head, and I struggled to maintain my composure.

My son nodded his head, apparently pleased with the answer I'd provided. I wanted to get out of there. I folded the drawing and put it in my pocket, and as quickly and calmly as I could, I began packing our things up. I stepped over Alex and to the window, moving the curtain aside. I peered out into the parking lot, which was populated by our car in front of our door and a different car in front of the office than had been there the night before.

In the opposite direction, the car that was there the night before was gone. I continued getting our things packed, quietly telling kids to put the things they were doing away and get ready, this time without the levity in my voice. Kimmy then stepped out of the bathroom and asked why I was in such a hurry, and at that moment, I made a decision I still regret today.

"I just...want to get an early start. We have a lot of ground to cover. And I'm super hungry."

I thought back to that night at her parent's house, of the fear in Kimmy's eyes. She had been more afraid than anyone I'd ever seen, and it was because of a predator, someone invading her life. I made what at the time seemed like the selfless decision to spare my wife that same fear, and I didn't tell her that the person who had broken into our vehicle and stolen our daughter's art portfolio had also followed us to the motel.

But then, as Kimmy turned to pack up her things, the cocktail of fear, hurry, worry, and anger swirling around in my head settled for a moment. It settled long enough for me to realize something.

It's there to keep heat and air conditioning in, and to keep leaves and snow out.

The rubber strip along the bottom of the door to Room 3 of the Whitmore Motel would make sliding something as delicate as a piece of paper underneath the door impossible.

Whoever was responsible had been inside our room while we slept.

Three

I

My family and I were out the door in about fifteen minutes. I knew Kimmy could tell something was wrong, but I played it off as excitement for the next part of our trip. After the kids were buckled into their seats and Kimmy and I got into ours, I lingered in my seat for a moment, just looking at the door to room 3 of the Whitmore Motel.

"You okay?" my wife asked as she settled into her seat.

"...yeah. I think I left my...I just feel like I'm forgetting something. You sure you got everything? I'm just gonna do a once over quick." I got out of the car without waiting for an answer and walked back to the room.

I unlocked the door and went inside, leaving it open behind me. To be convincing, I pretended to search all over the room for any items we might have forgotten. After I spent what I considered adequate time building my ruse, I turned towards the connecting door next to the dresser - my true purpose for reentering the place I was more than prepared to leave.

The door seemed more ominous now, even in the daylight. It felt like it was radiating a certain darkness as if the room on the other side that I'd seen with my own eyes the night before had been switched with some chasm of unknown terrors that threatened to swallow me whole if I opened the ingress to it.

What the entryway implied made my stomach turn. Images of a man cloaked in shadow, standing at the edge of the bed our children were in, looming over them with a sickening, satisfied smile on his face seared themselves in my mind's eye and brought with them a wave of nausea.

Until this moment, my brain had been doing somersaults trying to convince myself that I was wrong, that a piece of paper could be slid under the door after all. This, of course, would still leave us with a person who had followed us to the motel and left my daughter's drawing as some kind of sick joke, but at least we wouldn't have been at his whim as we slept, entirely vulnerable to whatever revolting proclivity he might want to subject us to.

I put my hand on the knob of the connecting door and took a quick breath, silently praying to whatever higher power would listen that the door be locked. I knew that even if it was locked, it didn't mean that no one had gone through it; anyone who had could just as easily have locked it again when they left. But I needed something. I needed something to cling onto to convince myself that my morbid thoughts weren't true, weren't necessary.

I twisted the knob and pulled, and I found myself staring into the abyss that was Room 2. It sat exactly as it had nine hours earlier, only now, the room's contents sent a chill down my spine. It was set up identically, only reversed, and with one bed instead of two. I wondered if the mysterious art fan had sat on the bed and stared at the wall, imagining us on the other side until he worked up the nerve to cross the threshold and invade our space.

Another part of me wondered if he second-guessed it at all.

I shut the connecting door and walked back out of the room, content to never return. I returned to the car and did my best to hide the shaken feeling coursing through my bones.

"Find anything we forgot?" Kimmy asked.

"Nope, I'm just being weird," I replied with a disingenuous laugh.

"What a unique, strange experience that must be for you." My wife's tone was sarcastic, and a smile crept across her face. I returned the smile and offered a sarcastic laugh, and that small moment made the horror I kept to myself a tiny bit easier to deal with.

I reversed out of our parking spot and pulled up to the office. Since a different car was parked next to the one I pulled into, I assumed that the man who had sold us the room the night before wouldn't be there. As I walked in to return the key, I found myself dreading the prospect of mentioning to Kimmy what I suspected had happened in our room the night before.

I knew that my wife would find out if I had to stand inside explaining everything that had happened the night before to whoever was working the counter. If that happened, I would most certainly come under fire for attempting to hide it, and rightfully so. But that wasn't nearly as dissuading as the prospect of dealing with the elder Officer Billings, who had shown us no hospitality when all this had started.

Ultimately, it was the girl sitting behind the counter, a girl who looked no older than seventeen and exhibited all the disinterest inherent in a young lady her age, that made me drop off the key, thank her and leave the Whitmore Motel forever.

II

The rest of our trip went without incident.

We spent another five days zigzagging around the country, heading as far north as Chicago, then traveling to Boston, then taking our time down the east coast until we finally reached Orlando, Florida. We spent three days at Disneyworld and another three at Universal Studios, enjoying all the rides and attractions that stood within its magical castle walls.

I worried about the events in northern Kansas less and less as the days went on, and the feeling in the pit of my stomach gradually got smaller. Although that uneasy notion never entirely dissipated, the idea that this was an isolated incident slowly started to grow and overtake it. I knew that what had happened was a very serious, very terrible thing, but it began to appear as though we'd left it behind when we drove away from that small town.

Because we'd taken a route through the Midwest on our way to Florida, we resolved to drive through the south and see all that the region had to offer on our way back. For the next seven days, we traversed the lower United States, making stops in Georgia, Alabama, Mississippi, and an especially fun stop in Louisiana. After stopping in Texas and New Mexico, we made the final stretch home, something that, despite all the fun we'd been having, all four of us were ready to do.

III

As we turned down Tanglewood Drive and our house came into view, that familiar feeling of worry, that ball of anxiety, returned to the pit of my stomach. Even still, I knew that I was being irrational. Doing something to terrify a family in an unfamiliar town was one thing; it would be an entirely different level of madness to go to their home halfway across the country to continue their campaign of fear. I pushed that nervous feeling out of my mind and laughed a bit on the inside at how ridiculous I was being.

"We're home!" I announced. The kids replied with quiet cheers. "I was talking to your mom, guys. I don't know what your plan is now that we're back. Where are you gonna live?"

Katie and Alex laughed harder than I expected. While they'd certainly had fun on our month-long trip, their readiness to get back home grew more and more on the final days of it.

"Dad!" Katie jokingly whined.

"You guys can stay with us, I guess," Kimmy added. "But you're gonna have to get jobs and start helping out around here. No more free rides!"

The clock read **4:43 P.M.** as we pulled into our driveway to the music that was my family's laughter.

Kimmy started putting together a quick dinner while I unloaded the car. I hauled the suitcases inside and reveled in the familiarity and warmth of the place I was at my happiest. As I stood in the foyer, I looked to my right and saw Katie already setting up shop at the coffee table in our living room while straight ahead, my wife bounced around the kitchen.

"Daddy, can we go outside?" I heard Alex's meek voice call out. To my left were the stairs leading to the second floor, at the top of which stood my son.

"We're gonna eat soon, bud. Go hang out with your sister till dinner's ready," I called back up to him, then turned my attention to his sister. "Kate Austen from Lost, you wanna put something on TV? Something your brother likes too?"

Katie looked up at me and nodded with a smile on her face, then stood up to get the remote. I continued bringing our things in from the car, and after two more trips, a thought popped into my head - I needed to get our mail. I'd asked our next-door neighbors, Ben and Amanda, to get our mail while we were out of town rather than having the post office stop our mail and restart it when we returned, which the couple graciously agreed to do.

I walked over to their house and rapped my knuckles against the door a few times. After a moment, the door opened, and before me stood Amanda.

"Oh my god, hey!" the short, blonde woman of thirty said, opening the door and inviting me in. "How was your trip?"

"Good, good, it was great. We went all over the place, spent some time at Disney and Universal. I think we hit like fifteen, sixteen states, something like that. Pretty much the whole lower half of the country. It was awesome."

"That sounds amazing. I'm trying to get Ben to take time off work to go visit my sister in Hawaii."

"Ah, that's where I wanna go next. Kimmy's been there a bunch of times. I told her she has to take me there next time."

"Hey, welcome back!" A deeper voice called out. I turned my head and saw Ben walking down the hallway toward his wife and me. He reached his arm out and I met it for a handshake. "Trip was good?"

"Yeah, it was a lot of fun...glad to be home, though."

"It's always like that, right?" Amanda asked rhetorically.

"It definitely is. I think two weeks is a good time limit for a trip. Three weeks tops if you're somewhere really good. I get like...anxious being away from real life for so long," I replied.

"Same for me," Ben chimed in. "I'm always thinking about things I have to do when I get back and things I didn't do before I left."

"Right, right."

"Ah, so you probably want your mail," Ben said as he turned and headed toward their kitchen.

"So, everything was good while we were gone?" I asked Amanda. "Cats were good? Didn't see anyone skulking around our house, figuring out ways to break in and steal our millions?"

Amanda laughed. "Nope, everything was quiet and boring around here, as usual. And your cats were adorable as always!"

"Boring and quiet is good," I laughed.

Ben returned a moment later with a small stack of envelopes and two catalogs, which he handed me.

"There you go, sir," he said.

"Thank you, guys, so much. This was a huge help, seriously."

"Oh, stop. It was nothing." Amanda brushed off my thanks as she linked her arm with her husband's.

"Well, if there's anything you guys ever need, you know not to hesitate," I insisted. I truly was appreciative of their favor; Ben and Amanda had always been wonderful neighbors, with whom Kimmy and I had a lot in common. The environmental engineer Ben had a comic book habit nearly as severe as mine, and our wives bonded over their nearly identical political ideologies.

"We should all get dinner one of these days!" Ben suggested. "And we'll definitely have to continue the Sunday night tradition when Thrones starts back up."

"Oh, I'm counting down the days," I replied.

"Tell Kim we say hi!" Amanda announced as I turned around to head out the door.

"I definitely will!" I smiled. "Have a good night, guys. We'll see you soon."

As I headed down the walkway and turned onto the sidewalk towards our house, I flipped through the envelopes. Most of it was junk mail, something I was expecting considering Kimmy and I do most of our important correspondence via email. But one envelope in particular caught my eye.

It was a plain white envelope labeled 'the nice family' in handwriting, just barely legible enough to read. What I noticed more than that, however, was the fact that there was no return address.

My heart sank to my stomach as I stopped at the end of our driveway and tore at the envelope in a mixture of confusion, fear, and rage. Once it was open, I pulled out two pieces of paper. One was a letter-sized piece of white paper folded in thirds, and the other was an index card, on which was written by the same hand as the envelope:

I like your house. The girl is vary good at pichures.

As the concrete beneath me seemed to give way, I felt bile travel from my stomach to my throat. I suddenly felt eyes on me. I looked around, and it now felt like behind every corner, inside every car, was the person responsible for this. Feeling exposed, I quickly shuffled up my driveway on wobbly legs until I was behind our car.

Tucking the man's message between my index and middle finger on one hand, I then unfolded the larger piece of paper and instantly recognized what it depicted.

Another of Katie's drawings, this one done in crayon nearly six months ago. It was a portrait of a black and brown puppy, the one that Katie had been saying she wanted for the past two years. The dog most closely resembled a German Shepard, and in this rendition, it sat happily on bright green grass with its tongue hanging out of its mouth, which itself was curved ever so slightly upwards in a hint of a smile.

The addition to this picture was the same smiling stick figure, much smaller than the dog itself, and the words **GOOD DOGGY**.

IV

I stared at the drawing for a moment that felt like an eternity, then quickly shoved it and the index card back into the envelope, tucked it in the back of my pants, and pulled my shirt over it. I took a few breaths, quickly cycled through the rest of the mail to ensure there were no more surprises, and headed back inside. Kimmy was tending to a pot of macaroni and cheese on the stove when I entered the kitchen and dropped the mail on the counter.

"Did you get everything inside?" my wife asked with a smile.

...

I almost immediately became lost in some morbid thought and stared out the sliding glass door that led to the backyard.

"Hey," she said, snapping me back to attention. "Is your secret wife out there again?"

"Yup! You caught me." I played off my worry as best I could. "Sorry, no, I just went over to Ben and Amanda's and got the mail. They say hi."

"Oh, nice. If you wanna leave the rest of the stuff in the car, I can get it later, as long as we have everything we need in."

I walked up behind Kimmy and put my hands on her hips, then planted a kiss on her cheek. "Nah, I got it. What kind of husband would I be if I ordered you to cook me dinner and empty the car? Now finish cooking my dinner, woman."

Kimmy quickly shoved her backside into my groin, and after I winced at the sudden attack, we both laughed.

"I'll be right back," I said as I finished laughing and walked towards the front door.

Once back at the car, I stood at the open trunk and gazed at the remaining luggage with the same blank stare I'd exhibited in the kitchen only moments earlier. I didn't know what to do.

On the one hand, something had to be done. This person who'd broken into our car in Kansas had apparently used information gleaned from what I suspected to be our vehicle's registration to come to our home. On the other hand, going to the police would almost certainly make my wife aware of my deception. This had snowballed into something in what felt like the blink of an eye, and it was eating away at me.

This was turning me into someone I did not want to be, and it was making me do something I absolutely did not want to be doing.

Four

Then

I sat in the chair next to the door in the Intensive Outpatient room at Roger's Memorial Hospital. The room was populated entirely (aside from the two counselors) with others like me - addicts, people seeking help for their mental health. Even still, I felt exposed, targeted. Next to me sat a young woman named Jocelyn, who had already been in the program for the previous two weeks and had done her best to introduce me to people who had also started before me.

I'd been introduced to Kyle, an opiate addict like myself, who displayed a temper nearly as short as my own, though he lacked my learned ability to distract from that rage with near-flawless manners. There was Sarah, who was in the program for help with an eating disorder tied to various mental health issues. There were others that made impressions, others that didn't, and more still who would come and go over the next six weeks.

But in the corner, next to the window, with a sketchbook open on her lap and a disdain for having to talk to anybody, was the most beautiful woman I'd ever laid eyes on, a tan-skinned Filipino artist with her long brunette hair hanging wavily past her shoulders, sitting pretzel-style in her chair in leggings and a top decidedly more fashionable than the highlighter yellow hoodie I was sporting in a misguided effort to quell the remaining cold sweats I was experiencing from detox.

As Jocelyn went around the room quietly pointing everyone out to me, she nodded to the quiet girl in the corner who had started the program the previous day, and a statement rose from my throat with no input from my brain:

"Holy shit, I'm going to marry her."

In retrospect, I must have sounded like a grade-A creep at that moment, not to mention wildly inappropriate given the setting. I hadn't intended to say it out loud; it was just a thought that had materialized in my mind with such force that it needed to be put out into the world.

My first day in that program saw me introduce myself to the group as a bipolar heroin addict with thirteen days clean. In the coming weeks, I would reveal that I had been a drug dealer, that I had been paid to hurt people and lied and stolen to get by, and that now, after finally deciding to get clean, I was broke and living at my mother's house.

All of my baggage, my entire past, was laid out in that room over that month and a half. My darkest secrets, my most shameful memories were put out into the open alongside those of everyone else, including the girl in the corner, Kimberly Hill. So when it came to her last day in the program, my second to last, she and I knew things about one another that not even our closest friends knew. And when I bashfully asked her to include her phone number when signing a painting she'd done for me, she did so knowing all the worst things about me.

I made good on my quiet, corny proclamation to Jocelyn: I married Kimmy.

It's because of that openness that I always felt our relationship worked; at least on my end, I had never lied to her, save for very infrequent small, inconsequential things for various reasons. This was the first substantial thing I'd ever kept from the woman I loved, and it was eating me up inside. I knew she deserved to know, and while a factor, the prospect of the fight that would surely arise wasn't the primary reason for my continued duplicitousness, nor was the primary reason for sparing my wife from a situation that could trigger memories of the most painful, traumatic time in her life.

I didn't want to admit that the streak was over. I didn't want to have to admit to Kimmy that I'd deceived her in a matter of such importance. It was selfish.

It was wrong.

Five

I

The day after we returned home and I found the note and picture amongst our mail, I told Kimmy I was going to the comic store, which I indeed was. I left out that I was going to the police station first. I had hidden the envelope and the drawing that was slid under the door of the Whitmore Motel under the seat in my car, and before I pulled out of the driveway, I reached under and retrieved them.

They sat on the seat next to me, and as we drove, they seemed to mock me. The person behind the intrusion of our motel room and this envelope's hand-delivery to our home was out there somewhere, walking around, smiling at the fact that I was so paranoid, so nervous, so impotent in my ability to do anything about it. That thought caused anger to temporarily overlap the anxiety, a feeling that, for a long time, I was more comfortable with being enveloped in.

I pulled into the Walnut Creek Police Department parking lot shortly after 1 pm. The three-story building loomed over me as if to taunt me, to shame me for the hole I'd been digging for myself. The air had that distinct, ineffable smell of summer, which offered a pleasant, albeit brief, reprieve from the nausea that had been terrorizing me.

My legs felt like they weighed a thousand pounds each as I walked across the parking lot and into the police station. Behind the bulletproof glass at the front counter sat a young male officer on the phone, who signaled for me to wait with his index finger. Further back into the police station were several offices, some occupied and others empty, and various law enforcement officials all walking around with determination in their eyes.

My hand trembled lightly as I gripped the evidence and stood awkwardly, waiting for the officer to finish his call. I tried to formulate what I was going to say in my head. I didn't want to stumble over my words; misplaced anxiety was causing me to worry about the police thinking I was lying. I tried to paint a picture of an ordered checklist in my mind, one that I could refer to as I explained what was going on.

"Can I help you, sir?" a voice called out, snapping me back to attention.

I looked up and saw the officer at the front desk no longer on the phone, now writing something down on a piece of paper. I took a few tentative steps forward and set the papers down. A silver name tag identified him as Officer Morris.

"I need to talk to someone...I think my family is being stalked. Or my daughter, I mean."

The officer didn't skip a beat.

"Can I have your name, please?"

"Yeah, Botic. Nick—Nicholas Botic."

"One moment," he said. He then picked the receiver of his phone back up, hit three buttons, and waited. "It's Morris. Would you have whoever's up next come up front? Yeah...yeah, name is Botic. Thanks."

I appreciated the urgency with which he responded to my issue. I was hesitant to go to the police; even beyond my foolish decision to keep the situation from my wife, I simply couldn't imagine what they could do for us.

"A detective will be right out, sir. He'll be coming from this door on your right, here." Officer Morris pointed to the door of which he spoke. I thanked him and walked over to a bank of uncomfortable-looking plastic chairs, only to pace alongside it. After about ten minutes, the door opened, and a detective ushered me through it.

II

Detective Hume was a man who might have been a model in his past life but was about thirty years and thirty pounds past that opportunity in this one. He attempted to hide his less-than-healthily maintained beer belly, making the buttons of his yellow-brown dress shirt work a little harder than they wanted to, but all things considered, he was remarkably in shape for a man of nearly fifty. Spots of silver tinted his full head of black hair, and his face seemed to be successfully repelling the attack of wrinkles that typically waged war on someone of his age.

He introduced himself as Detective Brian Hume and shook my hand with a firm but welcoming grip. He led me through the maze of cubicles to a small office nestled in the back corner of the station. As the detective shut the door behind him and walked around me to his desk chair, I took stock of his office.

His large, ornate desk occupied a great deal of the area. Atop the oak behemoth were a number of framed photographs, all of them featuring the same older woman and three young girls, whom I presumed to be Hume's wife and children. The five-drawer file cabinet in the corner stood nearly to the ceiling and showed the wear and tear that comes with being a veteran of a police station.

There was a kind of organized chaos about Hume's workspace; there were numerous stacks of paper piled up haphazardly all around the office, but I got the impression that Hume knew precisely what was in each of them.

"What can I do for you, Mr..." the detective started our conversation.

"Botic."

"Botic," he repeated, committing my surname to memory.

I spent the next few minutes giving Detective Hume the rundown of my family's predicament. He sat and listened intently, all the while jotting down notes and asking me to clarify things when necessary. When I reached the point of our plight that saw me walking into the police station to have this very conversation, Hume sat back in his chair and audibly sighed while interlacing his fingers over his gut.

"Well...that's a new one," he said, with a hint of exasperation in his voice.

I couldn't help but offer a monosyllabic ha. "So I'm guessing you've never dealt with anything like this?"

"I mean, I've seen a stalking case or two, sure, but I don't know if I'd even call this that—no..." he pondered for a moment. "...no, I'm sorry. This is a stalking case. It's just that the guy stalking you, or, the guy or lady stalking you, they're just doing it in a really...kind of a roundabout way."

He paused as if waiting for a response, but I had none to offer.

"I'll tell you what," he finally said, flipping back to the first page in his notes. "Let me track down the number of this PD down there in Kansas, see if we can't coordinate. I'll tell you right now - this is some bizarre shit, I'm not gonna lie to you. Like I said, I've seen a few stalking cases, but this just...it sounds like more than that."

I nodded in agreement.

"But I don't wanna, you know...that's just my gut feeling. I could be wrong. Hell, I hope I am. What I'm gonna do, though, is I'm gonna get in touch with them down there, see if we can't try to make sense of this."

"They didn't catch the guy who broke into our car," I noted. "How are you gonna, like...what's your first step when you get in touch with them down there?"

"In cases like these, with no real leads or any suspects or anything, we have a few things we do. I think the safest bet--" Detective Hume sat back in his chair. "--you said it was a real small town, right?"

"It seemed like it. I didn't see a population sign or anything, but it definitely seemed like the kind of place where everybody knew everybody."

"Alright, that's good. That's a good thing. That means when I get in touch with them, I'll be able to get a few names, see who might be into this kind of thing, you know, if there's anyone down there who's a little off. Or, well, 'off' relative to a bunch of people from small-town Kansas," he laughed, and I reciprocated.

"Alright, thank you. Is there anything I can do?"

"Just stay vigilant. Stay aware. Make sure your wife knows to keep her head on a swivel, maybe sit your kids down and have the old 'stranger danger' talk. Just make sure you're all staying on top of things, you know?"

"Yeah, I..." my shame almost kept me from being able to verbalize it. "...I haven't told my wife."

"Well, excuse me for saying, Mr. Botic, but why in the hell would you do something stupid like that?"

"I...I don't know. She dealt with a stalker when she was younger. And this shit, I should've said something right away, but I didn't want to bring up all that past stuff, you know? And now it feels like I waited too long, so it's all just...compounding."

"Man, I've been a police for a long time. Between me and my three closest cop buddies, we've got seven ex-wives. You don't have to explain lying to a wife to me, alright? But a word of advice? Just fess up. The longer you keep up the charade, the worse it'll be when she does find out. And she will find out. You know she will."

He plucked a card from a small plastic holder on the edge of his desk and leaned down to write something on it.

"Take my card. It's got my direct line here, but I wrote my cell on the back in case you can't get me here and you need me, alright?"

I nodded as I took the small white rectangle from him and absentmindedly looked it over.

"We'll get this squared away, alright? I'm gonna get to work now. I'll keep you posted every step of the way, no matter how small."

I thanked Detective Hume and shook his hand before walking out of his office and the station proper. It's difficult to explain, but at that moment, a part of me knew that this was going to get a whole lot worse before it got any better.

III

The following week, I found myself in a state close to paranoia. Every creaking door, every halfway shady-looking person sent my mind wandering. I was in a constant internal struggle with myself over my selfish decision to keep everything that was happening from my wife. As much as I wanted to protect her from having to relive the memories of her past trauma, a more significant part of me wanted to tell her. Every day I found the words nearly leaving my lips, but my tongue's cowardice would push them back down before they could escape.

A week to the day after I spoke to Detective Hume, my family and I returned home from a morning at the park. As we stepped into our home, Katie and Alex both made a beeline to the living room, where Katie picked up the remote and turned on the TV. Kimmy headed to the kitchen to make lunch for the kids while I went to my office to get some work done.

I was calm at that moment. As I opened my laptop, the only thing on my mind was the work I needed to get done, relaxed from a calming morning under the warm sun with the people I loved most in this world. But two words shattered that false sense of peace. Two words reminded me of the infant horror surrounding us, a horror that could do nothing but grow.

"Hey, Nick…?" Kimmy's voice rang out, dripping with uncertainty.

I got up and sauntered down the hall towards the kitchen, my anxiety consuming me in a cold, sweaty blanket. When I got to the kitchen, I found my wife standing in front of the sliding glass door that opened to the backyard.

Once again my mind wandered. All manner of horrific thoughts passed before my eyes, invisible to the rest of the world because of my secretiveness, monstrous and violent creations of this elusive stalker left for us to find.

"Y-yeah?" The word tried to stay hidden, but I managed to push it out. And that's when I heard it.

Yip! Yip, yip!

My brow furrowed as I stepped beside my wife and peered out into the backyard. There, bouncing and rolling around in the grass, was a brown and black German Shepard that looked to be a year old at most. Bile crept up my throat as I stood next to Kimmy, a sour blend of fear and hatred and unspoken truth. The words nearly began pouring out, the full explanation of everything that had happened since our car was broken into in that small Kansas town. But before I could open my mouth, the excited shrieks of my children pushed them back down.

Katie and Alex pushed past my wife and me and all but pressed their faces against the glass. Outside, the dog sniffed around, its tail wagging happily as if it had finally found its home. Katie was nearly shaking with excitement.

"Did you get me a dog?!" she hollered, excitedly stamping her feet against the kitchen floor tiles.

I looked at my wife, who returned my precarious gaze. Again, just as the muscles in my throat began to operate, Kimmy stole the silence and replaced it herself.

"You guys, wait here," she said to our kids as she slid the door open, allowing a warm breeze to squeeze itself through the spaces in the vinyl screen behind it.

Kimmy and I stepped outside and approached the exuberant puppy. I advised Kimmy to be careful as I nonchalantly peered all around us, part of me hoping I would find some shady individual observing us from afar, but a stronger - much stronger - part of me hoping I wouldn't.

"Hiiii!" my wife spoke in a voice reserved only for pets as she knelt down and let the pup sniff her hand. And sniffed her hand it did, before it began licking her. I wanted to grab Kimmy by the shoulders and tear her away from the dog, imagining it suddenly baring its teeth, foam dripping from its mouth, somehow turned into a weapon by whomever it was that had left it in our yard. "Oh, he's so nice!" Kimmy exclaimed, looking up at me.

The dog rolled over and presented its belly, which Kimmy gladly began rubbing, her fingers gliding through the short brown and black hair that covered it.

"How did it get in here?" I pondered, despite already knowing the answer. I looked around us, at the brown wooden fence that surrounded our home, at the closed door in the fence, the lock of which was securely in place.

"Jumped the fence, maybe?" Kimmy suggested. "Dug under it?"

My eyes followed the ground around the yard, finding no evidence that anything had burrowed under our fence. Just then, the sounds of tiny feet shuffling through the grass alerted me to our kids' arrival. They brushed past me and dropped to the ground beside their mother.

"Guys...be careful," I warned again, despite knowing in the back of my mind that what squirmed around in the sea of green grass, relishing the attention it was being given, was nothing more than a normal dog with no ulterior motive.

"Can I name him?!" Katie spoke so quickly that the words nearly tripped over one another.

I didn't say anything. My mind was halfway across the country in the parking lot of a small diner in the backwoods of Kansas.

"Sweetie, we don't know if he belongs to someone else. We don't want another family to be sad because they lost their puppy." Kimmy spoke with a soft tongue, the kind of tone of voice usually reserved for delivering bad news to a child, but also with a whisper of hope. My wife looked up at me with the eyes that had always had the strange power of bending me to their will, and I knew that if this dog entered this yard without an owner, it would enter the house connected to it with one. "But if we find out that he doesn't have a home..." she trailed off.

"We'll see." I relented, swallowing the true reason for my apprehension and storing it somewhere deep in the pit of my stomach. "We'll take him in and see if he's chipped...that's what we'll do first."

IV

"Well, this is a change!" Carrie, the veterinarian to whom we normally took our two cats, remarked upon seeing us with the black and brown canine.

"He was in our backyard!" My daughter blurted out. "He's just like the one I colored, but I don't have that picture anymore."

"Uh oh..." Dr. Carrie exaggerated her sadness at the loss of the picture she'd never seen in a way Kimmy and I appreciated. "I'm thinking maybe you can't find your picture because it up and came to life!"

Katie was delighted by the prospect. Dr. Carrie Simpson tucked away a few stray strands of brunette hair that had found their way behind her thick-lensed glasses.

"Can you lay on your back for me?" she asked the dog rhetorically, guiding it to the position she needed it in. "There's a good boy."

The gender of the dog hadn't occurred to me. I felt terrible, ashamed of my feelings toward it. I hadn't wondered at all if it were male or female; in my mind, it was nothing but a nightmare. But standing there with my family, watching the vet examine the gentle pup, I knew it wasn't a bad thing in and of itself; it was simply a pawn in someone's sick game.

Dr. Carrie continued looking him over while Kimmy - along with some interjections from Katie and Alex - explained how we'd come to have the dog in our possession. All the while, he wagged his tail and writhed on the table, carefully considering all of us. At that moment, I felt my feelings shift, a quick snap like an extra heartbeat.

I had been silently pleading to whatever higher power there might be for the dog to be chipped. That would mean we wouldn't be keeping him, but more importantly, depending on whom the owner was listed as, we would either learn who had been stalking us or learn that whoever that was had nothing to do with the dog at all.

But now I hoped the dog wasn't chipped. I wanted to make my family happy...and I wanted to show whoever was fucking with us that their plan hadn't worked. But perhaps more than anything, maybe I wanted to give the people I love most in this world something they wanted, an act that would perhaps alleviate some of the burdens of my deceit.

"Well, there's no chip..." Dr. Carrie said, to my conflicted delight. "But I did find something kind of funny."

Kimmy leaned down and explained to our kids what the dog not having a chip could mean, but being sure to clarify that it didn't necessarily mean we would be keeping him; after all, just because he didn't have a chip didn't mean he didn't belong to someone. To fully exhaust our options and welcome the dog into our family, we would need to contact the local Humane Society, post flyers, and make entries to local groups on Facebook. But even knowing all those things needed to happen, I knew in the pit of my stomach that there wouldn't be any results.

"Something funny?" I asked the vet.

"Yeah...there's a...a thing here, it looks like it's a scar, a light one..." she used both hands to frame a section of the right side of the dog's underside. I stepped in closer to get a better look. "It looks like it says--"

"Hi," I interrupted flatly, and I could feel the color drain from my face. "It says…'hi.'"

Six

|

Katie picked his name. We had done everything Kimmy had explained to the kids, put up flyers, made posts online, checked with shelters and the Humane Society to see if anyone had come around looking for a missing German Shepherd. Just as I'd suspected, no one had.

"Roscoe!" Katie called the dog over to her as she ran an orange marker around a large piece of poster board on the deck in our backyard. Kimmy sat in one of the deck's four chairs with her heels buried into the edge of the seat, with her sketchbook resting on her knees and a blue pen winding up and down and around, crafting an intricate design that had no proper form or reason.

In the almost three months that had passed since Roscoe had arrived, he'd become enamored with Katie more than any of us, which only made the entire situation sting that much more. But I couldn't kid myself. Roscoe made himself part of the family, and I came to care about him every bit as much as my wife and kids did. Even still, my subconscious waited for the other paw to drop. I felt as though this dog was doing exactly what the person who had "gifted" him to us wanted - acting as the centerpiece for the application of psychological pressure and keeping me on edge.

I found myself lying awake in bed some nights, wondering what the predator (if they could even be called such a thing) was doing. I wondered if he knew of my deception, knew that he wasn't terrorizing my entire family, only me. When I tried to picture the admirer of Katie's artwork, I saw little more than a vague shape of a thin man standing just past the point where some sourceless light stopped shining. He would open his mouth and smile a crooked grin, his decaying teeth barely visible, his eyes a jaundiced yellow.

He would be standing in the shadow, fidgeting, like he was about to jump out of my mind's eye and materialize in my daughter's room, looming over her bed with the most despicable of thoughts racing through his head.

But he never jumped. And the other shoe never dropped.

The time came for our annual trip to the cabin that had been bequeathed to me by my father when he passed nine years prior. Every part of me screamed that we shouldn't go, but nothing had happened since Roscoe had shown up in our backyard. The most stubborn part of my personality wanted to defy the fear that Roscoe's original owner was clearly trying to instill in me. So rather than putting into use any of the several excuses I'd conjured up not to go, I gritted my teeth and decided that I would keep my family safe no matter where we were.

II

The drive from our Northern California home to the cabin is an idyllic one. Much of the six-hour journey is spent on two-lane roads, surrounded by mountains and valleys and trees and bodies of water both natural and artificial. A long, winding road eventually takes us to the turn that leads straight to the tiny town.

Long Lake has a posted population of one hundred seventy-seven, but the area in which our cabin resides is almost exclusively used for vacationing. By this late in the year, I expected there to be next to no one there, if anyone at all. I was torn over this; on the one hand, fewer people meant fewer witnesses if the stalker decided to try something. On the other hand, anything out of the ordinary would be more readily apparent - at least, that's what I told myself.

The General Store, which connects to the lone restaurant and is run by the same people, is the only business that actually operates within the town of Long Lake proper. The employees for each drive the twenty-plus miles from the more populated surrounding towns (where, ironically, a good number of people staying at Long Lake go for grocery shopping and other activities) to come to work, and their dissatisfaction with that fact shines through with every syllable that passes their lips.

Our cabin, which was left to me when my father passed away, rests on the edge of the lake from which the town gets its name. It had sported the same hideous, weather-worn yellow-brown paint job since long before I first came here as a child. The matching shed sits ten yards east of the house, with a narrow dirt path cutting through the grass connecting the two.

As we turned from the main road on which the majority of the town's cabins are placed and onto the dirt driveway leading up to our annual retreat home, the first thing that caught my eye was the grass; it was taller than I expected. The length of time between our trips here had remained consistent over the years, but for whatever reason, the swaying sea of yellow-green seemed to stretch their thin bodies more than they appeared to have upon past arrivals. On the opposite side of the driveway, across a small plot of freshly mowed grass that sits between our cabin and the next, I saw a man whom I'd seen once a year every year since the very first time I'd ever come to Long Lake.

That man was Floyd.

Since I was a child, I have always admired Floyd. Whenever we would arrive, he would trudge across the grass and greet us with the same joke - Well, I guess they're just letting anybody up here! - and I would invariably laugh. That joke suddenly changed when I was thirteen, the summer after I'd recently had a growth spurt. "Jeez guys, there's enough trees up here, you didn't have to bring your own!"

As I grew into adulthood, so too did Floyd grow, only into his senior years. As a boy, I would often see our once-a-year neighbor bumbling about, fishing, fixing things in, on, and around his cabin, and later, playing with his grandchildren, but now as a man, I see that much less. Now, Floyd spends most of his time simply sitting in the rocking chair that acts as his throne on the enclosed porch on the face of his cabin.

I remember being afraid of that porch when I was younger. The screen that wrapped around the three sides of it only allows someone trying to look in to see vague shapes within, but whenever Floyd would see me peering apprehensively at it, he would pop out and say something along the lines of "Just me! I scared all the scary stuff away with this ugly mug!" while pointing to his head as he made a goofy face, which always adequately cured my fear, if only for that trip.

When Kimmy and I started bringing Katie (and then Alex) up to Long Lake, the "letting anyone come up" joke saw a resurgence in frequency as well as popularity, though as the years crept by, it took Floyd longer and longer to get across that grass to make it.

This year Floyd didn't cut across the grass at all.

As we pulled up to our cabin, we observed Floyd dragging a suitcase from his porch to his car, a vehicle I'd recognize if I were blind. It was three different colors. The front third of the sedan was an awful shade of yellow, the middle a pristine sky blue, and the rear third a terrible shit brown. I put our own vehicle in park and turned it off.

"Guys, you wanna go see Floyd, help him with his stuff?" I asked and was given an excited affirmation from the kids in return. We walked across the grass division, with Kimmy gripping the leash that bound the hyper, bouncing Roscoe, who seemed to be burning the built-up energy that had accumulated from the six-hour car ride with only a single ten-minute break.

"I thought there was a sign somewhere around here that said 'No Dogs Allowed'!" Floyd joked as we approached his cabin. "'Course, if that's the case, I better get, they might mistake me for a big ol' bulldog!"

My family and I all laughed, but Kimmy gave me a look that told me she was thinking the same thing I was - Floyd was in awful shape. He was never the most comely man, but from last year to this year, it looked as though ten had passed in between. He was frail; he walked as though the ground were collapsing under his feet with every step and had a slight tremble to him that I could tell he did his best to hide. But mostly, it was his face. The light behind his eyes had dimmed, and Floyd just looked...tired.

"Oh, he's a good boy, isn't he?" Floyd asked in the kind of voice you speak with when addressing an animal as he let Roscoe sniff and lick his shaking hand. "And I see that supermodel convention is back in town!"

Kimmy let out a boisterous "ha!". The sentiment was spot on, but she never has and will never acknowledge the objective fact that she is a remarkably attractive woman; the ability to do such a thing remained trapped behind a wall of insecurities that I silently vowed to dismantle, brick by brick, for the rest of my life. Although, my vows didn't feel particularly valuable at that moment.

"Floyd, what did I tell you? You keep talking like that in front of Nick and he's gonna start to suspect something," she laughed, wrapping her arms around the old man.

"Let him find out. I can take him!" Floyd replied, jokingly putting his hands up in a boxing stance.

"Oh, there's no way I'd even dare, Kimmy. Enjoy your new life," I laughed, wrapping my fingers around Floyd's feeble hand.

"Hi Floyd, this is Roscoe!" Katie suddenly blurted out. It was clear that she had been only barely containing her words while her mother and I greeted Floyd.

"Well, hello, Mr. Roscoe!" Floyd replied, but it was nearly cut short by the wet coughing fit that followed.

"Jesus, Floyd, you okay? You need some water?" I asked, taking a step closer. He pulled a black handkerchief from the breast pocket of his button-down shirt and finished the hacking flurry into it while his other hand waved my question away as if it were a persistent fly.

"You alright?" Kimmy asked again as the cough subsided.

"Yeah, yeah. Just a bug." Floyd presented it as nothing of concern, but I felt that if I were to have been able to see the handkerchief after his coughing fit ended, it would have been tinged with red.

"Where are your grandkids? They should be helping you with all this stuff." I pointed out their absence, looking past Floyd and at the collection of bags piled up just past the open door of the enclosed porch.

What little light remained behind Floyd's eyes was extinguished a little further yet.

"Eh, you know..." A follow-up cough acted like an aftershock to the first fit's earthquake. "They're...you know...they just think they're too old."

Despite how jovial Floyd was upon our arrival, it was apparent how devastating his grandkids' absence was for him. The time he spent at his cabin was what he looked most forward to every year, but when his grandchildren started accompanying him, that joy and anticipation increased a thousandfold.

But I understood. His grandkids were, if I was remembering correctly, fifteen and thirteen that summer, and I know that when I was their age, I felt the same way; they would learn with the benefit of hindsight how special their time up here was and how one week away every year may not have felt like much to them at the time, but it meant the world to their grandfather.

"I'm sorry, Floyd," I said. "Well, I know you're taking off today, but these two will be happy to keep you company next year," I said, tussling Alex's hair as he clung to his mom. "They don't have a choice. They're still our prisoners."

"Oh, I'm not leaving today. I'm just getting a few things packed up…" another brief storm of coughs interrupted him. "…just a few things I know I won't be using anymore this weekend. No, I'm gonna spend tonight and tomorrow in my favorite spot with my book, enjoy the weather, head back the day after tomorrow."

"That sounds like a plan. We'll be sure to keep out of your hair," I said as the kids started to pull us away, no longer entertained with the conversation (if ever they were).

"Oh, you're always welcome, you know that. So's this little fella." He winced as he bent down slightly again to scratch behind Roscoe's ear.

After helping Floyd pack the rest of his bags in his car, we turned back towards our cabin and made our way back to the car, at which point I depressed a button on the key fob. The tail lights flashed twice, and a quiet chirp sounded as the trunk began opening.

"You wanna get it opened up and get the electricity and water on while we bring everything in?" Kimmy proposed.

I agreed and gave my wife a kiss and a playful slap on her backside, much to her chagrin. I broke off from my family and headed up the side of the cabin towards the door while digging the keys to the cabin from my pocket. I became aware of my surroundings at that moment. The trees were alive with vibrant emerald accessories; past them, the sky shone like the ocean, with only the occasional weightless white ship sailing through it.

It was peaceful. For the first time in what felt like ages, I breathed a sigh of relief. Up here, I thought, I didn't need to worry. The location of the cabin wasn't something readily available, be it on documents or otherwise; it was just something that my dad had known and that I'd memorized as I grew up and went up every summer. Even the deed of ownership was in a safe deposit box at our bank. On top of that, I'd made sure we weren't followed on our way up (Kimmy had remarked as my constantly shifting eyes darted back and forth as though the rearview mirror and the road ahead were ping-pong paddles).

I dragged my fingertips along the faded mustard-brown exterior, bringing small flakes of the decades-old paint up in the wake. The wooden door of the cabin was solid, but it, too, had been ravaged by the elements. I felt at ease. I felt protected by the crisp autumn air, calmed by the gentle lapping of the lake against the dock behind the cabin. It was a—

The door was unlocked.

III

My heart crashed to the bottom of my stomach. It was impossible. I looked around; the ground in every direction was undisturbed save for the trail of footprints I'd left myself. A visible layer of dust had congregated on the screen door, on its handle, on the main entrance...on the doorknob.

I looked at my hand and found that some of the dust from the knob had migrated to my fingers and palm. I leaned in for a better look; in reality, it was impossible to tell, but at that moment, despite being inclined to lean toward the worst possible scenario, I thought it looked as though my hand was the only thing that had smudged the rusting brass doorknob,

I suddenly remembered the end of our trip the previous year. As we were pulling out of the dirt driveway, Kimmy blurted out, "wait!" and revealed that she'd forgotten her phone charger. I went back in to retrieve it from the wall outlet behind the bed, and as I went back out…

…I forgot to re-lock the door. If my memory of an entirely unremarkable moment from a year prior could be trusted, it meant that nothing was amiss, that my family and I were the only ones up there. I filled my lungs with that fresh lake air and held it there as I turned the knob and pushed the door open.

Sunlight snuck through the spaces between the blinds, making it appear as if the strips of golden light were busy roads crowded by the cabin's dense population of floating dust.

Everything appeared to be in order. Upon stepping into the cabin, to the immediate right is a long window that faces the lake, with a shelf running along its entire length just below it. To the left is the living room with its barebones couch/tv/coffee table setup, and connected to it is the kitchen. Along the far wall opposite the bay window are the two bedrooms.

I cut diagonally across the carpet and then the linoleum to the larger bedroom, which housed the cabin's fuse box on the far wall. I flipped the small metal door open and plugged in the fuse that provided the other slots the option to provide power to the rest of the building and then plugged those in.

Next came the water, and by the time that was done, there were only a few bags left to bring in. Katie and Alex were thrilled to stay in the bunk beds in their room again, laughing when I retold them what was supposed to be the cautionary tale of when I fell from the top bunk and split my head on the dresser, resulting in seven stitches. It didn't matter to them, in the way danger doesn't matter to kids (not that bunk beds are especially dangerous). It was a luxury they were only afforded once a year, so they loved it.

We sat down and ate a dinner of macaroni and cheese with bits of chicken and bacon sprinkled in, which, if you let Alex tell it, is the best meal the human mind has ever conceived. I remember sitting back in my chair as I swallowed the last bite from my plate, and I think that at that moment, I was truly free from the binds of fear and paranoia. My beautiful wife was joking around with our son, and their laughter was intoxicating.

As a joke, Katie ate the last bite and looked at me with a funny face, exaggeratedly chewing her food. I laughed, she laughed, and Kimmy and Alex laughed. Even Roscoe sat impatiently at Katie's feet and had his tongue hanging out of his mouth with what seemed to be the best rendition of a smile a dog can have.

There was peace at that moment.

There was contentment.

There was happiness.

IV

The following morning, we let Roscoe out to do his business. In (what I considered to be) another impressive feat for a dog we'd had for such a short time, Roscoe had fallen into the routine of sitting at the door when he needed to go out and offering us a "hey guys, I'm done" in the form of single barks until we opened the door for him to come back inside. This was no different at the cabin than it was at home, only there wasn't a fence here to keep Roscoe inside, so we attached a leash to a small post I'd impaled and secured into the ground in the center of the lawn.

After a quick breakfast, Kimmy and I discussed our plans for the day, then set about seeing them through. After getting ourselves and the kids ready, we took a trip into town. To save room in the car on our drive up we, as we did every time we visited Long Lake, opted not to bring a cooler full of food and other groceries with us, instead going into town and the nearby larger town (the same that the employees of the General Store come from) to do an extensive shopping.

That was first on our list. After getting what seemed to essentially be an absurd amount of bacon with some other foods to accompany it, we headed back to Long Lake, stopping at a gas station on the way to pick up a gallon of gasoline for the lawnmower. Once back in Long Lake, our final stop was the General Store.

I was almost certain that much of the inventory that the General Store kept on the shelf was wholly illegal for them to be selling. Lining the shelves were all manner of products that had poorly done logos of major companies on them; shirts with a crooked Game of Thrones logo, a set of plastic dishes with stickers featuring characters from Disney's Frozen, coffee mugs with stickers of the Marvel Comics logo or the company's characters. That's what it mostly was - regular items with stickers on them being presented as officially licensed merchandise.

It had worked on me for a few years when I was a child, the same way it had worked on Katie for a couple of trips, and the same way it was working on Alex now. He clamored for a notebook that was adorned with ill-placed Pokémon stickers they were trying to sell for six dollars. While Kimmy did her best to dissuade our son from this soon-to-be outrageous, frivolous purchase, Katie and I walked up and down the aisles, taking in all the General Store had to offer.

Aside from unlicensed officially licensed products of major entertainment brands, the Store boasted an impressive array of products one could purchase. Next to a rocking chair that had chips of its green paint flaking off it sat a short shelf with what seemed to be a collection of months-old magazines from a variety of people's homes and businesses, and next to those were individually labeled Ziplock bags of dog and cat food (and some with both, for some reason). Behind the counter, one could find a wall of cigarettes and cigarillos, seemingly randomly obtained bottles of liquor (with no liquor license anywhere to be found), and knives. So many knives.

We picked up two foam noodles for the kids to use in the lake, and when Katie expressed her absolute, unwavering need for some of the fireworks that sat on a small table just behind the counter, I relented and bought some, much to Kimmy's dismay. The woman operating the General Store that day was Colleen, a woman in her late fifties with gray hair that hung down to the small of her back.

Ever since the ten-cent Tootsie Rolls had only cost a penny, whenever I'd come to the General Store, it had been run by either Colleen or her father, Judd, but Judd had passed away four years prior. In keeping with tradition, their son Jedd was now the one to share shifts with his mother.

We made some small talk with Colleen, asking how she was doing, how her family was, and all the typical pleasantries shared between people who see each other once a year and who aren't particularly invested in the answers they get. She, like every year, remarked how we'd made it just in time, as she was getting ready to close the General Store until spring, and I, like every year, joked about how we'd come up specifically to patronize the Store before that happened.

After we bought the pool noodles and fireworks and the traditional single Tootsie Roll for each of us, we left the General Store to make the forty second drive back to the cabin. But as it came into view, something felt off. For a moment, I couldn't tell what it was; I just knew that something about it had changed between the time we left and now. What was it? Why did it seem like something shifted? What was

—

Then it hit me.
The grass had been cut.

V

It had been over three feet tall when we'd arrived the day before, but now it stood no higher than the soles of my shoes.

I panicked.

All of that previously alleviated dread came flooding back, breaking down the dam of comfort I thought had been erected. But at that same moment, I felt conflicted. Sure, the grass could have been cut by someone else, some random good samaritan doing his one good deed for the day. However, even if it was this elusive stalker, what had he done to us so far? Given us a wonderful dog? Taken care of the chore I was least looking forward to?

"Guess you got the gas for nothing," Kimmy remarked, naturally unfazed.

We all piled out of the car. Katie immediately took off towards the front door, not realizing that she wouldn't get inside without a key. As I handed the cabin keys to Kimmy, I glanced over toward Floyd's cabin. On his front porch, past the thick, obstructive screen that stretched around it, I could see his silhouette rocking back and forth in the chair in the corner.

"Hey, Floyd!" I announced my arrival as I made my way across the grass that separated our places. The rocking stopped and the silhouette rose to its feet, making slow, difficult steps to the rickety screen door on the enclosure. The door opened with a screech that seemed to echo across the lake.

"Two visits in one trip? I must have won the lottery!" he coughed into his handkerchief, a worrisome punctuation to the man's affable proclamation.

"Weird question for you. You didn't happen to mow our lawn, did you? Or see who did?"

Floyd denied having mowed the lawn and had seen no one else on our property, noting that he was a heavy sleeper. I left after he told me to accept the favor someone had bestowed upon us and that he needed to sit down and rest a bit longer if he was going to make his three-hour drive back home shortly after that. I said goodbye to him for myself and my family, and I couldn't help but think that that may have been the last interaction I'd ever have with the old man.

I headed back into our cabin and found my family getting ready for the rest of the day's activities. Once we were all packed up and dressed appropriately, we ventured out yet again. Much of the rest of the day was spent at the small beach just down the street from the cabin, one that I'd been frequenting since I was a boy. The water was dirty and cold, but it was Long Lake, so I looked past the drawbacks, as did Katie and Alex.

Katie was particularly excited since she was now a strong enough swimmer to make her way out to the raft that bobbed about a short distance from shore. Kimmy or I still accompanied her, of course, but this was the first time that she was able to swim out by herself with no floaties wrapped around her small biceps. As she, Kimmy, and Roscoe swam out to the raft, Alex and I sat on the dirty sand, having found a small space without crushed leaves and snapped twigs.

As we built a sand castle, Alex began regaling me with tales of the structure, that a king lived there with his queen and a prince and princess, but that another king, "a mean mean man" who wanted to castle all for himself, was sneaking around. He called this other man "The Stealing King." It was then that I heard rustling coming from the trees behind us. I couldn't be sure, but some part of me felt like I'd been hearing such sounds since we'd gotten there.

My wife and daughter jumped off of the raft, sending it careening to one side before they leaped and bouncing back into place once they'd launched. The raft had been there longer than my dad had had the cabin. It was oddly built; the frame was wood, with what I'm relatively certain were pieces of bicycle racks underneath it along the two longer sides of the weathered, oblong rectangle. The top was carpeted...carpeted...with a dark green overlay that had been ruined the first day the raft was open for use. Underneath, it was anchored by a long chain that connected to some weight on the floor of the lake, allowing the raft to drift back and forth and side to side without any occupants really even noticing as it happened.

Roscoe spent his time running in and out of the water, swimming out to Katie and Kimmy and back to Alex and me over and over again, even once jumping off the raft with Katie; he only got the opportunity to do this once, as it wasn't worth the considerable effort it took to get him up there.

"Daddy, are there animals here?" Alex's question snapped my attention back to him and our project. He too had noticed the rustling in the woods to our rear, and I could tell that his imagination was running wild with all manner of horrifying beasts. But only one such monster materialized in my mind.

I scanned the trees and bushes, in equal parts hoping my eyes would meet someone else's and hoping they wouldn't. But there was nothing there, at least not so far as I could tell. I turned back to Alex, who was looking up at me, and I realized I hadn't answered him.

"Yeah." I cleared my throat. "Sorry buddy, yeah, there's animals over there. Squirrels, rabbits, stuff like that. Maybe even a gorilla, a giraffe." Alex laughed and told me I was lying, to which I jokingly replied that I wasn't sure one way or the other but that if any wild animals gave us any trouble, we would just have Roscoe talk to them and get them to leave us alone.

The rustling in the bushes persisted for a while, but the rest of our day went by just fine. We packed up and left the beach, returning to the cabin around dinnertime. While Kimmy took the kids inside to get cleaned up, I stayed outside with Roscoe, building a fire. Soon after that, I cooked us dinner on that fire. Burgers, hot dogs, corn, all the mainstays of a meal cooked over an open fire.

As we ate, Kimmy pointed out that Floyd's car was gone; we were all a bit dejected that we hadn't gotten to see the old man off, especially with Floyd's wet, hacking cough acting as a kind of grim signal that he may not return.

Darkness swept over Long Lake as we ate, and by the time the sun had retired behind the mountains to the west, it was time for the kids' favorite part of coming up to the cabin: s'mores. Two years earlier, during that trip's designated s'more time, Katie had had the idea to put something other than the Hershey's chocolate we usually used in between the graham crackers and marshmallows.

We'd tried a few variations like Kit Kats, Crunch bars, and a few of the fun-size Krackels, but one of them stood high above the others: the Reese's Peanut Butter Cup. They quickly became the only kind of s'mores we ate.

After s'mores, we played a few rounds of the kids' favorite board game, Sorry!, and then it was time for bed. It had been...off-putting...turning into the driveway and realizing the grass was cut, but the more I thought about it, the less I worried. Thus far, this family had a "stalker" who had given us a dog that had quickly become ingratiated with our family, whom we all loved and who loved us. And then, after the gift that was Roscoe, this person had mowed the lawn at our cabin, affording me even more time to spend with my family.

I knew that this was still a dangerous situation. I knew that. But at that moment, as I lay in bed next to my beautiful wife, listening to the symphonies of the cicadas and ballads of the bullfrogs, the worry melted away. I closed my eyes and got the best night's sleep I'd had in ages.

VI

The following morning, I was the first to wake. Roscoe greeted me with a flurry of licks and circled my feet as I plodded to the front door of the cabin. Roscoe followed me outside and happily accepted the leash I attached to his collar. Kimmy had seemingly woken up when I did, and after she brushed her teeth, she started breakfast.

It was more than I had been expecting. The kids awoke to a breakfast of pancakes, eggs, bacon, sausage patties, and hash browns. Katie drew in her sketchbook as she ate, and for the first time since everything had begun, her artwork hadn't twisted the pit of my stomach into a knot. It had been months since another drawing had been sent to us.

But then, as we all sat back in our chairs, our stomachs full of the wonderful breakfast Kimmy had provided us, the world came crashing down in a single question. Two words, my son spoke. Two words, and the cabin became a suffocating tomb. Two words, and I knew that things were never going to be the same.

"Where's Roscoe?"

He hadn't barked to come back in. It had been nearly forty-five minutes since I'd put him outside, and he hadn't barked to come back in. There was, of course, the possibility that he was simply enjoying the fresh air, but in the nearly three months that we'd had Roscoe, I had never seen him able to be apart from the kids for this long.

I slid my chair out from the table and walked on wobbly legs to the door.

"I'll g-get him." I choked out, the words feeling like acid on my tongue. They felt like a lie, but I didn't know if I was indeed lying or not.

I closed my eyes and opened the door to step outside. With my eyes shut tight, I closed the door behind me and listened for a moment. I wanted to hear him panting. I wanted to hear his paws shuffling through the short grass. I wanted to hear him amongst the whistling of the wind, the gentle crash of water against the dock in the rear of the cabin, the chittering of insects. I just wanted to hear him.

But I didn't.

When I opened my eyes, I nearly vomited. It took me a moment to understand the situation laid out before me.

Mostly there was red. Red stained the grass; red was splattered across the shed; red clumped at the edge of the dirt driveway. And red, along with brown and black, was piled up on the ground next to the fire pit.

My legs felt like they weighed a thousand pounds each as I took shaky, uncertain steps toward him. He had been cut from his testicles to his throat with what appeared to be a dull, serrated blade, judging by the rough edges of his massive wound. His innards had been removed from his body and hung from a nearby tree like tinsel on a December fir.

There were more wounds, but I can't bring myself to relate them; in truth, they hardly matter. He was butchered. The only thing that gave me one tiny shred of peace of mind was the idea that he must not have suffered; he would've been near enough to the cabin that we would've heard his...his cries as we ate breakfast. But there were no cries. There were no yelps. There was no struggle. I suspected that the range of the scene, how far the blood had traveled (and indeed the tree's "decoration"), had been staged afterward as if to add insult to injury.

I snapped into "take care of it" mode. I walked briskly back to the cabin, carefully opened the door so no one would see outside if there were near it, and shut it tight behind me. Kimmy, noticing Roscoe's absence, gave me a puzzled look. I closed the blinds and stepped over to her, leaning forward so closely that my lips nearly touched her ear.

"Get everything packed. We need to leave," I whispered as sternly as I could manage without letting the tears take control. "Do NOT look outside until I come back in, and do NOT let the kids look outside, okay?"

Typically Kimmy would balk at any order someone gave her, let alone one this brusque, but I think she understood the urgency of the situation, even if she didn't know what that situation was. She simply nodded and got to work. Meanwhile, I went back outside. As I neared the shed from which I planned to retrieve a shovel, I saw a note scrawled across the opposite side.

Big, red, dripping letters taunted me, screamed at me, chided me.

GOOD DOGGY :)

As the tears stung my eyes, I opened the shed and grabbed a shovel, then slung the circle of the long, green hose over my shoulder. The world felt like it turned in slow motion as I dug a hole near the tree line, yet I got through it exceptionally fast. I retrieved a rolled-up bit of carpet from the shed and rolled Roscoe up into it. I gently placed

Roscoe in the grave; his head hadn't been damaged in the brutal attack, and I could almost feel his warm breath against my chin as I pressed my forehead against his.

I wept like I hadn't since I was a child. Nearly everything that had happened until now could've been explained away, but this was more than that. This was an escalation.

I cleaned up the yard. I removed the innards from the tree and placed them in the grave alongside the dog inside of whom they belonged. I sprayed down the red grass, the red dirt. I sprayed down the message Roscoe's killer had left for me, for us. I did all I could to make the outside look as normal as I could for when I walked my wife and children through it. When I was finished, I stepped back inside and saw my family sitting impatiently with all of our belongings at their feet at the same table we'd been eating at only a short time prior.

"Um..." I cleared my throat as I joined them at the table. I wanted to jump out of my skin; we needed to leave, but I knew this must be addressed. "So...Roscoe, he..." a tear streamed down my cheek. "There must have been a big animal...out there. He—it..."

I turned to Katie, who was doing her damnedest to stifle the tears that were welling up in her eyes. I took her hand in mine as my own dam broke.

"Roscoe had to...he had to go to doggie heaven." Speaking it out into the world brought the weight of my message down on my family. We sat there for a short while to a soundtrack of our sniffles and whimpers. I held Kimmy's hand. Katie hugged her brother and comforted him. It was the most somber moment in our shared history, and when that moment ended, fear surged through me like electricity.

We carried all of our luggage out to the car, and before long, I turned the key and put it in reverse. As we neared the mouth of the driveway, I looked towards Floyd's cabin, and for a moment, I would've sworn that through the thick mesh screen that surrounded the front of his cabin, I saw the garbled shape of his chair rocking back and forth to a standstill as if someone had just gotten up from it.

But I couldn't be sure.

As we drove down the desolate street towards Long Lake's exit, we drove past a thicket of trees and a steep downhill decline. At the bottom of that hill, I would've sworn that through the obstruction of tall, brown pine bodies and prickly green hair, I saw a wrecked vehicle, one that was yellow in the front, blue in the middle, and brown at the rear.

But I couldn't be sure.

As we left Long Lake in our silent car, I took Kimmy's hand in mine and looked at her, and she at me.

"When we get home...we need to talk."

Seven

I

The first short leg of our return trip was set to a soundtrack composed solely of whimpers and the hum of the tires beneath us. That is, until Alex's declaration that he needed to go to the bathroom. I couldn't blame him; usually, we'd have ensured everyone went before we left, but our haste didn't afford us that luxury this time. I pulled into the gas station just outside Long Lake, put the car in park, and looked solemnly at my family.

"Be quick. Alex, you and I are going to the men's room. Katie, you stay with your mom." I turned to Kimmy and lowered my voice. "Do not let her out of your sight, not even for a second."

"What is going on?!" my wife yelled at me in a hushed whisper.

"Not now. We just need to get in and out and get home." I took her hand in mine. "I promise I'll explain everything once we're home. I'm sorry. I love you."

She looked at me, deciding whether or not she wanted to press the issue now. Ultimately, she relented. We followed my plan. Alex's hand stayed firmly in my grasp while we hurried to the back of the gas station and into the men's room, with my wife and daughter keeping our pace toward their destination, their hands intertwined.

Alex and I exited into the small alcove that separated the bathrooms first, with Kimmy and Katie emerging soon after that. On our way out, the cooler full of cold beverages caught Alex's eye, and it was only then that I realized we had brought nothing to drink for the kids.

I reasoned that they had just eaten breakfast, so there was no need for food, but in an internal struggle that lasted all of the blink of an eye, I thought that it wouldn't be a bad idea to get some drinks. I hurried them along, grabbing a handful of drinks from the icy refrigerators and putting them on the counter in front of a boy of maybe seventeen who proudly supported a head of greasy, ill-cut hair and a wiry mustache that couldn't decide if it truly wanted to grow in or not.

As I reached into my back pocket to get my wallet, my eyes drifted out the clear double doors, between sticker ads for Newport cigarettes and Monster energy drinks, and landed on our car as it sat idle at the gas pump closest to the building.

The world started spinning. I felt like I was going to pass out. Plainly visible on the windshield of the car, nestled under the right windshield wiper, was an envelope. I dropped my wallet and turned toward my family as I walked backward out of the gas station.

"Stay together. Don't move. DON'T MOVE!"

Outside, I peered left down the long two-lane road, then right. It was empty - no cars headed in either direction. I sprinted to the side of the gas station, finding nothing but a field of grass and distant mountains. I ran around the gas station once, glanced through the glass to see my family inside afraid - but safe - then turned around and circled the building a second time the opposite way. There was no one.

At the car, I kept my eyes trained on my family inside as I yanked the envelope from under the windshield wiper. The envelope was blank, with the fold tucked into the body of the envelope rather than licked and sealed. From it, I pulled the twice-folded piece of paper out and opened it to find, of course, another of Katie's works.

I remembered this drawing well; it was the last work of art she'd made before we left on our vacation, the cross-country road trip on which this nightmare had been born. I remember it because I'd happily put it up on our refrigerator, to Katie's delight, only for her to take it down the next day to put it in her portfolio.

The colored pencil illustration depicted herself, me, Kimmy, and Alex in our backyard at home, swimming in our pool. Like the others, this one too had a crudely drawn addition applied to it. In black colored pencil was a man who appeared to be hiding behind the fence with several multicolored wrapped gifts at his feet. Above him, a message had been scratched into the page by what looked to be a hand trying out writing for the first time.

We are a hapy famly :)

Instinct nearly made me crumple the paper in my fist, but I knew I'd need to give it to Detective Hume, so I didn't want to damage it in any way that might prevent him from catching the person responsible for all of this. I turned back to the gas station and stormed inside to find my family nearly shaking with worry and the wide-eyed attendant confused as to what was happening.

"Cameras!" I said before I even realized I was talking.

"Wh—wh--" the attendant, whose name tag read Billy, tripped over his words.

"Cameras! I saw the cameras on the sides of the building. I need to see the recording."

"I—they--" Billy tried again, and Billy failed again.

"Now!"

"They don't work! I—they don't work. I'm not supposed to tell anyone, the owner does--" he cleared his throat. "--he doesn't think it's worth getting them fixed because we don't get many people here anyway, so--"

"Of course they don't work." I pinched the bridge of my nose and reached into my back pocket, finding nothing but air. "Where the fu--"

"Here," Kimmy interjected, holding my wallet out to me.

I quickly snapped back to hurrying. I took out a twenty-dollar bill and slapped it on the counter in exchange for the seven dollars' worth of drinks we'd grabbed.

"Alright, let's go." I rushed my family out the door and followed closely behind them.

"You—your change!" Billy called out.

"Keep it! Sorry for yelling at you." The door closed with the ring of a bell.

Kimmy and I got the kids secured in the backseat while I checked the rear of the vehicle to make sure no one was hiding in it, snickering to myself that I was earnestly looking to make sure an urban legend hadn't occurred while we were in the gas station. In the car, I looked at Kimmy, trying to gauge what and how she was feeling; her face told a story of fear, confusion, and anxiety, a story I was all too familiar with by now.

I was worried. I didn't know what would happen when my wife and I sat down and I revealed my deception to her and told her of the phantom that was haunting our family. Would she scream at me? Would she divorce me? Would she not say another word to me? As these thoughts crossed my mind, I placed a shaking hand on the shifter and put the vehicle in drive.

I closed my eyes and took a deep breath, but opened them when I felt Kimmy's warm hand on my own. I looked down and saw her hand covering mine as it rested on the shifter, and at that moment, for that one brief instance, it was all okay. However fleeting it was, I found peace for a second. I looked at my wife with my eyes full of tears, and as the first broke free and traveled down my cheek, I lifted the folded drawing from my lap and handed it to her.

II

After we hurried them inside, Katie sat in her room to paint and Alex plopped down in front of the TV. Once they were situated, Kimmy and I went to our room. I went into my closet and pulled out a manilla folder, the one that contained the two drawings I'd kept hidden from her until now. I sat down on the edge of the bed next to Kimmy and apprehensively handed it to her.

"Tell me what's going on," she said, her voice void of any inflection.

I sighed and ran my fingers through my hair, my jaw clenching and unclenching and clenching again - the telltale sign of my anxiety.

"After--" The word caught in my throat like it didn't want to be set free. I cleared away the obstruction and continued. "After our car got broken into...in Kansas...they took Katie's folder with all of her artwork. They've been...there's been three of them so far."

Kimmy opened the folder and examined the two pieces of Katie's art that had been returned to us. She looked at Katie's depiction of our family, which I feared might be - understandably - shattered by the end of this conversation. She folded the first picture back into thirds and opened the picture of the dog, and I heard a barely audible gasp escape her lips. She covered her mouth as if she were trying to prevent another from crawling out, and her eyes welled up with tears.

"Roscoe..." she whispered.

"Yeah. I'm pretty sure he didn't just wander into our backyard. I think whoever...whoever did this gave him to us just so he could take him away."

"So—so there wasn't any 'big animal'?"

"No. There wasn't. He...it doesn't matter what he did to him. He wrote...that..." I placed a finger on the page where it said **GOOD DOGGY**. "...on the side of the shed."

"Oh my god..." Kimmy's voice trembled.

We sat in silence for a few moments, almost as if in remembrance of the dog, who had quickly become a member of our family but had been a pawn sacrificed in this one-sided game of chess.

"I'm so sorry." I barely managed to get the words out. Kimmy ignored the apology.

"These are copies," she sniffled. "Did he keep the originals?"

"No, the cops have them. I went to them as soon as we got back from our road trip. I don't know for sure, but..." my voice drifted as I stared absentmindedly at the first piece of the returned artwork. The feeling I got when I first realized that this person had been in our motel room returned to the pit of my stomach.

"Don't know what?"

"I think...this picture, the first one, of all of us, it might have been slid under the door in our motel, the one we stayed in after the car got broken into, but...there's a chance that whoever put it in our room...like...actually came into the room and put it there."

Another quiet gasp emanated from Kimmy's mouth. I could tell she was measuring every word I said, getting as firm a grasp as she could on the entire situation. We sat in silence again, this time for longer. Once again, I broke the silence with a meek apology, one that again went unacknowledged. Finally, Kimmy turned towards me.

"I get why you didn't tell me," she started. "It's not right, and you shouldn't have kept this from me. You should not have fucking kept this from me. I'm fucking mad at you, but I get it."

"I just didn--"

"I'm not some delicate fucking flower. I don't need protecting. I'm a grown woman. Since we've met, has there been any part of you that thought I was some fragile little thing that needed to be handled with care?"

"You're the strongest person I know," I answered, my words heavy with regret.

"And you're the strongest person I know. Yes, I was stalked. I was terrorized. It was a difficult time, but I made it through. And no, I don't like talking about it, but you don't need to tiptoe around it, at least not when it's something like...like this." She held up the papers to make her point. "This...this is bad. We need to be together on this. We need to keep our kids safe."

I felt it was more appropriate to offer a silent reply rather than a verbal one. Kimmy sighed.

"I get why you didn't tell me," she repeated. "But no more secrets. No more keeping anything from me, okay?"

I had been staring at the hardwood floor upon which my feet nervously bounced, but looked up to meet Kimmy's eyes. They were still damp with tears, but they'd taken on a new attribute: a kind of determination, a resolve to end this nightmare entirely. I shamefully nodded.

"You said you already talked to the police?" she asked.

"Yeah, this detective...Hume, I think his name is."

"Alright. Tomorrow, we're going to go talk to him, make sure all three of us are on the same page."

I nodded again and returned my gaze to the floor.

"Hey," Kimmy reached over and turned my head towards her own. "It's okay. I know you were just trying to keep me safe."

She leaned in and pressed her lips against mine, then took a slightly firmer grip on my jaw.

"You've done a good job of it for the last...however long we've been together. But I don't need a protector. We'll deal with this together."

I kissed my wife again and felt a surge of optimism flow through me. I had been so painfully nervous about that conversation, so anxious that it would blow up my family. What I had failed to take into consideration, however, was the fact that the love of my life was as inviolable a woman as there has ever been. I'd realized at the cabin that I was incapable of handling this situation on my own, and now that Kimmy was aware of everything, I was eager to finally get to the bottom of it and put an end to the madness.

III

The following day, Kimmy and I went to see Detective Hume. His first observation was that I'd finally told my wife about the situation and immediately informed her that he had urged me to do so as soon as possible, which Kimmy absentmindedly thanked him for. She was laser-focused on addressing this problem; being reminded of my deception was something she didn't have time for.

For everything we talked about, the conversation went by quickly. After Kimmy told Hume the story of her own stalker years prior, we gave him the picture that had been left under our windshield, which he promptly made a copy of for us to keep while, like with the others, he held on to the original. We talked about what this latest picture meant; had this man been spying on us while we enjoyed our pool at home those past months?

In my opinion, the pool was likely a stand-in for the lake, and the fence replaced a tree that this unhinged fuck had observed us from while we were at the small beach - I was reminded of the rustling in the trees that Alex and I had both heard that day. It was the only thing that made sense. We had spent a bit of time in our pool between the road trip and the trip to Long Lake, during which I was on high alert; I can confidently say no one was spying on us while we were swimming at home.

Most curious, however, were the gifts at the scribbled black addition's feet. Kimmy posited that Roscoe had been the gift, which seemed to be the only scenario that made sense, as we had gotten nothing else from this monster, just the amended drawings and our late dog.

We also explained to Hume that in our haste, we hadn't called the local police in Long Lake. He said that while it would've been better if we had, but that he would contact them himself and see if any information could be gleaned.

The detective said that he'd gotten in touch with the police in that small Kansas town where this had all started, but that they had been little help. I shared my opinion on the elder Bennett cop I'd dealt with outside Daisy's Diner, and Hume shared my sentiment, having spoken to the same man. Bennett had told Hume that the notion of the person who broke into our car and the person stalking us being one and the same was ludicrous. The Kansan lawman had listened impatiently as Hume laid out the case and the very clear connection between the break-in and the stalking, but when it came time for Bennett's thoughts, he had made a very thinly veiled insinuation that we were making the entire stalking situation up.

We left after Hume assured us that he wouldn't stop pursuing our stalker. As we exited the station, he told us to call him if we needed anything at all and clambered back to his cramped office.

IV

A week later, it was time for the kids to start school. Kimmy and I were, of course, apprehensive about leaving them without either of us for eight hours a day while the sick bastard who'd taken a dangerous interest in us was still out there, but we thought that that was what he wanted - he wanted us afraid. He wanted us to second-guess our every step.

Kimmy and I first sat Katie and Alex down and gave them a refresher course on the topic of 'stranger danger.' We hammered it home; typically, we would take a softer approach, letting them know that not all strangers were harmful or dangerous or had malicious intent, but these were typical times. We told them that their teachers and other school officials were the only adults they should talk to aside from us. And really, there was no reason for that not to be the case, anyway; they were only six and four years old at the time.

Then, on the first day of school, after we'd seen our kids off to their respective classrooms, Kimmy and I sat down with the principal of their school, a woman who looked to be not much older than us named Jenna Katzen. She sported an expensive-looking ombre haircut that accented her natural brunette with blonde. She wasn't much taller than Kimmy and wore a grey power suit. We regaled Jenna, as she insisted we call her, with the details of our recent tribulations, her eyes widening with every new aspect revealed. Once we'd gotten the principal up to speed, she sat there for a moment, pondering, then sat forward with an exasperated "wow."

From there, we developed a plan. Jenna herself would wait at the front doors of the school in the morning and, from a short distance away so as not to embarrass our kids, oversee our drop-off and ensure Katie and Alex got to their respective classrooms.

After school would be similar. Katie knew to meet her brother at a designated spot immediately after the bell rang. Once they were together, Jenna would again oversee their short walk to either me or

Kimmy outside. In the event that Jenna was unavailable to do what she'd selflessly volunteered to do, she would have her vice principal step into the role. Furthermore, unless given express permission from me or Kimmy (using a security question we'd conjured up during that meeting in Principal Katzen's office for verification), it was made clear that our kids would not be released to anybody besides us under any circumstances.

We left school with the genuine feeling that our kids would be safe while they were there. Principal Katzen had gone above and beyond her role as the head of the kids' school, something my wife and I were unspeakably thankful for. We'd needed something positive, and though it was born out of something negative, having this layer of security we otherwise wouldn't have had felt like a win.

V

Jenna Katzen kept her word. Every day that Kimmy or I dropped the kids off at school, we were able to spot Jenna and observe her as she monitored our children making their way to their classrooms. That act of kindness was a kind of cherry on top of the next peaceful few months, where no more drawings were returned, and no more pain was inflicted on us.

Then came winter break.

If I hadn't known any better, I might have thought that everything was over, that our stalker had decided we weren't worth the trouble and scurried off back to Kansas.

If I wouldn't have known better.

Like any children, Alex and Katie greatly anticipated Christmas, but our son was particularly fascinated by how elaborate the visual celebration was in our neighborhood. Our neighbors' houses were adorned with lights, some multi-colored and others plain white, giving them the appearance of so many glowing icicles. Roofs were topped with vibrant reindeer and elves and sleighs, and the yards were populated with plastic and inflatable snowmen of all sizes.

Because of our geographic location in the southwestern United States, we don't often get snow. So seldom, in fact, that our kids have never once looked out their bedroom windows to see the ground covered in a pillowy white blanket. They'd seen snow elsewhere, such as when we returned to my and Kimmy's hometown in Wisconsin and at Kimmy's parents' in Colorado, but the only white Christmas either of our kids had seen was the first Christmas after Katie had been born, which she, of course, had no recollection of.

But despite the trees shedding their oranges and reds and greens and yellows, giving the entire area a more monochromatic palette, we excitedly planned for the holiday. We decorated our house with lights the kids picked out and put up several plastic and inflatable characters, creating something of a wintery scene on our lawn. We even rented a snow machine, initially intending to give only our yard a light dusting to create a faux-frozen landscape, but ending up giving several houses around ours the same.

The tree was Katie's favorite part. We went to a lot that had rows and rows of spruces, pines, and firs, and, like with the directions, we let the kids pick which tree we got. The first tree they chose was an absurdly large pine tree that wouldn't have possibly fit in our living room, even with our tall ceilings. Their second pick was the one that ended up in our home, the one that, not long after, we were hanging ornaments on.

Every year for a Christmas gift, my mom got me an ornament, from my first Christmas to this one. In a funny coincidence, Kimmy's parents had done the same for her. Those ornaments were kept separate in a small plastic bin with a white lid, along with the decorations Kimmy and I got for Katie and Alex every year, continuing the tradition. Before long, the large number of ornaments my wife and I had collected throughout our lives hung next to the ones from our parents, and all of them were surrounded by a variable bevy of generic ornaments of myriad shapes and colors, and all of it accented by strings of multicolored lights. The last thing we needed was that which topped the tree and had been a mainstay of our decorations for the past four years.

"Kate Bishop, protégé of Clint Barton, otherwise known as the second Hawkeye, since your brother put it up last year, would you like to do the honors of putting our favorite angel on the tree?" I asked.

My daughter's eyes lit up, and she hurried to her feet with a flurry of excited acknowledgments that she did indeed want to do so. I reached into a bin, withdrew the wrapped tree topper, and began removing the paper around it. When it was finally free of the restraints that contained it during non-Christmastime, I handed it to Katie, then lifted her where she could reach to put it on top of the tree.

We stepped back and admired her placement of it. While many homes find their Christmas trees adorned by angels of biblical origin, we went a slightly different route. Atop our tree was a wax Castiel, the angel from the long-running television series Supernatural, of which Kimmy and I, and in the previous year (despite our best efforts) Katie, were huge fans.

"What do you think, sweetie?" Kimmy asked, bending down to meet Alex at eye level. "Think it needs anything else?"

"Actually, you know what I think would look great?" I interjected. They all looked at me. "I think we should take Cas down and let Alex be the tree topper this year. What do you say, man?"

Alex gave an exaggerated declination as we all laughed. For a good long while, that was the last memory I had of us all happy. The sound of that laughter replayed in my head like a never-ending playlist with only that one song in what I suspect was some kind of coping mechanism my brain had conjured up. I would've given anything to have stayed in that moment forever because what came next shattered any illusion of safety and security I may have had. It crushed the very idea of happiness.

Eight

|

It was two nights after we'd decorated the tree that I woke up shortly after 3 A.M., parched. I looked at my nightstand and just then remembered that I'd finished the soda I usually kept beside the bed for moments such as this, too tired to leave the comfort of our bed and get a fresh one. I groggily plodded my way through the dark hallway and downstairs.

The living room was cast in the stale yellow glow from the streetlights outside as they crept in through the spaces between the blinds, mingling with the reds and greens of the lights on our Christmas tree. Moonlight poured in through the kitchen window on the other side of the house. That moonlight guided me through half-closed eyes as I made my way to the refrigerator and grabbed another bottle of Pepsi. After taking a drink, I turned to head back upstairs, but as I neared the steps, I froze in my tracks.

I hadn't seen it on my way down, but now, the dull amber light glinted off of it just enough that it caught my eye.

There was something under the tree.

We didn't typically put gifts under the tree until a few nights before Christmas. Somewhere around the twenty-first or twenty-second, we would crowd the floor at the base of the tree with the presents the kids knew were from us, and then the night of the twenty-fourth, after the kids were asleep, we would add the gifts that were dropped off by "Santa." We'd done it that way since Katie was born.

That night was December eighteenth. There weren't supposed to be any presents under the tree yet, but there it was: a box covered in shining green wrapping paper with a red bow on top.

I knew I needed to move. I knew something was wrong, but my half-awake brain hadn't determined what exactly that something was yet. I stood there for a moment, soda in my hand, just staring until I finally snapped out of it.

The bottle of soda hit the hardwood floor with a dull thud as I dropped it and climbed the stairs two at a time. Alex's room was the first door on the left and was slightly ajar, as he insisted we leave it every night. I pushed it open, just barely catching it before it slammed into the wall.

Alex was asleep in his bed.

The first door on the right of the upstairs hallway led into Katie's room and was wide open. Did I leave it all the way open when I put her to bed? I couldn't remember. I barged in and found her fast asleep.

After checking her room for intruders, I sprinted to our bedroom and did my best not to wake up the kids as I yelled for Kimmy to wake up. She leaped out of my bed and followed my direction to get Alex and go into Katie's room, call the police, tell them our home was broken into, and wait for me. As she did so, I did a quick search of the rest of the upstairs and found nothing, so I went back to ground level.

I searched everywhere. Inside, outside, basement, garage. There was no one. No windows were broken, no doors were pried open. It was as though no one had been in our house at all. Only then did I realize that I hadn't even checked to see if whatever was under the tree was indeed from the art enthusiast.

I checked on my family, finding Kimmy standing guard just inside the doorway to Katie's room with a serrated Ka-Bar knife clutched in her hand, ready to strike. Alex had fallen back asleep next to his sister, who, as far as I could tell, hadn't woken up at all. I updated Kimmy on the situation: someone had been in our house, there was a "gift" under the tree, and I'd searched everywhere I could think of to look for the sick fuck who had invaded our home.

I went back downstairs and into the living room. The green paper seemed to stare at me, to taunt me. The corner of a small to/from card atop the box was tucked underneath the red bow, and though I knew Detective Hume would scold me, I went to the kitchen, grabbed a pair of latex gloves, and tore at the wrapping paper before I'd even read the card on top of it. Before pulling the cardboard flaps that waited underneath, I held the card up to the light.

"**TO: KATIE**" and "**FROM: :)**."

II

I shuddered in disgust. In the face of the truly unknown, the mind does its most sinister work. Against my will, my brain conjured up all the things that might await me within that box. Body parts, a piece of Roscoe he'd taken as a trophy, a bomb, or maybe it was something not outwardly grotesque or threatening but rather implied some horrible deed.

I pulled the flaps open, finding a large piece of folded paper and a small one on top of it. Without the slightest bit of surprise, the larger of the two was a piece of Katie's artwork - a painting she'd done of a princess entitled "Princess Penelope." By now, I was as used to this person perverting my daughter's passion as one could be, but this one stung in a way the others hadn't. I found myself wondering if our stalker was envisioning Katie as the princess and hoped against hope that he wasn't.

Because what made this one the worst yet, worse even than the image of the dog we had come to love and had ripped away from us, was the predator's additions.

The smiling watercolor princess was dressed in a pink ball gown with a blue tiara and matching wand with a star on the end of it. It was the product of a child's wonder, something pure, something innocent. And underneath it, in the same medium, was a pool of red. Off to the side, much smaller than the princess, was another crayon man in scratchy black, holding what seemed to be a knife with blood dripping from it.

I nearly crumpled the paper in my fist, but in my effort to preserve it as best I could for the police, I relented. I picked up the other, smaller piece of paper. Scrawled in the same awful handwriting as the other notes was a message:

Their are 2 becuse you will have to give 1 to the polise but I no you will want too see your wellcome :)

Under the papers was a small white cloth placed over something on the bottom of the shallow box. The fabric was clean and white; so far as I could tell, it wasn't covering anything bloody. I tore off the proverbial Band-Aid and found two videotapes, one right next to the other. My mind attempted to flood itself with a new wave of horrific possibilities, but it was thankfully cut short when there was a pounding on our front door followed by a loud "Police Department!" from just outside.

I quickly grabbed one of the tapes and shoved it into a drawer beneath the TV. I figured they were going to search the house, but I also figured they wouldn't look for an intruder in the drawer of an entertainment center. Similarly, I kept the note that would have otherwise informed the police of that second tape. I opened the door and let the police in, finding two squad cars outside, red and blue lights illuminating the neighborhood's houses.

III

The police did their search of our house, finding nothing. They weren't able to discern how an intruder may have gotten in - the doors and windows were all locked and undisturbed. Small puddles of water on the hardwood floor led from the foyer to the living room, remnants of snow falling from the shoes of our stalker. These were obviously of no help, but they did make clear to the police that what we were dealing with was serious.

The lead responding officer did indeed chastise me for ripping open the box that had been left under our tree, but in the same breath, commended me for having the forethought to wear gloves when I did. Another officer took my statement, and another yet bagged up the box, and Detective Hume showed up just as I was finishing up relaying what had happened to the young officer.

I gave Hume a quick rundown of what I'd just explained in detail, and after he took a quick look around our home, he assured us that he would be going to the station straightaway to log the evidence personally and learn what he could from it, including watching the video. As he turned to leave, he said that he would call as soon as he got a handle on this particular chapter of our developing ordeal.

The sun was rising as the last of the police personnel pulled away from our house, and after I closed and locked our front door, I headed upstairs.

"There's a tape," I said to Kimmy as she exited Alex's room after finally getting him back to sleep in his own bed. "Or, well, there were two, but apparently they're the same. I kept one from the cops. He wanted us to see."

Kimmy rubbed the tired from her eyes and looked at me with a face that screamed a shriek of exhaustion.

"Okay...no drawing, painting, whatever?"

I hesitated to relay the contents of the returned artwork to her but quickly extinguished the apprehension. We were in this together. Not sharing everything wasn't an option.

"Do--" It was as though my throat did its best to suppress the words from materializing. I cleared my throat. "--do you remember the princess picture she painted?"

Kimmy looked at me with knowing eyes.

"She, uh—the guy, whoever is doing this...it's that one, but he drew blood all around the princess and drew himself holding a knife. I mean, I think it's supposed to be him. I don't know."

My wife's face went white, but the color returned as she steeled her resolve and looked me in the eye.

"Let's watch the video."

IV

The pull-down ladder groaned and scratched a symphony of wood on wood as I lowered it from the ceiling in the second-floor hallway, and the warped steps bent under my weight as I ascended into the dark, windowless attic. The ray of light projecting from my phone brought to life innumerable specks of dust, all dancing around one another as they floated on the stale air.

As I pointed the light in various directions in search of a particular box, I suddenly felt very exposed. I was walled in on all sides, but it felt as though the eyes of some omnipresent being were trained on me, watching my every move. I suppose, in a way, that there was.

The feeling of being watched made me do a survey of the attic from my spot just inside the opening. I peered past stacks of boxes and bins to the far corners of the abyss, half-expecting to find a makeshift living area, a spot from which our tormenter operated, composed of old blankets and stained pillows, littered with empty chips bags and bottles of piss.

But there was no hideout. Of course there wasn't. There were just boxes and bins and dust and darkness.

After I calmed myself down, I resumed my hunt for the box I needed. I slid a stack of purple Rubbermaid bins off to the side, and there it was.

The DVD/VCR combo unit.

On top of the box it was supposed to be in.

My brain cycled through the possibilities, the most invasive being the one in which our stalker had been in our attic and found it, leaving it for us to find, but then I remembered that nearly two years earlier, I had transferred some old tapes to DVDs for my grandparents. I must have just not put it back in the box when I was done.

That had to be it..it had to.

I quickly grabbed the combo unit and made my way back down the weak steps and into the hallway, where Kimmy was anxiously waiting.

"Are you okay?" she asked, noticing my nervous disposition.

"Yeah, the..." I lifted the ladder and aided it as it folded into itself and ended its upward journey flush with the ceiling, a short string hanging down from its face. "...the VCR was out of the box...but I'm pretty sure it's from the last time I used it. I think I just didn't put it back."

"Few things would surprise me more." Kimmy's smile on that unbearably tense morning could've rid the attic of its darkness entirely.

We went to our bedroom, where I connected the DVD/VCR unit to the TV and apprehensively inserted the tape. I hit 'play' and sat down next to my wife, who had positioned herself to be able to see down the hall through our doorway. I absentmindedly held my breath as the tape began playing and a poor-quality image burst onto the screen.

The camera seemed to be on its side and remained stationary for the first thirty-five seconds of the video. What we could see was a poorly lit room with concrete walls, the rear and left of which were in the frame. The wall directly ahead had a filthy white sheet hanging over it, suspended from the ceiling like a rudimentary photography studio. When the video started, footsteps could be heard walking away from the camera towards the right, followed by rustling noises and grunts that preceded a dragging sound. Then, from the right of the frame emerged a girl roughly Katie's age, if not a bit younger.

I felt a hole open in the pit of my stomach and my heart plummeting to meet it, followed by the foul, acidic taste of bile crawling up my throat.

The girl wore a pink ball gown, stained with dirt and grime and god knows what else. Atop her head was a silver tiara, and a matching wand was loosely gripped in her small hand.

It was her.

The princess, inspired by Katie's painting.

"I don't wanna…" the little girl sounded as though she were in the middle of sobbing, something made only apparent by the tone of her voice, as the quality of the video and the distance between her and the camera was significantly obscuring any finer details.

"Shut the fuck up," a voice replied in a harsh whisper. "Do it. Do it."

Footsteps to the right of the frame gradually got louder, and the camera was then lifted by the unseen person to whom those footsteps belonged. The grainy image was straightened and lingered on the girl from the same distance for a few moments before the cameraman moved in closer. We were then able to see the "princess" up close.

Shoulder-length brown hair that appeared to, in reality, be blonde with a poorly done dye job was matted with a handful of patches missing, and what loose strands there were found themselves slicked against her face with tears. The parts of her arms visible below the puffed sleeves of the dress sported bruises caused by what I believed to be large hands gripping her much too tight.

"Do it. Do what you're supposed to do," the voice behind the camera whispered again, but this time it was much less aggressive. This time it was more...anticipatory, almost...giddy.

The girl broke into a full-on sob, and my heart shattered a little more. Tears filled my eyes and my jaw repeatedly clenched as I looked at Kimmy, just as a tear fell from her right eye and rolled down her cheek, but she didn't break her gaze from the television. A hand reached out from behind the camera and slapped the child across the face, making me wince and turn away in disgust. I looked back to Kimmy again, who had a steady stream of tears running down her face now, but her expression wasn't that of sadness or disgust.

Kimmy's face sported an emotion I hadn't seen her display with such intensity in all the years I'd known her.

Her face was that of pure, unadulterated rage.

"GO! Like we practiced." The voice's hushed whisper seemed to scream at the girl, and at that point, she reluctantly composed herself, curtsied, and began to "act."

"I...My name is Princess Penelope. I am—I was rescued by the prince, and now I live in a big—a huge castle to live happ—happily ever after." She began to sob again and recoiled as the man shifted his position, fearful of another strike.

"Keep...going." The voice sounded as if it were seething through clenched teeth.

The poor girl sniffled and continued. "My—my daddy was mean, though. He didn't want the p-prince to rescue me."

I felt like I was going to vomit. This child was being forced to narrate this situation as her captor saw it. It was morbid. It was bizarre. It was heartbreaking.

"But I w-wanted the p-prince to rescue me, and so he did, but my-my daddy was mean, and so now the pr—prince is going to show..." she trailed off, looking above the camera frame. The camera wobbles the two steps forward and suddenly points at the ground. Indiscernible whispering from the deeper voice of the cameraman is barely audible, and then the camera raises again and takes a half step back. "So now...now the prince is going to show mean daddies what happens to princesses when daddies are mean."

No sooner than the last words left the little girl's lips did the camera - and the man holding it - rush the little girl, who let out a single, solitary yelp as he...as the man began violently stabbing the girl in the princess dress about the face and arms and torso. The sounds of squelching flesh began emanating from our television's speakers and I leaped up from the bed to turn it off.

"Don't," Kimmy said, her voice teeming with fury. I looked at her just as my stomach's contents began to rise to the back of my mouth. "Leave it on."

I wasn't able to reply. I lunged to my side of the bed and reached for the small garbage can I kept on the floor between it and my night table, vomiting with an intensity I hadn't felt since I was in the throes of active addiction. So immediate was my body's need to represent the utter revulsion toward the video that I missed, with a good amount of liquid and bile landing on the carpet with a wet splat.

Tears streamed down my face as I sat on my knees with my head facing downwards into the garbage can, the room a quiet din of thuds, squishes, and grunts. When the noises ceased and were replaced by the heavy breaths of a single source, I looked back up towards the TV. The lens had been hit with blood, obscuring much of the left side of the frame, while the right side was a mess of pinks and reds.

The screen then turned blue, indicating that the recording had stopped.

Kimmy and I sat in silence for a while...a long while. I vomited again, and again, and then a fourth time. At one point, Kimmy broke down in tears. It was the most revolting thing either of us had ever seen. I finally rose from the floor, and I went downstairs to the kitchen without a word.

V

As I sat at the kitchen table, my phone rang with the name Detective Hume glowing on the screen.

"Hello?" I answered.

There was a momentary delay before Hume responded, and when he did, he spoke with a tone as sorrowful as it was brusque.

"You need to come in."

"Did you find something? Do you know who it is?" Of course, I wasn't expecting that Detective Hume would actually have learned anything as to the identity of our tormenter. I could tell by his tone that he'd seen the video, but I couldn't let him know that I had too.

"No, I—just...just come in. Can you come in right now? You and your wife?"

"We're not really wanting to leave the kids without either of--"

"Bring them." Hume cut me off. "We have a kid's area, or we can have someone sit with them right outside my office while we talk, so you can keep an eye on them yourselves."

"Alright...yeah. We'll be there as soon as we can."

I hung up the phone and told Kimmy we'd been summoned to the police station, and after getting the kids ready, we made the short trip. Hume met us in the lobby and led us through the bullpen without saying a word. As we reached his office, we saw that a number of toys, as well as crayons and markers and a stack of printer paper, had been set up on a small folding table just outside a large window through which we could see them while we talked to the detective.

We left Alex and Katie at the table under the watch of a comely young officer whose name, coincidentally, was Katherine, which she said was always shortened to Katie. Our daughter was instantly taken with the young officer, and if I didn't know any better, I might have thought that Alex had developed his first crush that day.

Once we were in his office, Detective Hume gestured towards the chairs opposite his own, and Kimmy and I saw in the same spots we had during our first visit. The detective looked pale, his hair disheveled, his eyes puffy and bloodshot. He melted into his chair, ran his fingers through his messy, thinning hair, and let his palm fall to his desk with an unintentionally loud thud.

"I watched—a few of us watched the video," he choked out.

Kimmy leaned forward, feigning hope. "Did it show them? Do you know who it is?" Her performance should have been brought up during awards season.

"Unfortunately not." Hume let out a heavy, exhausted sigh. "I, uh...I said I would keep you informed of every development, and as much as I wish I didn't have to make you aware of what was on that tape, you...you need to be aware of the kind of person we're dealing with."

I understood his hesitancy. If it were me in his spot, I would have likely said the same thing, verbatim. Kimmy and I looked at each other and then back at Hume with a manufactured curiosity accented with a very real, very genuine - and seemingly perpetual - worry.

"The video was...Christ..." Hume rubbed his eyes with the heels of his palms, cutting off the tears that had begun to form before they had a chance to fall. "The video showed a little girl dressed like...like the princess in the pictures that they left. And how there was that little drawing of the guy with the knife? The person, uh, filming, he...he stabbed the little girl...killed her, looks like."

We sat there in silence. Tears flowed down all three of our faces, and none of them were for show.

"Jesus Christ..." I broke the silence. "Did he say anything?"

"Just to the girl. He had her recite this...this speech, I guess, about how he was a prince and he'd brought the princess to his castle, but her dad was mean, so he was punishing her for it. The guy in the video, I mean. The dad she talked about...I'm thinking that's gotta be you, right?"

I didn't answer.

"Anyway, the point is that this guy is...he's more dangerous than we anticipated."

"So what are you going to do about it?" Kimmy's tone dripped with acid.

"Well, Mrs. Botic," Hume leaned forward. "I think that there's a case to be made for federal authorities stepping in. I can't say for certain, but this guy is obviously crossing state lines to fuck with-- excuse me, to harass you, right? So with your permission, I'd like to call a fed buddy of mine, see what we can't make happen."

"That would be great," I said, looking at my wife.

"Now, I'm going to be honest with you. This is a very difficult case. We don't know this guy's base of operations. I mean, presumably, it's in Kansas, but the local PD down there isn't any help. If he were using the postal service, we could follow the mail trail, but he's not. There isn't a whole lot more even the feds can do, but they would be able to check that town out, so..." the detective trailed off with a look on his face that begged for an answer.

"Yeah, call them," I said. Kimmy didn't look hopeful, and I couldn't blame her. The detective was right. This was like finding a malevolent needle in the most enormous pile of malevolent needles ever collected.

After we met with Hume, I left with my family, heading home to await the next chapter of the perpetual torture we were being subjected to. Every day was spent in crippling anxiety while Kimmy and I continued to try to protect our children, to keep them from the knowledge that Katie had acquired a dangerous fanatic.

But the day her biggest fan finally made contact with her was always going to happen.

Our luck was always going to run out.

Nine

I

Three months had passed since we'd received the tape, the contents of which stayed at the forefront of my mind's eye day in and day out. I wanted to know who the girl was...I wanted her parents to have closure, however painful it might be to learn of their daughter's fate.

The end of the month quickly approached, and Katie's birthday with it. For her eighth birthday party, she had elected to have an arts and crafts-themed party, something which every bone in my body told me to object to, but not wanting to disappoint my daughter and not wanting to submit under the boot of our aggressor, I acquiesced, and we set up the party she asked for.

Her birthday that year fell on a Saturday, so we had her party on the day of, and all of her friends showed up, piling gifts and cards on a table under a pop-up canopy. My wife and I both helped Katie host the party with our heads on swivels, but we felt at least a modicum of security with the number of parents who had stayed for the party instead of simply dropping their kids off as others had. A guest with whom no one was familiar would stick out, and we knew that if nothing else, our stalker liked his anonymity.

Our backyard was bustling for the better part of the afternoon, with different stations set up for different art projects. The party was the spurred all the children into fervent creative action, with all eleven in attendance having what appeared to be a wonderful time painting, drawing, and making jewelry. They ran around our backyard and through our house; the liveliness of the day proved to ease our perpetual stress, however minimally.

Katie had made the final decision on the food that would be offered at her party, landing on a spread of hot dogs, burgers, brats, pizza, and mashed potatoes. The kids sat on either side of two long folding tables and ate, each of them trying to finish their meals as quickly as possible in order to get to the main attraction - the dessert.

We'd told Katie that she could have whatever cake she wanted. We presented her with a variety of options from yellow to chocolate to confetti, with chocolate frosting or vanilla or fruit-filled, with characters on it or not, but our daughter had chosen to go a different route - cupcakes. A local bakery that specialized in cupcakes large enough to be meals in and of themselves had filled our order - thirty-six cupcakes of a variety of flavors and combinations. Kimmy had set them up at the end of the food table, a multi-tiered display of sugary heaven that the kids had wanted to invade so fiercely that we needed to have a parent stationed to protect it.

And once that table had become a barren wasteland of crumbs and wrappers, it was time for the main attraction of any child's birthday party: presents. Kimmy, Alex, and I sat next to our daughter as she tore the wrapping paper from box after box and ripped open the envelopes atop them. Katie reveled in the new art supplies she would put to use in the coming days, in the stuffed animals of her favorite characters she would sleep with, and in the new books she would read.

Nearing the bottom of the pile, Katie picked up a small box wrapped in a sheen green wrapping paper - wrapping paper that was immediately recognizable as the same that had covered the box I'd found under our Christmas tree months earlier. I locked eyes with my wife, and she returned my look of terror.

He had won.

We didn't know what our stalker's ultimate goal was, but getting something directly into our daughter's hands felt like something they would consider a victory. The uncertainty of their motives was as terrifying as anything. At this point, it seemed as though their intention was simply to terrify us as much as possible. They had had ample opportunity to cause us physical harm, but none of those opportunities had been seized. And if their goal was just to scare us, it was working.

II

Kimmy and I were frozen in shock, staring at one another, silently screaming in fear, frustration, and defeat. Before we knew what was happening, Katie had torn open the unmarked envelope.

As she unfolded the piece of paper within, it felt like everything was happening in slow motion. The last thing we'd received from this person was a video of a child being brutally murdered; anything even remotely close to that was nothing I would ever want my daughter to see. Kimmy quickly sat up to take the paper and box from Katie, but she wasn't quick enough.

"Awesome!" Katie exclaimed, turning the paper to show everyone. "It's one of my pictures I lost!"

The few parents paying enough attention saw my and Kimmy's fear, and their expressions turned to concern.

"Let me see that, honey," Kimmy said, not giving our daughter a choice as she quickly snatched the paper from her hand.

"Someone drew something on--" Katie began, then looked at her mom, confused.

"Sorry honey, this..." Kimmy searched for something to say. "...this is the wrong gift. It was supposed to be something different."

Kimmy picked up the shimmering green box and hurried over to me.

"Will you keep an eye on everything for just a minute?" I asked a group of concerned parents next to whom I'd been standing during the gift opening.

"Sure, of course," Jacob Myers said. His daughter Kayla was arguably Katie's best friend. "You guys okay?"

"Yeah, we just..." I trailed off as Kimmy and I turned to go inside. "Yeah."

Once inside, I called Detective Hume to report this newest instance of our nightmare while Kimmy inspected the unwanted delivery. I watched the color leave her face as I left the detective a voicemail.

The picture that had been returned this time was of the youngest member of our family, Alex. It had originally been a painting of him standing in front of our house with a big smile on his face.

But the addition to this image made me nauseous. Everything around me spun as I locked eyes with the poor rendition of a man next to my son, also smiling.

"Oh god." Kimmy's voice shook as she turned the paper around to show me a message scrawled on the back in red pen:

Me and your brother are frends now when will we be frends :)

The anxiety nearly made me vomit. I rushed back through the sliding glass door that led from our kitchen onto our back patio and brushed past adults and kids alike with a tunnel vision I'd never before experienced. I reached my son just as he was going to begin a game of 'tag' with the only other two boys in attendance. Alex objected as I took him by the hand and hurried him back into the house.

By this point, all of the adults there knew something was wrong. Once I got Alex inside, I went back out to get Katie.

"Hey, hey, hey," Jacob Myers summoned me as I was breezing by him. "Something's obviously up. Do you want me to clear people out?"

"No, no, just—we just have a little family emergency. I just gotta talk to Katie quick, but no, if you could just keep everyone having fun, that'd be great. Start a game or something? I'd appreciate it."

"Of course." Jacob's voice was filled with doubt. I continued to Katie, who had opened her final two presents but was aware something was amiss.

"Come here, sweetie, come inside for a sec," I said. She slid off her chair and joined my brisk walk back into our house, where Kimmy was already talking to our son.

"Are you sure?" she asked as she knelt to meet him at his eye level. Alex meekly nodded his head. "It's okay if they have, honey, you're not in any trouble at all. We just need to know."

Knowing what she'd asked without having to hear her ask it, and ignoring the fact that the message from the stalker had implied there had been no contact with her, I knelt down to Katie.

"Has anyone tried talking to you? Any adults you didn't know? Like mom said, no one is in trouble. We promise, okay?"

"No," Katie looked me in the eye as she replied. "I promise."

I kissed her on her forehead and turned to Alex.

"Buddy? You're sure no one has tried talking to you? Have you noticed anyone, maybe, watching you when you play outside or when you're at school?"

"Uh-uh."

"And you remember what to do if that does happen?"

"Run and find a grown-up we know!" Katie answered, seemingly excited that she'd beaten her brother to the answer.

"Honey?" Kimmy looked at our son.

"Run and find a grown-up," Alex confirmed.

"What about if they say we sent them, if they say they're friends with your mom and dad?" Kimmy continued questioning our kids' familiarity with the 'stranger-danger' policy.

"Still...still find a grown-up we know?" Alex treated the question like it was meant to trick him, but answered correctly nonetheless.

"That's right," I said, leaning down and wrapping my arms around Katie while Kimmy did the same to Alex. "Go have fun."

Alex bolted back outside, but Katie took slow, careful steps toward the sliding glass door, then turned around to face us.

"You're being weird and it's scaring me," she said, and it broke my heart. Kimmy and I knelt.

"We're sorry, sweetie. There's just grown-up stuff going on and we're trying to make sure it stays away from you guys," Kimmy assured her.

"I'm surprised you were able to tell. I mean with me, sure, but your mom is always weird. Good eye." I smiled, and it was returned by my two girls, along with a playful punch in the arm by Kimmy.

She and I watched Katie return to her party and then looked each other in the eyes.

"How did he get the present in there?" Kimmy asked.

"I have no idea."

"He was in our fucking yard today. I could've been standing right next to him."

"I know."

We stood in tense silence for a moment before the green wrapping paper shined in my periphery. "Should we open the box?" I asked. "Or wait for the cops?"

"Let's just wear gloves. He hasn't left fingerprints on anything else. I doubt he got sloppy now."

And so we did. After putting on blue latex gloves, I carefully unwrapped the gift, doing my best to touch it as little as possible. The flaps on the brown cardboard box underneath gave me pause. They felt more like the gateway to some dreadful place I had no desire to go, but a place I needed to nonetheless. It was the only way I could learn more about our enemy. Even if it was on his terms, information and insight were information and insight, however minuscule.

I don't know what I expected to find in that box, but it certainly wasn't what actually happened to be in it:

A set of brand-new charcoal pencils.

Resting on top of the plastic holding case that contained the new instruments was a note written on a piece of paper the size of a business card. It was written in black ink, with a much more steady, focused hand than when he scribbled his note with red ink.

Never stop drawing.

It sent a chill down my spine. The way it was written made us feel like this person was somehow becoming more determined, like the worst was still yet to come. I gripped a flap of the cardboard box in my right hand and squeezed it, my jaw clenching over and over. I was nearing the end of my rope. The long periods of peace between each contact had kept it below the surface, but this made me want to hurt the person doing this. Since it all began, and up to a few moments before this, I simply wanted it to stop, and if I had any kind of luck, for the person doing it to see some kind of consequence.

Not anymore. Now I wanted to make this person feel the physical equivalent of the emotional terror he had wrought over us for so long. I wanted to make him feel true pain.

III

We spent the rest of the party on high alert. We considered ending it early, but the damage had already been done. In retrospect, it was foolish to think that just because he had gotten the present where he wanted it he wouldn't do anything else; it was just luck that he didn't.

Kimmy and I dodged questions about what was going on from the other parents, who were as yearning for gossip as they were genuinely concerned.

As night fell and our house began emptying, my phone buzzed in my pocket. After explaining to Detective Hume what had happened, he told us he would be by our home within the hour. As Kimmy put the kids down to bed and I cleaned up around our house, the doorbell rang. I opened the front door, and before me stood a tired Detective Hume and two uniformed officers, one male and one female. I invited them then, and the four of us made our way to the kitchen, where the 'gift' still sat on the table.

"Too tempted to wait again, huh?" Hume chuckled to himself.

"Why not? It's not like he's gonna get sloppy now." I echoed Kimmy's earlier words.

"Yeah...probably not." Hume and the other police put their latex gloves on and placed the note, the pencils, the box, and the wrapping paper in individual evidence receptacles.

"The detective mentioned that this has been going on for a while now?" the young male cop asked.

"About a year, yeah, little under."

"Huh." He seemed to contemplate that revelation for a moment while Hume, the other officer, and I waited for him to continue. "You should talk to your friends, could be someone taking a joke too far."

Detective Hume scoffed and looked down at his shoes, shaking his head, while my expression shifted from incredulity to anger.

"'Someone taking a joke too far?' Are you fucking joking?" I looked at Hume. "Is he fucking kidding?"

The officer about whom I was talking placed his hand on his holster. "You need to watch your language, sir."

"And you need to go back to the fucking academy. Maybe ask the kid he fucking killed if this is all a big joke, see what she has to say!"

"Alright, alright, enough." Hume stepped between us. "Mr. Botic, please forgive our young Officer Haas here. He doesn't have all the facts on your case."

I didn't offer a response. Instead, I just stood there, clenching and unclenching my jaw, glaring at Officer Haas. I knew he meant well, but I had nowhere to direct my rage. I realized at that moment that this entire ordeal had been chipping away at me and that I was beginning to slip back into old behaviors, old habits, old ways of thinking. Even recognizing this, I couldn't stop it. Every bone in my body was screaming to apologize, but I was blinded.

The tension dissolved fairly quickly as Hume asked me more questions, and before long he and the other officers left our home, though I knew we would be speaking soon one way or the other.

But there was a month of tense peace. No further contact from our aggressor was made, but we never let our guard down anymore, and we certainly never made the mistake of assuming things were over. This made life an endlessly anxious affair. We checked the mail with our breath held; we eyed every person walking past our house with suspicion, and we kept a closer watch over our kids than ever before.

And of course, while we were no less frightened and furious, we weren't surprised when that brief period came to an end.

IV

It was the middle of April when I picked the kids up from school and we walked back into our house. Alex trudged after Katie as she ran upstairs while I went to the kitchen. Kimmy was spending the afternoon at a gallery that was to feature her work in an exhibit in a few months, and I had decided to surprise her by (likely very poorly) cooking dinner for her. I had barely gotten the first pan out of the cabinet when Katie's voice startled me, her words weighing so heavily on my ears that they physically hurt.

"Did you put this on my bed?"

I spun around and found my daughter standing on the other side of the kitchen, holding a twice-folded piece of paper. A lump so large I thought it would stop my breathing formed in my throat instantly, but I swallowed it and hurriedly walked over to Katie and gently took the paper from her. The familiar cycling of my brain resumed again, the game of one-upmanship that all the ideas of terrible things play in my mind started another match. I didn't know what would be on that paper, but I was at least somewhat relieved when it was words instead of a picture.

Dear Katie,

I would like so much to be your frend. I don't have a lot of frends, but youre pichures make me so happy and they are so good! You are a vary vary good artist and to be a friend with someone so tallented would be so fun. I dont think youre mommy and daddy would want us to be frends thow so maybe it could be a fun secrit. I want you to draw

*me lots and lots and lots and lots of pichures so that I can look at
them all the time. I hope we can be frends.*

The letter was left unsigned.

I called Kimmy, who told me she would come home immediately. After
I hung up with her I called Hume, and after a short while he was back
in my house with another uniformed officer, and the envelope was
taken as evidence and to be fingerprinted, which we naturally didn't
expect any results from. That night, after putting the kids to bed,
Kimmy and I sat down at our kitchen table, which after everything that
day hadn't seen the meal I was supposed to prepare.

"So...I think it could've been said a long time ago, but this has
gone too far," I began.

Kimmy didn't offer a reply, instead just scoffed. I could see that
she was tired, exhausted, that looking over her shoulder every minute
of every day was wearing her down both physically and emotionally. I
knew this because it was doing the same to me.

"So the way I see it is that we have two options," I continued. "We
either take the kids out of school, stop Katie's dance, Alex's tee-ball,
all the extracurriculars, and we keep them in our line of sight twenty-
four seven. They sleep in our room, they don't play in the backyard
unless at least one of us is out there too, and they don't see their
friends.

"Or...we move. We put the house up for sale, and find something
in another city, another state. Cover our tracks, make it so whoever
the fuck is doing this can't find us. With our jobs, I figure both options
are as feasible as the other, one might just be easier. It's your call,

though. We'll do whatever you want, whatever you think will keep the kids the safest."

Kimmy's eyes welled with tears; it was visible that she had been holding everything inside for so long, and the dam was beginning to crumble. She put her face in her hands and rubbed her eyes, then looked at me with a face I'd never seen her wear before, one of pure despair, anguish. I grabbed her hand and looked her in her damp eyes.

"Whatever we do, they're gonna be okay." I did my best to sound reassuring, but I was as uncertain as she was.

My wife returned my gaze, sniffled, and replied with a shaky voice. "We have to move."

V

The following night, we sat Katie and Alex down for dinner. We told them that we needed to leave, that it meant they would be changing schools, that they wouldn't be seeing their friends anymore, and that their entire lives were about to change.

Tears were coming from all sides of the table, and Katie pleaded for us to stay; she apologized for showing me the letter, and my heart shattered inside my chest. I took her hand and told her that she had nothing to apologize for, that nothing she had done had influenced our decision to move. I told her that it was just something we needed to do to keep her and her brother safe.

I called Detective Hume and informed him of our plans to leave the state, which he understood. He advised us that wherever we move, we go to the local police and put them in contact with him, so if anything else happened in our new surroundings, they would be up to speed. He also assured us he would continue looking into everything. And while I appreciated his assurance, it wasn't especially reassuring. It felt like there wasn't anything that could be done. I'd gone through a hundred different ways our predator could have been operating so elusive, each way less combatable than the last.

But we were moving, and we took great precautions in making sure our new location was known only to us.

We first went next door to Ben and Amanda's house and told them we were moving to a small town in Arizona. We went to the kids' school and told the wonderful principal, Jenna Katzen, that the kids would no longer be attending as a result of our impending move to Milwaukee, Wisconsin. Phone calls were placed to my mom, Kimmy's parents, and a select few others, and we told each of them that we were headed to a different place.

Before we left, Kimmy baked a pan of brownies. She lined a tin with five envelopes addressed to the aforementioned people along with a note that read:

Amanda & Ben,

I know this is strange, and I will explain someday, but could you please deliver these envelopes to the post office next month? Please don't say anything about this to anyone, and at the risk of sounding paranoid, please don't even speak out loud about this at all.

I promise we will be in touch soon. Thank you for being such great friends.

Please destroy this letter.

*   -*

*   N & K*

She put a protective layer of plastic wrap over the envelopes and proceeded to transfer the brownies from the pan to the tin, successfully hiding the letters in which we had included the actual address to which we were moving.

And that actual address was located in Colorado, a small town roughly two hours from Kimmy's parents. After speaking with them, we collectively decided that having them closer was worth the risk of having them become targets should our stalker learn of our new surroundings. My wife and I were reluctant to potentially involve them, but they were insistent, noting Shawn's healthy connection with the police force in their town as well as being involved in the state's politics, which could afford them better opportunities for protection than the average person could rely on.

We operated under the assumption that our house was under twenty-four-hour surveillance, however unlikely that may have been. Over the course of a week, whenever we had to go somewhere, we would take a few of our things out to the car in gym bags. While at the gym, we would take empty identical bags into the gym, while Kimmy's friend Katrina would stop by and remove the full bags from our car and take them to her house. Earlier in the week, we had ordered three sets of luggage and had them delivered to Katrina's. She was incredibly helpful in aiding us with our convoluted plan.

All week, Kimmy and I would occasionally wonder if what we were doing was overkill. All the subversion, the sneaking around, the elusivity. But any time those thoughts would infiltrate our minds, I pictured the little girl from the videotape we'd gotten at Christmas; her bruised arms, her matted hair, her visage of pure fear. To keep our daughter from a similar fate, nothing would be too much.

When moving day came, we enacted the last part of our plan.

Katrina had been instructed to load all of our luggage into a U-Haul truck I had paid for but was under her name. While she drove to a prearranged location roughly fifty miles outside of the city, my family and I left our house under the verbally-expressed pretense that we were going to go get breakfast. I calmly explained to the kids that it was going to be a weird morning and that they needed to trust mom and dad and do everything we said when we said it, to which they obliged.

I called the Capitol Cafe and placed our regular order, but I placed it as a carryout order. We arrived, parking in the building's rear as we always did. I then wondered if our car might have a listening device in it and treated it as though our next move would be heard by the stalker.

"You know what? We should just eat here," I said, looking at Kimmy. "I mean, we're already here, right?"

"Yeah, whatever's fine with me," she replied, then turned in her seat to look at Katie and Alex. "Do you two want to eat here?"

They responded enthusiastically.

We walked in through the front doors like normal. I approached the owner, who stood at the hostess station, an organized mess of menus, printouts of the specials for all the days of the week, and ticket pads all sitting around two paper bags, which I suspected held our order. Joanna, the Greek woman of about forty who owned our favorite restaurant, turned around and flashed a welcoming smile.

"You guys change your mind? Wanna eat here?" she asked, then looked down at the kids. "Hi, honey!"

Joanna looked back up and met my eyes.

"Sadly, no," I answered, and readied myself to ask the favor, hoping that my (and later our) once-a-week patronage of the restaurant for the last thirteen years had built up enough goodwill for Joanna to grant it. "I have a very strange request, one that I truly do not have time to explain."

As I retrieved two hundred-dollar bills from my wallet, Joanna eyed me curiously.

"This is for our food, your tip, and the opportunity to leave through the kitchen door," I said, laying the bills down on the counter.

Joanna's eyes widened. "Are you okay?"

"We will be if we can leave through that door."

She pondered for the briefest of moments, then snapped to action, picking up the bills, folding them once, and shoving them back into my hand.

"Keep it," she said, grabbing the two paper bags by their handles.

"No, no, Joanna--"

"How much money have you spent here? You guys are my favorite, and it sounds like you won't be back anytime soon. It's a goodbye present. Come on." She turned around and started toward the door that led to the kitchen.

I took Alex's hand and ushered him between the booths to our left and the bar to our right, with the girls a step behind us. Joanna pushed through the swinging and started veering to the right, but I stopped her.

"Joanna," I said, and she turned around to face me. "It's gotta be that one." I pointed to a door that was very clearly seldom used, as evidenced by the sparsely populated metal rack that stood in front of it. The restaurant's kitchen staff looked at us with curious eyes.

Joanna pondered for another moment, this one even quicker than the last. "Help me move it."

She set the bags down and moved to the right side of the rack. I grabbed the left and we lifted it half an inch off the floor and out, just enough for us to squeeze through the door behind it.

"Thank you, Joanna," I said, repositioning a large metal can of French dressing I had noticed was wobbling on the rack's warped spokes. "We'll be back someday."

"I hope so," Joanna pulled on the door, which objected to being opened but ultimately afforded us enough space to pass through it. "I need more of this little lady's artwork to hang in my office."

Katie smiled up at Joanna.

"Be safe," the Greek woman said.

"Thank you so much," Kimmy reiterated as she lifted the bags off the kitchen floor and shuffled out the door.

That door had been the lynchpin of the entire endeavor. When we walked through it, if we would have turned to our left and taken a single step forward we would've gone face-first into the wall of trees that not only blocked the view from the street but also stretched the short distance from the restaurant to the next structure over - the parking garage for the office building next door. Instead, we hustled forward and covered that distance in seconds, at which point Kimmy and I helped the kids onto the concrete wall, jumped over, and helped them down.

The spot at which we'd crossed into the parking garage had placed us next to a silver Toyota Camry, a car that belonged to Katrina's sister. I reached down and felt around under the passenger's side wheel well until my fingers finally brushed against the cold, magnetic key holder underneath. I retrieved the key, and we were pulling out of the parking garage on the opposite side of the restaurant in under a minute.

VI

We all devoured our food in the car, and around forty minutes later, we took an exit off the freeway that led to long, desolate roads and farmland, an area in which we would see if anyone was following. We took a series of turns, the last taking us down a dirt road. After a mile, we crested a hill, and at the bottom, we saw the U-Haul box truck idling on the side of the road. As we pulled up behind it, the driver's side door opened and Katrina jumped down.

"Babies!" she yelled to the kids as we all piled out of the car, crouching down and extending her slender arms out for hugs.

The kids loved Katrina, referring to her affectionately as "Auntie Kit-Kat".

"Hey! You changed it again!" Katie remarked about Katrina's hair, which had long been a vibrant purple but was now a sky blue cut off at the middle of her neck. Katie took a strand and let it slide between her thumb and finger.

"I sure did!" Katrina replied, smiling. "Just for a little while, though. It'll be purple again by the next time I see you. I know it's your favorite color."

Katie returned the smile and stepped back.

"Thank you, Kat, for everything," Kimmy said as the two hugged.

"Stop, it's nothing," Katrina said, releasing my wife from her arms and taking me into them.

"It's really not," I countered. "We owe you. A lot."

"All you owe me is your new address, so I can visit you."

"Give us a little while. We'll get it to you."

"No rush." she smiled. "Now go. Drive safe. I'll follow for a few miles in case there is actually someone watching, but it doesn't look like there is."

"Better safe than sorry," I said as she and I traded keys and headed to the corresponding vehicles.

Kimmy and I got the kids into the cramped backseat of the box truck's cab. Alex watched a show I'd put on his tablet while Katie opened her sketchbook and took out a sky-blue colored pencil. Kimmy took my hand in hers and kept her eyes forward, a look of determination on her face.

As we barreled down the road toward our new life in Colorado, I wondered again if all of our attempts at stealthiness over the past week had been necessary, if there was anyone following us at all, if it had been worth all that effort.

And then I pictured that little girl's face.

Ten

I

We spent our first month in Colorado on the seventh floor of an Extended Stay America until we were able to close on the house we'd bought through her parents. Katie and Alex wouldn't have minded another year with their nearly unlimited access to the pool and hot tub and complimentary breakfasts, but when the time came to move into our new home, Kimmy and I were more than ready.

Our heads were on swivels at all times, but even under our increased scrutiny of every situation, every car that drove behind us, every place we went, it appeared that we weren't followed to the Centennial State. Regardless, we didn't take any unnecessary chances. We refused to be lured into another false sense of security.

Our new home was a ranch house with, oddly enough, the exact same square footage as the home we'd fled from in California. Despite that fact, this house felt bigger when we walked into it for the first time, and that feeling persisted even after we filled it with new furniture and all of the belongings we'd managed to bring.

It had been two months when Kimmy's phone buzzed in the middle of the night. It took three calls before she woke up, but when she did, her phone screen read **Amanda Jensen**.

"Hello?" she said, nudging me awake. I rolled over and looked up at her as she sat with her back to the wall at the head of our bed. "What's g--"

Kimmy nudged me again, and this time I became alert enough to realize I should be worried - nothing good has ever come from a phone call made at 3 A.M. I sat up in bed, bathed in the flashing blue glow of an episode of Archer. Kimmy took the phone from her ear and looked at it, then tapped the screen, putting Amanda on speakerphone.

"...house. It sounds like they're breaking a bunch of stuff. Ben is on the phone with the cops right now. I just thought I should call you."

"No, oh my god, thank you," Kimmy said, looking at me.

I pieced together that someone was in our old house, apparently destroying things.

"Can you see anybody in there?" I asked. "Like are there lights on anywhere?"

"Umm, yes. Upstairs, it looks like there are lights on in two rooms. The middle window and the one towards the back of the house. That's all I can see from here."

Katie's room and the art studio. Why wasn't I surprised?

"Is there anything there with your new address?" Amanda asked.

"No, we went through our house with a fine-tooth comb and made sure we got anything important out of there," Kimmy answered. "Whatever he's breaking can be replaced."

"Oh my god," Amanda said, to nothing in particular, just addressing the situation as a whole.

"Hey," Ben's voice poured through the speaker on my wife's phone. "They're on their way. Is that them?"

"Yeah," Amanda replied.

"Hey guys, uh, yeah. I was up getting some work done, up in my office, and I saw the light upstairs in your house go on, so I started watching, saw someone up in that room. Obviously, I didn't see any, like, details or whatever, but there's definitely someone over there. We got a window open and it sounds like he's just destroying shit."

"He can destroy whatever he wants," I said. "As long as he's there and not here. By the way, did you guys happen to do that thing?"

"We did. Last month," Amanda confirmed that they had mailed the letter we'd left for them.

"You guys are the best," Kimmy said, taking my hand in her own.

"What's he doing?" I asked our old neighbors.

"I don't know..." Ben had that halfway-distracted tone a person gets when observing something. "Only those two lights are on, far as I can tell."

A smirk unconsciously crept across my face, and I found myself picturing what was going on inside our Walnut Creek home. I envisioned a faceless figure, slovenly and furious, storming through our old house, irate over having been outsmarted. The smile also marked my satisfaction at the fact that our elaborate exit from the Golden State hadn't been for naught, that it had worked. Kimmy was right - all the things he might be dismantling or taking, it was all worthless when held up against our family being safe.

"Tell them the cops are right around the corner." I heard Ben tell his wife, who then relayed the same message to us.

Kimmy and I sat in our bed, eagerly awaiting the conclusion of this chapter in our painful stalking saga. My mind raced with images of that same faceless monster being dragged away in handcuffs, ranting and raving nonsense about Katie's artwork, until Amanda's voice drew me back.

"Oh, wait...Ben, look, he's--" she cut herself off.

Kimmy and I looked at each other. "What's happening?" she asked.

"There! Look!" Amanda exclaimed, and we heard shuffling on the other end of the phone. "Someone just ran out your backdoor and through your yard. I think he jumped the fence towards the Casie's house. Ben, tell them."

We heard Ben talking to the police on his phone in the background. I turned over and grabbed my phone from my nightstand, scrolled through my contacts, and called Detective Hume. The phone rang once before it was picked up.

"Mr. Botic, everything okay?" he asked.

"With us, yeah, we're in our new house, but we're on the phone with our old neighbors and I guess somebody was over there breaking shit, I don't know. Cops are there, or almost there, I mean, so...yeah, I don't know. I obviously don't know for sure if it's the guy who's been fucking with us, but I doubt it's just a random break-in."

"Yeah, no, I doubt that, too. I'll get on the horn and make my way over there. I'll keep you posted."

"Alright, thank you." I hung up the phone.

"--over. Oh, hang on, he's off the phone." Kimmy said, turning to me. "That was fast."

"Yeah, he said he's gonna get over there and call me later," I said.

"Oh, hey, one second," Amanda said through the speaker, and we heard Ben's voice follow but couldn't make out what he was saying. She returned a moment later. "Okay, well, the cops are here, and the 9-1-1 person said they're gonna want to talk to us, so…"

"Okay, thank you so much, Amanda, for everything. Thank you for letting us know," Kimmy said.

"Of course, talk soon."

"Bye."

Kimmy ended the call and looked at me.

"So do you think they caught the guy and he's going away to prison for a long time, and our horror is over?" I asked with half a smile, and Kimmy replied with half a scoff.

Later that morning, my phone buzzed as the detective called me back.

"Mr. Botic," he replied after I answered the call. "So, first things first, the guy was gone by the time our unis got there. They searched the area but didn't come up with anything. But since this is in connection with your ongoing case, the break-in is getting a lot more…you know, oomf than any random break-in would. Our guys are looking for fingerprints, but…I mean, to be honest, this guy's never left any before, so…"

"Yeah…" I said, already having assumed that. "How bad is the damage?"

"Well, it looks like he only screwed with two rooms. They're the--"

"The two rooms upstairs, right."

"Yeah. Looks like he just went through them like a tornado. The stuff that was left in the room is pretty much all smashed. Looks like he used something to hit the walls, maybe a bat, crowbar, something; bunch of drywall is torn out. Looks like you really pissed him off."

"Yeah, I think we actually managed to sneak away without him knowing where we went."

"Good, that's good news."

Silence lingered between us, though it wasn't awkward.

"Well, I'm gonna stay on this regardless," Hume assured me. "Just because you guys got away doesn't mean this son of a bitch doesn't have to pay for what he's done. And Mr. Botic?"

"Yeah?" I said, listening intently.

"Don't let your guard down. Not for a second. He might not know where you're at, but he's still out there."

"Believe me, I don't think my guard will ever go down again."

"Oh, it will. We'll catch this piece of shit, one way or the other."

II

Our guards did indeed stay up throughout the entire nine months of peace. Instead of our annual road trip, we spent the summer getting settled into our new house, and it quickly felt like home. We got the kids enrolled in school and explained our situation to their new principal, who was very receptive and understanding and helpful.

The thought lingered in the back of my mind like the shadows of a memory you can only see the outlines of. With every day that passed, it threatened to rise to the surface, but I didn't allow it. I couldn't allow it.

I couldn't let myself think that it was over.

III

Kimmy walked into the kitchen and set down her purse. In her hands was the day's mail. As she flipped through it, I suddenly became aware of how casually she was doing so; her hands didn't tremble as she sifted through the envelopes, waiting for the next scene of our tormentor's sick production.

"Uh oh, you got a letter from a lawyer's office," she said in a light-hearted tone, pulling my attention back. "Did you burn down another orphanage? We talked about that."

I smiled at the morbid sense of humor that had made me fall in love with her all those years ago. "No, no, nothing like that. Probably just something about the divorce I filed, no big deal."

Kimmy slapped me on my arm with the envelope, a mischievous smile plastered across her gorgeous face. I took the envelope, the return address of which read Law Offices of Nelson, Nelson, Brunner, and Roux.

"Seriously though, I have no idea what this is," I said, carefully tearing along the top of the envelope. "Maybe some distant billionaire relative I've never heard of died and left his fortune to me."

"Ooh, if that's the case, I'll have to tell my lawyer to hold off a bit on the divorce I was filing."

I laughed as I withdrew the twice-folded piece of paper from the envelope, but the smile left my face as I read its contents.

"What is it?" Kimmy asked as my eyes filled with tears. "Penguin, what's wrong?"

My hands began shaking as anxiety filled my body, spreading outwards from my stomach-bound heart.

"Where's my phone?" The paper fell to the floor as I patted my pockets, feeling only the absence of anything within them. "Where the fuck is my fucking phone?!"

Kimmy placed her hands on my tear-streaked face, both to calm me and to keep me from unintentionally scaring the kids who were in the living room, just around the corner.

"Hey," she said, her voice stern with concern. "It's charging by the couch. Breathe."

I looked into her eyes as I tried to calm down, but I couldn't.

"I need my phone." My voice quivered as I stepped aside and hurried to the living room. "I need my phone."

The words on that piece of paper clouded my mind as I rushed behind Katie and Alex, who sat on the floor watching a show on TV.

"To whom it may concern,

We understand that this is a difficult time..."

I picked up my phone from the side table next to the couch, yanking the charger from its port.

"...but we hope that as you grieve..."

I scrolled through my contacts and called. With every ring, my heart beat faster.

"...the reading of your loved one's will and bequeathal of their possessions will help you stay connected with them until you meet again..."

Voicemail.

Everything was spinning. I felt like I was going to vomit or scream or pass out or hit something or all of them. I called the house phone. It rang.

And rang.

And rang.

"...please contact us so we may schedule the reading of the last will and testament..."

The fucking answering machine.

Kimmy rushed into the hallway where I stood trembling, her eyes wet.

"I can't get--" my voice broke. "I can't get a hold of her."

"Oh god..." Kimmy grabbed my hand, squeezed.

I scrolled through my contacts and called the only other number that might prove this nightmare false.

One ring.

Two.

"General surgery, this is Amber. How may I help you?"

"...of Amber Patricia Botic."

"...Mom?" I asked, my heart thumping in my ears.

"I'm sorry?"

"Mom? It's Nick."

"Oh, hi! What's going on? Are you okay?"

"Are you--" my mouth was bone-dry. "Are you okay?"

"Of course I am. What's going on?"

"I'm sorry I haven't talked to you in a few weeks."

"Well, that's okay, you're a grown man, you don't need to check in every day." Her voice cleared the fog that clouded my head as I broke down, just for a moment, into Kimmy's shoulder.

"I'm sorry to bother you at work," I said after a deep breath. "I got this thing in the mail that s--"

The words froze in my mouth as I realized what was happening.

He had done this. Sure, however unlikely it was, maybe there could have been another Amber Patricia Botic somewhere in the country, and maybe this law office had mistakenly sent this to me. But I knew. This was him.

He had found us.

"Mom, I'm sorry. Can I call you back? I'll explain everything later, okay? I'll call you back tonight."

"Sure, are you sure you're okay?"

"I am, but I'll be calling you back soon, okay?"

"Okay. I love you."

"I love you too, mom."

I went back to the kitchen and found the few envelopes Kimmy hadn't yet cycled through. At the bottom of the pile was one that had indeed been mailed, though it was addressed to Katie.

Inside was a picture she'd drawn of Grandma. Over the eyes were two black X's, furiously scratched into the paper so roughly it's a miracle it didn't tear.

The picture made me physically ill. It had only dawned on me then that it wasn't only my wife and kids that were at risk, but apparently everyone I cared about. I realized that by leaving California to protect Kimmy and Katie and Alex, I had left my mom vulnerable. It hadn't occurred to me that the rest of our lives, not simply that which was in the immediate vicinity, were eligible to be terrorized too.

IV

I called Detective Hume and explained to him what had happened, and we met with the Colorado detective that had been assigned our case after we'd moved, Alina Morgan. The detectives coordinated again, as they had immediately following our uprooting.

The conclusion they came to, one that was difficult to accept at the time but was ostensibly accurate in hindsight, was that this instance had been some kind of sick joke, our stalker's way of informing us that he knew where we were.

Even so, my mom was advised on how to keep herself safe, and her hospital and its security staff were made aware of the situation, as was the security at her condominium.

I followed through on my internally declared promise of keeping in better touch with my mom over the next seven months, throughout which we were granted another reprieve from the nightmare. But we knew it wasn't over. It wouldn't be over until he was dead or in prison. A decade could have gone by with no contact from him and our defenses wouldn't have relaxed; it was always just a matter of time.

And this time ended with a box that sat on our porch waiting for us when we got home from an afternoon at the park near our house. As the kids shuffled inside and Kimmy went to the restroom, I cut through the brown tape on the box. Flipping open the flaps, I was met with a piece of eight-by-eleven paper with a sad face drawn in permanent marker and a foul odor.

I knew I should have closed the box and called the police. The piece of paper told me that it wasn't anything on our never-ending list of things we were waiting to have delivered at any given moment, but it didn't stop me. I lifted the paper by its upper right corner and pulled up, revealing the true contents of the box.

There was a polaroid picture of a little girl with a smile on her face. I recognized her instantly as the girl from the video we'd received under our tree. And underneath the photograph was the grim centerpiece of this latest display:

The small, decaying right hand of a child.

Eleven

I

I walked into the Colorado police station with black latex gloves on my hands, carefully holding the box out in front of me.

As I used my shoulder to push through the second set of doors, I spotted Detective Alina Morgan moving swiftly toward the lobby from behind the long front counter. Detective Morgan was Hispanic and of an age with me; she was attractive, an olive-skinned, petite woman with bold brown eyes and brunette hair so dark it was almost black, with a jawline that could cut glass.

She rushed up to me, her own gloves already on her hands, with an exasperated look.

"Jesus," she said, taking the box from me. "Are you okay? Your family?"

"Good as I can be. Thank you for letting me bring it here. The kids get so scared every time the cops are at our house, and it's happened so much since this all started."

"Of course, of course." She took the box from me.

"I know I shouldn't have done anything after I realized it was from...from him. I'm sorry. I didn't touch the actual...you know. But yeah, there's not going to be any fingerprints or DNA or whatever it is you're going to do with it. Only thing I can think of is fingerprinting the..." I couldn't bring myself to say what it was out loud. The hand, I thought, maybe you can fingerprint the hand that was severed from a child and delivered to my doorstep.

Detective Morgan led me to her office, which was markedly cleaner than that of her California counterpart. Various piles of paper were stacked neatly about her meticulously organized desk. She kept three pens - one black, one blue, one red, evenly spaced apart to the right of her chair near the top of the desk, labels all facing up, caps all in the same position. Also on her desk was a plastic slip, the kind you use to file away papers you need to protect.

She stepped to the side of her desk and set the box down atop it. I stood next to the chair reserved for people summoned to Detective Morgan's office, not needing another look into the parcel. Bile rose to the back of my throat as she opened the flaps and took the piece of paper out, eyeing the sad face with an expression consisting of curiosity, horror, and disgust. Holding it by a corner, she placed it into the laminated sleeve and set it aside.

Looking back into the box, Detective Morgan's countenance shifted to one of equal parts anger and sorrow. She reached into the box and gently lifted the small hand from it, the skin decaying, the sinew long, dried, and hardened. The smell was powerful, but neither of us reacted to it. She eyed the extremity, turning it, holding it up to the light.

"God..." she muttered under her breath.

"Yeah," I replied.

"I wonder if he painted the nails before he...or if he did it after..." she gazed at the purple polish that covered the nails on the green fingers, a feature that seemed to darken an already impossibly grim situation. She wasn't talking directly to me, just thinking out loud. She flipped the hand over so its palm faced the ceiling. "He burnt the fingerprints. This...this was a child. There more than likely wouldn't have been any prints on file for a..."

A silence lingered between us for a moment before Detective Alina Morgan turned to me.

"I want to get this motherfucker," she said, her voice filled with disgust and violence before she turned, set the hand back down, composed herself, and turned back. "Detective Hume made an inquiry to the FBI, correct?"

"Uh, yeah, but they said that since the drawings and everything aren't being mailed, that it's not crossing state lines or something," I explained, recalling a conversation I'd had with the California lawman some time ago.

She pondered a moment. "I'm wondering if now that you're here, new state and everything, if they'll pay attention now, because something has got to give."

"It really does," I said, exhausted in every sense of the word.

Even if it didn't end, I just wanted something. I wanted to put a point on the board and end our stalker's scoring streak. I wanted to be on offense after such a long time on defense. I wanted to cause him even a fraction of the pain he'd caused us...us and that little girl.

I wanted him to be afraid.

II

I woke up and looked at the clock - **3:17 A.M.**

Something felt wrong. I couldn't say what, but I was sweating with anxiety. My chest heaved as I took fast, constricted breaths. I looked to my left and found Kimmy sleeping on her side. Straight ahead was the TV, an episode of Archer playing quietly, giving our bedroom a constantly shifting glow.

A look to my right made me leap up from our bed, absentmindedly pulling the blankets enough to wake up my wife.

"Katie!!" I hollered as I started towards our bedroom door. As I passed through the threshold, a sickening crunch sounded out, my right pinky toe hitting the doorframe. "Fuck!! Alex!!"

Ignoring the shooting pain in the right foot, I rushed to the first door on the right, finding Alex stirring in his bed, no doubt as a result of my shouting. I surveyed his room in a split second - empty but for him.

I passed the door across the hall that led into the girls' studio and darted to the door next to it.

"Katie!" I yelled again, though not quite so loud. I pushed her door open and found my daughter scooting up in her bed, rubbing her eye with a loose fist.

"Dad?" she asked, still half-asleep.

"Are you okay?"

"Uh huh…" Katie's eyelids fought against her will to stay awake. Suddenly, Kimmy rushed beside me.

"What's--" she started, but I cut her off.

"Get Alex, get in here."

She didn't respond, instead stepped across the hall and into our son's room, emerging seconds later with him slung over her shoulder. "Should I call Morgan?" she asked, laying Alex on Katie's bed. With a nod, I kissed her on the top of her head, turned, and shut the door behind me as I went back out to the hallway.

I descended the stairs two at a time and searched every room, every closet, every corner. I went outside, looking for any sign, any indicator at all, and found nothing. Back inside, I climbed back up the steps, realizing halfway up that I hadn't checked the most obvious room besides Katie's: the studio. I moved swiftly down the hallway to the second door on the right and pushed it open without a moment of hesitation.

The left side of the room had been ignored entirely. Kimmy's various projects, both in-progress and completed, were in their rightful places amongst the controlled chaos that was her workspace. But the opposite side of the room, Katie's side, had been rummaged.

Finished pieces from the replacement portfolio she'd been building over the last while were scattered on the floor, the accordion folder itself sitting on her desk, empty. Next to it sat an unopened box of high-quality colored pencils with a blue bow on top. I noticed the pencils first, and then the note stuck to the wall to my right.

You are so talented you are my favrite. I wanted all of them but I only took my favrite one but they are all vary good. If your mean mom and dad ever stop being mean you can come and do art for me. You are so talented. Keep drawing I want more.

I seethed with a wave of disgusted, confused anger and threw my fist into the note and through the drywall to which a thumbtack had affixed it.

"Nick?!" I heard Kimmy shout from the other side of that wall in response to the sound of the punch and the falling plaster that followed it.

"Yeah. It's fine," I replied, not sure if I'd said it loud enough for her to hear me. I quickly picked up the misplaced works of art from the floor and put them back on Katie's desk, then went to her bedroom to give my family the all-clear. Only then did I return to the master bedroom to take a closer look at what had caused me to leap up from bed and frantically search the house in the first place.

A piece of paper on my nightstand folded once in the middle and propped up like a tent with a ":(" scrawled in permanent marker on the side facing our bed. I picked it up and flipped it over. On the inside was a message composed of three words that held the weight of three thousand:

I AM EVERYWHERE

III

A cold sweat dampened my forehead. I sat on the edge of the bed, a scream fighting its way up from the pit of my stomach, but it retreated when Kimmy, Katie, and Alex walked into the room.

The kids quickly fell back asleep in our bed beside their mom, who, like me, would not be getting any more rest that night. I called the alarm company whom we had contracted for our home security system when we relocated.

For as vigilant as we had been, that night's intrusion had, frustratingly, been made infinitely easier by a simple miscommunication: I thought Kimmy had set the alarm, and she thought I had. Detective Morgan came by and looked everything over; the note by the bed, the drywall dust-covered note in Katie's room, the box of pencils with the UPC barcode cut out of it to make tracking its purchase impossible, the jimmied-open window in the bathroom.

Given how long this person had been tormenting us and the periods between his making contact, as well as the aggravating and expected lack of evidence he'd left behind, we had gotten to the point of avoiding the spectacle of blue and red and white lights illuminating our street, instead just contacting the detective directly. Everything was still given the same amount of attention and investigated with the same thoroughness, but the predictability of our stalker's careful nature almost negated any need for alacrity.

And this time was no different in that regard. What was different, however, was the empty feeling that night had left me with. It wasn't the first time he had been in our home; he had left his sick home movie in a gift-wrapped box under our Christmas tree almost two years ago. But tonight, he had explored our home, the home we only lived in because we needed to get away from him.

He had walked our halls. He had spent enough time in our house to sift through my daughter's artwork, to write her a note. He had stood next to the bed I shared with my wife, close enough to touch me, close enough to utter the quietest of whispers and have me hear it.

All the emotions I had felt since it all began, the rage, the confusion, the fear, the concern, the despair, they had all joined together to create a feeling that had been lurking in the shadows, a feeling that I had done my damnedest to stave off.

I felt completely, utterly, and entirely helpless.

But that helplessness gave way to a kind of willingness, a willingness to go beyond any defensive measures we'd taken up to that point and finally go on the offensive.

I was going to go back to where it all started.

Twelve

I

I didn't have a plan. All I had was a place in mind where I could start. I just thought that, since the police local to me couldn't do anything, and the police where this all began wouldn't do anything, maybe I could go back to the origin point and see what I could dig up.

The debate raging inside Kimmy was evident in her face, her words, her overall demeanor. On the one hand, this was exactly the kind of recklessness she was uniquely suited to helping me curb. On the other, she was as fed up with it all as I was. She would tell me that without us getting proactive, we were at the mercy of the stalker, and in the same breath express her reluctance in that very same idea.

But we ultimately agreed that, for better or for worse, it was something I should do.

For obvious reasons, we didn't apprise Detective Alina Morgan of my intention of returning to that small Kansas town, but we did tell her I was leaving on a business trip.

The danger in this plan didn't just rest with my returning - alone - to the home of a deranged, dog-and-child-murdering monster, but also with leaving our home short of one of its two primary protectors. To supplement this, Kimmy's dad drove the couple of hours down to stay with his daughter and grandchildren.

I packed minimally, rolling my clothes into small, tight tubes and storing them in a single duffle bag. I didn't know how long I was going to be gone, but if it ended up being longer than the three days' worth of clothes I packed, I would address that issue when I came to it. Kimmy, Katie, Alex, and Shawn Hill waited by the door as I exited the kitchen with my keys in my hand and the duffle bag slung over my shoulder. I pecked Kimmy on the lips and said goodbye, and as I pulled away, she grabbed my hand and placed her other palm on my cheek.

"Be. Careful," she said in a stern voice.

"Always am, doll." I said in a poor imitation of Humphrey Bogart, then smirked and turned my head to kiss her palm.

"Oh god." She rolled her eyes with a half-laugh as I turned to her dad and offered my hand.

"She's not going to be there to keep you from doing anything stupid," he said, accepting my hand and giving it three solid shakes. Shawn Hill knew of my past, once describing me as a very bright young man who just happened to make every worst, dumbest possible decision for a few years, and he knew the details of all of those decisions.

"I'll be good," I told him, then looked back at Kimmy. "I promise."

I knelt down and hugged both of our kids at the same time.

"Kate Beckinsale from Underworld, keep an eye on your brother, okay?" I kissed the top of her head as she smiled and nodded, and then I addressed the youngest human member of our family. "Alexander de Large from A Clockwork Orange, while Katie is keeping an eye on you, you keep an eye on Millie and His Royal Fatness, yeah?"

Our cats Millie and Mr. Fat loved Alex more than anyone else, so it was more likely that they would be watching him.

"I'll be back soon," I said to the group. "I love you guys."

They all reciprocated my sentiment and watched with nervous eyes as I threw my duffle bag into the back seat of the vehicle that had been burgled in the same place I was heading to now. Then I got into the driver's seat and started towards the place I figured would be best to begin - Daisy's Diner.

II

I left that Wednesday and spent the eleven-and-a-half-hour drive forcing myself not to turn around and go back home. About halfway there, I put a copy I'd made of the polaroid of the little girl on the dashboard next to the pictures of Katie and Alex that already adorned it. This felt too much like a plan from a bad action movie, the vengeful return of the wronged protagonist. That's exactly what this was, except I didn't even know who it was that had wronged me.

My GPS told me I was only seven minutes from my destination, but I recognized none of my surroundings and that familiar feeling of being exposed returned in the form of a malignant emptiness in the pit of my stomach. It had been dark the first time I drove these roads, roads I never expected having to drive again.

I was in his territory now. Despite having no evidence to support the idea, I had to assume that the man responsible for our misery lived somewhere along these roads, just as I had to assume he was aware of my traversing them now. For as terrifying as this had all been, it had been equally frustrating. We did regular sweeps of our home in California and our new house once we moved in search of listening or recording devices. We took every precaution we could take, but even so, he somehow stayed a step ahead.

I rounded a bend, and everything suddenly got much more familiar. On my left sat Daisy's Diner, its small parking lot holding two pickup trucks and two sedans, each parked next to one another. That made the closest available spot that one next to the spot in which our car had been parked when Katie's art had been discovered by the cruel admirer. I pulled into the spot and parked the car. I lifted my phone from the cupholder next to me, pausing the audiobook that had been playing but which I hadn't heard a word of for the duration of the drive. As I composed a text to Kimmy, I felt a bead of sweat travel down the back of my neck.

I just pulled into Daisy's.
Wish me luck. I love you.
Tell the kids I

I stopped typing and erased the words, then called Kimmy, who picked up before the first ring had ceased.

"Hey. I just pulled into Daisy's Diner. I just wanted to hear your voice before I go in."

"Remember: no matter what, don't you dare make any horror movie decisions," she said.

"No horror movie decisions," I offered a dry laugh as I repeated her words back to her, but we both took the mantra seriously. "I'm going to send you a pin for...in case something happens."

Kimmy was under no illusions that this trip was without its dangers, but she spoke with a surety in her voice that was far beyond optimism. "I'll see you soon."

And after saying our "I love you"s, I took a deep breath and stepped out of my car. The smell was exactly as I remembered it, but instead of being mouth-watering, as it was my first time there, it now made me want to gag.

The bell dinged as I pushed it open, and it was once again like nails on a chalkboard. A few heads turned instinctively towards me as I walked into the restaurant, their absent and uninterested gazes quickly turning back to their food. None of the patrons that day - two men at a booth, a man and woman in the next booth, and two men and a woman all eating separately at the counter - looked familiar to me, and I had pictured the faces of everyone that had been there during our first visit over two years ago.

And then out from the kitchen walked a portly woman with a look on her face that told the world she was tired of her job, and a name tag that read **Roberta**.

"Hiya, hun. Take a seat wherever you like. I'll be right with you," she said as she strolled by and lifted a coffee pot from the warmer behind the counter, then tended to the three people sitting at it.

I didn't reply, instead just standing there, waiting for the server to be finished. After checking on the people at the two booths, she walked back behind the counter and up to me.

"Help you with something?" she asked, determining that I wasn't there for a meal. I studied her face, looking for any tell that she recognized me, but there was none. To her, I was stepping into Daisy's Diner for the first time.

I held up the picture of the little girl whose beautiful smile was forever snuffed out. "By some miracle, do you have any idea who this is? This little girl?"

She looked at the picture for longer than I expected her to, and for a moment I could swear her expression shifted, ever so slightly, to one containing some modicum of familiarity, before steeling itself over once again.

"Can't say I do," she finally answered, almost defiantly.

"Are you su--" I was about to press her, but I was cut off by one of the two men at the booth next to the couple's.

"The hell's goin' on out there?" he said, loud enough for everyone to hear.

I looked over at him, then followed his line of sight outside. In the parking lot, with their back turned to me, was a person in a gray hoodie, standing at the passenger's side door of my car, attempting to break in.

"No FUCKING way," I yelled, incredulously. At that moment, with the anxiety of being there and the pure shock and disbelief that it was happening, I thought, Someone's breaking into my car at Daisy's Diner AGAIN, but in retrospect, it was very obviously a trap, one that I foolishly fell into.

I turned around and barreled through the door. The sounds of the world seemed muffled, and the DING of the door didn't register for me, but it must have for the person trying to break into my car. As I pushed through the door, he took off running, heading for the side of the building. I pursued, running as fast as I could, nearly falling when my foot slipped as I rounded the corner.

I caught a glimpse of the hooded person as they turned the next corner and fled behind Daisy's Diner. My heart was in my throat as my feet swiftly pounded against the pavement.

It was him.

It had to be.

It was him, and I was only a few paces behind him. I could end this nightmare right now, end our torment, and get back to a life that wasn't ruled by fear. The end of our ordeal was literally just around the corner.

And when I turned that corner, my field of vision narrowed and for the first time, after more than two years of his terrorizing us, I was face-to-face with the person responsible for our ever-present feeling of unease.

I saw the white mask that had HI scribbled on it in crayons of all different colors and a variety of sizes for all of a split second. As I turned to the rear of the building, the man in the mask swung something at me. I heard a dry, metallic *CRACK* and everything went white.

III

I suddenly jolted awake and scurried to my feet...

...and then nearly collapsed under the pressure of the most vicious headache I had ever experienced. Wherever I was, it was pitch black. I instinctively squinted my eyes as if there were some light I was sensitive to and began to feel around for a wall, a door, something, anything.

I had only just begun my search when the entire area to my left burst to life with a hellish mix of blinding light and screaming static. I squeezed my eyes shut and covered my ears until the static din suddenly ceased. I could see through my eyelids that the light had dimmed, so despite the disorienting pounding on the left side of my head, I risked opening my eyes just a crack.

On the opposite side of whatever this structure was stood a collection of televisions, some big, some small, but all of them older-style tube TVs. What I assumed had been static on the screen had now given way to video, the setting of which I recognized immediately.

The backdrop was still stained with the blood of the little girl who smiled happily in the picture on my dashboard, and whom I watched die in the video that was left in our house two Christmases ago.

In the dull, silver glow of the televisions, I found myself in a construct as wide and as tall as the tower of screens before me. The walls looked to be made of wood, and I saw no door to my left or right. As I turned further to my right to look behind me, I saw only a glimpse of the wall to my rear, maybe four feet behind me, before my attention was ripped back to the wall of TVs.

So suddenly that it made me jump, a quick brushing sound played from each of the TVs, the volumes of which were all apparently on full blast.

A man came into the frame but kept his back to me for the entirety of the video. He spoke to me in a high-pitched, yet gravelly voice. The best way I can describe his tone is that it was childlike. He spoke like an excited kid, and the volume of the cacophony made my already-pounding head feel as though it was going to implode.

"Hi Katie's daddy. I'm glad you got my present. I don't wanna do no harm to your daughter, the great artist. I just want her to be my friend and draw me pictures!"

Something out of frame to the right seemed to capture the man's attention for a moment, and while I can't be sure, he seemed to offer an almost imperceptible nod before continuing.

"I sent back the ones that weren't my favorite, but I've kept the ones that are my favorites and those are mine now. All I want is a friendship with Katie. Katie Katie Katie. She's such a very good artist."

Another pause, another something off to the right, and his tone then changed, now markedly angrier.

"But you won't let her be friends with me! You're making me get you out of the way and I don't want to do that because friends don't hurt friends' daddies! I want to be a good friend and not a bad friend! So, I'm going to make this simple. Simple simple easy peasy. If you promise to let your daughter the artist be my friend, I'll leave you alone. But if you still won't be nice, I'm gonna get really angry. Do you promise to be nice?"

I muttered "Y—yes?" unsure as to if this was a video or a live feed, or if I was being watched or not.

There were a few long moments of silence, and then he spoke again, this time calmed down.

"Good. But since you were such a mean mean person, I'm not gonna tell you how to get out!" He let out a sickening, childlike laughter. Then, the video simply cut off.

Now once again in complete darkness, I felt the walls around me for some kind of door, hoping to come across one I hadn't noticed anywhere when I was able to see. I tried my best to move the TVs, but there were some old fifty and sixty-inch sets that couldn't be easily moved. Still dazed from the attack, I wasn't thinking properly. Being knocked unconscious isn't like in movies and TV, where you're knocked out until the enemy is gone, at which point you're right back to a hundred percent. Rather, it took me longer than I care to admit to realize I hadn't seen the wall behind me in its entirety.

I walked the few feet from the TVs to the rear wall and felt around for a door, a hinge, a crack, something, anything.

There was nothing.

I began panicking at that point. I was in a room with no doors. Beyond the televisions had been a wall, and I felt behind the ones I was able to maneuver around for those same things, still finding nothing. The floor was similarly devoid of any egresses, so my last option was the ceiling.

The ceiling above me couldn't have been any more than seven feet high, which, being six-foot-five, I was able to reach with ease. I started from the televisions and worked my way back, moving side to side along the wide structure, until finally, at what I was pretty sure was above nearly the exact spot at which I'd awoken, was a doorknob.

I hurriedly turned the knob, prepared to push with all my might to flip it up and over so it would stay open. However, as I turned the knob, the weight of the door threw me off. It wasn't a heavy door, but I wasn't expecting it to open downwards. It swung down, nearly hitting me in the head, but my arm blocked it at the last moment, leaving it with stinging pain.

Sunlight poured in through the doorway, and as I looked up, I saw the blue sky and the branches of a tree. I slid one of the lighter TVs below the door and used it to boost myself up, reemerging into the world and finding myself atop the wooden structure, which was in the middle of the woods. At the base of the tree whose branches I'd seen from inside the room was a small bag, which contained my belongings.

I retrieved my wallet, phone, and my inhaler. I tried to call nine-one-one but was unsuccessful as my phone had no signal, so I opened the compass app and arbitrarily headed west, a direction in which I walked for nearly ninety minutes until I came to a road, at which point I decided to go north.

I looked through my phone, and in addition to several missed calls, I found a text message that had been sent to Kimmy, one that hadn't been sent by me.

**Hey, sorry, I barely have
any signal. I might be out
of reach for a bit. I think I'm
on to something. I love
you guys, and I'll talk to
you soon. I promise.**

The text had been sent late the night before and had gotten a wary acknowledgment from my wife. I decided I would call her after I was able to call the cops. Even still, I typed another text out so it would be ready to send the moment I had even a single bar of signal.

**It's me. I'm okay. I'll explain
as soon as I can call you.
I'll be back tomorrow.
I'm sorry. I love you.**

After staying on that road for another forty-five minutes, a truck approached me from behind and honked twice as he drove past and pulled over as I stopped in my tracks.

The door on the red, mid-nineties pickup opened and out stepped a chubby man in his fifties dressed in a white and red flannel shirt and blue jeans held up by a belt that appeared to have been constructed before he was even born.

"You okay?" he called out. I didn't respond. "I just ask because I've been driving this road every day for 'bout thirty years and I never seen anybody walkin' on it. Where you headed?"

I hesitated to answer, but I realized I had no idea where I was, no idea how to get where I needed to go, and no means of figuring either of those things out.

I cleared my throat. "Daisy—Daisy's Diner."

"I'm headin' right past Daisy's. I can drop you there, you want. I promise I'm not a pervert or anything." he chuckled to himself, which I did not return. I warily walked up to the truck as the man eyed me curiously.

I opened the passenger's side door and climbed into the rusted chariot of my apparent savior. "How far are we?"

"Bout a half hour, thereabout," the man replied. I guess I'd picked the right direction to walk after all.

I put my seatbelt on and kept my peripheral vision trained on the man in the driver's seat, ready to react if this was all some elaborate setup.

He didn't say anything else on the ride, surely sensing my desire to not answer anything. As we drove, I fought to stay awake. Remembering that with a concussion, falling asleep is the one big no-no, I ignored my exhaustion, at one point sticking my head out the window.

Almost thirty minutes later we pulled into the parking lot of Daisy's Diner, at which point I thanked the man for the ride, who nodded in place of a verbal goodbye, and waved his hand when I brought up the offer of gas money.

I got in my car and looked in the mirror, finding a cut on my forehead that had been stitched up and cared for, just adding to the confusion of this entire ordeal.

I realized that I finally had a signal on my phone, so I sent the text I'd prepared to Kimmy and then called the police, praying I wouldn't have to deal with the endlessly unhelpful older Officer Billings. After explaining the entire situation to Dave, the same person I'd spoken to initially when our car was burgled, I was told an Officer Billings would be there to meet me shortly, which irritated me to no end.

After hanging up, I went back into Daisy's, finding Roberta there yet again.

"Back again?" she asked, as though I hadn't simply disappeared earlier that day.

"What?" I asked, almost unintentionally. I realized then how foggy my mind was - it was hard to think, and I couldn't recall having actually thought of anything at all between that TV building and Daisy's.

"You're back again. Two days in a row."

"Two..." I looked at my phone's lock screen and found that it was indeed Friday. I looked up at Roberta with fire in my eyes. "I've been gone for...did you call the cops?" Somehow, I already knew the answer.

"The police? Why?" Roberta asked.

"Because I sprinted out of here yesterday and fucking disappeared, that's why. That wasn't fuckin' suspicious to you? You didn't think me running out of here like this shithole was on fire and leaving my fuckin' car here was out of the fuckin' ordinary?"

I realized then that there were other people in the restaurant. Three unfamiliar men sat at two booths and the counter, respectively, all of whom were looking at me as I went on my tirade. Roberta looked at them, then back at me.

"Okay, you're gonna need to calm down, sir."

"Fuck you I need to calm down. Are you kidding me?" I snapped back. "I was fuckin' abducted right behind this fuckin' building, and what? What did you do? Not a goddamn thing apparently, because that's just what happens around here, I guess, right? Someone gets attacked outside Daisy's Diner, and the dipshits of this country ass town just go about their business!"

"Okay, I don't know about any of that, but I'm gonna need to ask you to leave," Roberta said, looking at the men to her right and my left, two of whom were slowly rising to their feet.

"Oh, you need me to leave? Is that right?! Maybe I should just wait two minutes for somebody to hit me over the head with a brick and drag me away! Not that you'd notice, since apparently, you're fucking blind!" I turned my head towards the men who were now standing up and pointed at the one nearest me. "SIT THE FUCK DOWN!"

One man looked at the other and then back at me, not making a move at all.

"Yeah, don't worry, you dumb bitch, I'm leaving. Careful when you leave, guys! The people here won't give a shit if you get kidnapped on your way out!' I turned toward the door and cocked my arm back, sending my fist flying forward into the glass, making a spiderweb crack throughout the upper pane. I pushed the door open and stepped outside, then waited in my car for what I expected to be the man that would arrest me for punching the window and ignore the fact that I'd been taken against my will.

That just seemed to be the way things worked around here.

IV

I seethed in my car, watching as the waitress and her customers eyed me cautiously from inside the restaurant. Roberta retrieved a cordless phone and made a call, and rather than get pulled over on the side of an empty road, I simply sat and waited. Before long, a police cruiser arrived, and in the first stroke of luck in two days, the younger Officer Billings stepped out and walked up to my window, which I opened only enough for us to hear one another.

"How we doin'?" he asked.

"Oh, wonderful! I'm fucking fantastic." I said, still excessively sarcastic, then got a hold of myself. "Sorry. I'm not doing good."

"Well, talk to me, what's goin'—wait, I know you?" the cop asked as his eyes worked with his brain to place me.

I gave the younger Billings a quick breakdown of everything that had happened up to that point, and he seemed to be listening intently. When I finished, he sighed.

"Well...hell...sounds like you've had a real go of it," he said. I didn't offer a reply. "You said you don't know how you got patched up there?"

My hand instinctively reached up to the stitches on my hairline, which stung to the touch. After I winced, I said, "No idea. Just seems like whoever it was wanted to make sure I'm healthy as can be while he fucks with my family. Goddamnit."

"We should get you checked out by our doctor here. We don't have a whole big hospital or anything, but our people are the best of the best. Why don't we--"

"No, no. I'm fine. It's fine. Seriously." My declination was accompanied by a wave of my hand.

"You sure? You know I have to offer."

"No. I mean yeah, I'm sure. I'm good."

"Right then. Well...can you show me where you were held?"

It occurred to me that while I knew the general route I'd wandered from the TV House; I wasn't sure I'd actually be able to direct us there with any accuracy.

"I...I mean maybe? I thought I had a concussion, but I don't know...I think I might have been drugged or something. I know the direction of where it is, but I don't know like, exactly. I walked for a long time."

We got into Billings' cruiser and drove towards where I thought the odd, off-kilter TV House would be. The young police officer asked me more perfunctory questions about how I was feeling, insisting that he would prefer I get checked out by their doctor, which I continued to decline. After a pregnant silence that lasted for a short while, a question burst forth from my lips, independent of my brain's influence.

"Why won't you guys work with the detectives on my case?"

Billings turned his head toward me for a moment before putting his eyes back on the road. "Say again?"

"Since all this shit started, the detectives we've been working with, first the one in California and now the one in Colorado, they've tried getting in touch with you guys, and they said you've been completely unwilling to help."

Billings' eyebrows furrowed and he glanced at me again with an expression of total incredulity.

"All I can say about that is that I haven't personally spoken to anyone about you or your case. If they've talked to anyone, it would probably be my old man, and, if I'm remembering right, you got a glimpse of what he's like when you were here that first time." He looked over to me again, allowing me to disparage the man he evidently felt the same way about as I did, but I opted to stay silent. "He's got this whole weird 'keep outsiders on the outside' bullshit like he's something out of an old Western or something. He sure didn't even tell me anyone had tried. And Dave, hell, he's about as yes as a yes man you can get when it comes to my pops, so I'm not surprised he kept it secret. Tell you what, why don't you give me these detective's numbers, and I'll reach out to them?"

Those words were as pleasant a surprise as I ever could've hoped for in that stuffy Crown Victoria. Billings pulled his cell phone from the front pocket of his brown button-down shirt as I pulled mine from my jeans pocket. He handed me his phone and told me his passcode - **0911**, so original - and told me to program the detective's numbers in it, which I did.

Until now this trip had been a complete, unmitigated disaster, but knowing that there would finally be some much-needed cooperation between Detectives Morgan and Hume and the police in the town everything began, even if it was just this one officer, made it all worth it. I returned Billings' phone and sat back in my seat, keeping an eye out for anything that might be familiar.

But then, as we rounded a bend down the long, two-lane road the man in the truck had driven me up, a tower of smoke became visible over the trees. We noticed it at the same time, and I just knew. "That's it."

V

Billings told me to hang on and quickly but carefully turned the steering wheel hard to the left, cutting across the two solid yellow lines and the empty lane next to ours and taking us back into the apparently uncharted wilderness I'd escaped from only hours earlier.

We slowly made our way through the thinly populated trees using the gray and black portal in the sky as our North Star, and after fifteen minutes or so, we finally arrived and found the TV House (as I've come to refer to it) ablaze. The wood creaked and snapped and smoke rose high into the sky in a black and gray cyclone.

"I'm guessing this wasn't your doing." Billings observed. Again, I didn't respond. I just slowly exited the police cruiser, defeated.

I stood before the crumbling structure, my temples throbbing. As though it were timed for effect, the wall that faced us, which to the best of my knowledge was the wall that all the TVs had rested against on the inside of the structure, groaned as it collapsed into itself, revealing the smoldering tower of televisions all stacked up on one another.

In the car, I heard Officer Billings on his radio calling for fire services. When he was done, he got out of the car and stepped next to me.

"Are those the--"

"TVs, yeah." I finished the cop's question and gave him his answer all in one fell swoop.

Billings walked a wide berth around the blaze, then reached down to the ground and lifted something.

I approached him and saw that he was holding a thick bundle of cords that had all been tied together and, presumably later, severed.

"When you got out, did you see a generator or anything? Some kind of power source? Anything?" he shouted. I still struggled to hear him over the roars of the burning structure.

I shook my head and hollered back. "No. I was pretty out of it, but I feel like I would've seen a big ass generator powering a thousand TVs."

He pondered for a moment, then dropped the bundle of cords to the ground and walked back.

"There's nothing else out here," he said. "I mean nothing. Just these woods for...for miles. It had to be a video, I think. You said he was standing in front of the same background as that other video you mentioned, that it looked like a house, basement? Before right now, I would've told you that there were no standing structures out here at all, and I would've been telling you the truth as I knew it. I don't think it could've been live, not unless they ran miles worth of extension cords. This is...this is something."

VI

The fire department from the next town, a much larger town, made quick work of the burning TV House. When they were done, the younger Officer Billings and I drove back to Daisy's Diner, where we sat in his car for nearly another hour while he made his report. By the time we were done, night had fallen, and I didn't feel confident that I could drive for the next ten minutes, let alone the next ten hours, so I went to the closest place for lodging that I knew of: The Whitmore Motel.

VII

It was the same shithole it was almost three years earlier, with the same old man sitting behind the counter. My body weighed a thousand pounds, my eyelids a thousand more. I was in no mood for pleasantries, so I was in and out of the office in under five minutes.

I did note, however, that at almost the same moment I stepped back outside with the key to Room 5 (which was not a connecting room) dangling from the key tag I clutched in my hand, the man in the office picked up the phone and made a call.

I stopped and had an internal debate for a moment, and what snapped me out of it was my knuckles cracking from squeezing the flexible plastic tag so hard. I figured I had already caused one scene in this backwoods town today, I may as well go two for two. I stomped back to the door and flung the door open, that *ding* sounding just as it had minutes earlier.

"Yes, ma'am," the man behind the counter said. "Yeh. I will. You too, darlin'. Yeh. Yeh. I'll see yeh in the mernin' then. Goodnaght." He hung up the phone and looked up at me, adjusting his glasses. "Help yeh?"

"Who did you just call?"

"Beg pardon?"

"On the phone just now. Who did you call? As soon as I walked out, you called someone."

"Well, I...I called my wife," he said, seemingly confused.

"Your wife?"

"Yeh. I call her evry night't ten on the dot, cust'mers er' none."

I looked at the clock on the wall behind him, the hands of which did indeed point to 10:01. The manager looked up at me from his seat with an expression consisting of half concern and half annoyance. I held his gaze, not entirely convinced that he wasn't just an especially talented actor, but ultimately relented, leaving the office of the Whitmore Motel for the second time that night.

I backed my car into the space just outside the door to room 5, just in case, for whatever reason, I might need to make a hasty exit. I grabbed my bag and went inside, triple and quadruple-checking that the doors on my car were locked and the alarm was set.

I then set the poorly constructed chair up against the doorknob on the inside of the door to the room, locked the lock on the knob, and fastened the chain. I was as secure as I could be in this place, but I didn't feel any safer than if I'd left the door wide open. The person who was doing this seemed to have superhuman abilities of evasion, like he was able to appear and disappear at will, like no amount of locks would or could deter him.

I finally sat down and called Kimmy, who answered on the first ring with "what the fuck is going on, are you okay?"

I recounted the previous day's events to her, the brief chase, my being incapacitated, the TV House and its subsequent burning, and the welcome positivity from Officer Billings, and could hear her sniffles as I did. I asked how she was doing, how the kids were doing, how her dad was doing. When each of us was as confident as we could be that we would both survive until the morning we ended the call, with my assuring her I'd be back the next day.

Still not certain I should go to sleep, and not sure I even could due to the adrenaline that seemed to be coursing through my veins on a perpetual loop since I'd started this trip, I turned on an episode of The Office on my laptop and decided to wait another few hours.

I was asleep before the opening jingle.

Thirteen

I

When I awoke the next morning, the chair I'd propped underneath the doorknob was still in place. All of my things were where I'd left them the night before, and I was relieved to be able to know with no real doubt that no one had been in the room with me. I placed a quick call to Kimmy, who reported no disturbances on their end, either. I told her I would be on my way home within the hour, and we exchanged 'I love you's and hung up.

As I stood up from the uncomfortable bed, I stepped to the window, using two fingers to create a space in the blinds, letting a river of golden sunlight into the room. As I looked the left side of the car over, I couldn't help but laugh. I moved the chair, unlocked the door, and stepped outside. Looking at the right side of the vehicle, I laughed even harder.

All four of my tires had been slashed to ribbons.

It was an impediment, to be sure. I wanted to get home, and this was keeping me from doing just that. Nevertheless, this just seemed so...juvenile. This man had been in our house. He had murdered a child. He had been so elusive that there was hardly even an official investigation into him at all. And now...he cuts my tires. He did what a vengeful ex does. His follow-up to abducting me by force and holding me in a bizarre structure was to take inspiration from something Carrie Underwood would sing about.

A call to AAA and the subsequent wait for them to arrive and then replace all my tires made me three hours late getting back on the road. As I pulled out of the parking lot of the Whitmore Motel, I peered into the office, and like our first night there, a young girl (who now looked around twenty years old) sat behind the counter, her thumbs twiddling away on her phone.

I arrived home just shy of ten hours later and the smile on my face when my wife and children greeted me at the door could've been seen from space. It was nearly time for the kids to go to sleep, but because it had been a few days, we all stayed up and watched a movie, my father-in-law included.

It was a peaceful night, and a peaceful nine months followed. It was just like the other periods of inactivity from the person who had loomed over our lives for so long. His influence was apparent in all of our decisions, all of our movements. We didn't take any unnecessary chances or risks.

We just waited.

Waited for the other shoe to drop.

Waited for the nightmare to continue.

II

The clock read **2:07 A.M.** when I was woken up. It was one of those things when you can hear a noise happening in real life in your dream. I was never able to recall what the dream had been about, but the noise had been that of a soft knocking.

I had been sleeping on my side, so when my eyes opened, the first thing I had seen was the screen on our Alexa, and for whatever reason, the time imprinted itself on my brain. From waking up and seeing the clock to being on my feet, only a second had passed, at most. I listened for it again, but all I heard was the soft wind blowing leaves around outside. Still, I could feel that something was wrong. I didn't know what that something was, but there was a heaviness in the air, negative electricity flowing through my body, making my hands shake.

I stood there for too long. If I had acted quicker, maybe it wouldn't have happened.

I stood there for maybe a full minute before I leaned over the bed and gently shook Kimmy awake. The sleepiness in her eyes gave way to a vicious cocktail of concern, fear, and determination. I put my index finger to my lip and signaled for her to listen.

We listened for too long. If I had acted quicker, and not had my wife listen for the sound that never came again, maybe it wouldn't have happened.

After we listened for close to another minute and heard nothing but our breathing, Kimmy looked at me with eyes that said 'what now?' I took the knife I kept next to our bed from its sheath and nodded my head to the side, indicating that our plan for such a situation was now in motion.

I hurried down the hall, glancing into the kids' rooms through the cracks in their doors as I moved towards the front door. Behind me, Kimmy went into Alex's room. The plan, one which we had enacted at another point earlier in our years-long ordeal, was for Kimmy to first get our son and then move into Katie's room while I addressed whatever was going on.

I stood at the front door to our Colorado home and took a deep breath, my fingers wrapped tightly about the tang of the knife. I peered through the peephole and saw nothing but the walkway up to our home, cast in a pale yellow glow from the streetlights. With my free hand, I disarmed our alarm, turned the knob, and yanked the door open, as ready as I could be for whatever awaited me.

Then I heard the scream.

As the breeze from outside poured into our home, Kimmy let out a shriek. There had been something on the ground in front of the door, but I only saw it peripherally as I swung the door closed and sprinted back down the hall. In Katie's room, Alex stood crying next to the door while Kimmy frantically threw the closet door open and tore through what was in it. On the bed, Katie's pillows had been set up to make it appear that Katie was sleeping, but Katie wasn't sleeping.

Katie was gone.

My mouth went dry as Kimmy screamed, asking the world where her daughter was. My knees felt like they might give out at any second, and the floor felt like it was dropping from underneath me all at the same time.

I pushed off the door frame and ran back to our bedroom, getting my phone from the nightstand on my side of the bed and calling nine-one-one.

As I did my best to relay the information to the operator, I absently walked back to the front door, where on the welcome mat at my feet sat a twice-folded piece of paper under a small rock. I reached down and pulled it out from under the small makeshift paperweight and unfolded it.

A picture drawn in colored pencil. A full-body portrait Katie had done of herself. Above it, the word **ME**, but with a red **X** through it.

An addition, drawn poorly in crayon, due to the limited space in which it was able to be placed. But the message was clear. A man, holding her hand. A man wearing a smiley face mask.

Next to the crossed-out **ME** was its replacement.

US

I put the paper on the table next to the door and went back to my wife and son. I didn't know how to console them. I didn't know how to console myself. It had all been leading to this.

Our daughter had been kidnapped.

III

The police arrived quickly, and Detective Alina Morgan followed close behind them.

The standard response to an abducted child was enacted. Over the next two months, people gathered and searched the area. Police worked tirelessly trying to find whatever they could. And they found nothing.

After giving our permission to the home security company that handled our alarms, Detective Morgan found that our passcode had been entered at 2:03 A.M. She posited the kidnapper had somehow gotten our alarm code, abducted Katie, and then doubled back to leave the drawing on the porch.

It was also found that Katie's window was unlocked, which it never, ever was. This led the detective to believe that at some point when my family and I were gone, the kidnapper went into our home and unlocked it. When the time came, he opened our front door, took the one step inside that it took to get to the alarm, disarmed it, then went around to the window and took her, ostensibly to avoid walking all the way through the house to get to her and having to walk her all the way back through the house to get her out.

We had no way of knowing for sure what exactly had happened that night.

All we knew was that Katie was gone.

Fourteen

I

Ninety-seven days had passed since our little girl was taken from her bedroom.

Detective Morgan had done all she could to try to gain the cooperation of the police in that small Kansas town, and while the younger Officer Billings had been as helpful as he could, he seemed to be hindered by his father, who at one point had said to Detective Morgan, "Sure, tell you what, we'll go through every house and business out here with a fine-tooth comb, just for you," in a tone I can only imagine was dripping with sarcasm.

A palpable tension hung in the air between the walls of our home. I felt it, Kimmy felt it, Alex felt it. We were fractured. A puzzle with the final piece missing. Kimmy had slipped into an intense depression, at points not leaving bed for days at a time except to use the restroom. She didn't want to eat, didn't want to talk to anyone. And I couldn't blame her.

I was living in the same perpetual anger Kimmy had helped me escape all those years before. I felt like a stick of dynamite with the fuse so low it was no longer visible, and I found myself hoping someone would give me an excuse to explode, to make themselves the unfortunate target of my anger, my confusion.

After a month of sleeping in our room, Alex had taken to spending the night in Katie's bed with Millie and Mr. Fat. Kimmy and I did our best to make sure he was okay, but like us, a piece of him was gone. He loved his sister as much as any sibling has ever loved another, and he was lost without her.

On the afternoon of that ninety-seventh day after Katie was taken from us, Kimmy was in her studio. I was happy to see she had gotten up that day and hoped that she might be able to relieve some of the stress through her art. Seeing her up and going into the room to do the thing she loved to do most put me at ease, in a way. I was worried about her - not that she would harm herself, but rather that she might start thinking a drink wouldn't be the worst thing in the world - so the fact that she wasn't just laying there, dwelling, pondering, trapped with nothing but her thoughts, it was good.

I had gone outside to get the mail around a half hour after Kimmy had gone into her studio, and as I stepped back onto the porch, I heard the first crash. Offering a glance at Alex as he sat watching TV in the living room, I shuffled down the hallway, nearly slipping as I tried to stop, all the while hearing crashes and smashes and screams. I turned the knob and pushed open the door to the art studio we had set up for the ladies of the house, just in time to see my wife smash an easel against the wall.

Various pieces she'd been working on were strewn about the room, paints of a variety of colors splashed and spilled and staining the walls and wooden floor. She let out an animalistic scream, the years of horror and worry and pain and fear and anger and the past months of desperation and regret and confusion and hope and the taking away of hope all converging and coming out in a single scream that would shred her vocal cords if she held it too long.

I jumped over a canvas that was folded like a book against its will and wrapped my arms around Kimmy. I half-expected her to push me away, but instead, she went something close to limp, using only enough energy to stay standing with my help, and cried into my chest. The mail fell to the floor as I gently squeezed my wife into me.

"It's okay. You're okay," I said in as soft a voice as I could, then kissed her on the top of her head.

"I just want her back," she said.

"I know. I know. So do I. We'll get her. I know we will."

"You can't say that. You don't know."

"I know that she's a smart girl. And I know that she has parents who have taught her well. We are going to f--" I stopped mid-sentence. Kimmy sniffled and looked up at me, and saw that I was staring at the floor.

The envelopes from the mail had hit the floor and landed in a small collage. Underneath a catalog, the cover of which featured a collection of snow globes, sat an envelope. Four letters were visible on the face: **MO**, and below those, **DA**.

Kimmy turned her head around and followed my line of sight to behind her feet.

"Oh my god," she whispered, looked back up at me, and turned around.

I released her from my embrace, and she stepped aside. She gently brushed aside the other envelopes with her foot, revealing the one labeled **MOMMY AND DADDY**, which appeared to have been written in magic marker. She hurriedly stepped over to her desk and took out two pairs of clear latex gloves, handing one of them to me. I leaned down and picked the letter up, and my tear-filled eyes met Kimmy's own.

We both had the same thought at the same time. The fact that I held that envelope in my hands answered a question that had plagued us every day, every hour, every second since Katie had been gone: Is our daughter still alive?

I handed the envelope to Kimmy, and she used a fingernail to slice along the top of it. From it, she pulled two folded pieces of paper. On the first page, written on the outside of the first of the two folds, was a three-word message written in graphite pencil, a message that made my blood run cold and my legs want to give out from beneath me:

I'm home now

II

My wife and I looked at each other but didn't say anything. She unfolded the piece of paper and, little to our surprise, found that it was a drawing. But it was one neither of us had seen before. This particular piece was done in colored pencil, full of bright, vibrant colors, and showing off the progression of our daughter's talent since this whole situation had begun.

It depicted a landscape - green grass, a full blue sky, small birds flying through the air. In the middle was Katie, holding hands with the man who had abducted her. And for the first time, that part of the image wasn't included by the man himself - he had made her do it. The visage of the man was a bit overweight, wearing overalls with no shirt on underneath, and a mask with red and black stripes and what seemed to be spikes of various colors coming out from the sides.

What warmed my blood again, rather what made it boil, was the heart that had been drawn around the two of them. A sickening montage of horrors played through my mind all in the blink of an eye, all of the miseries that our beautiful daughter might be suffering at the hands of this mask-wearing monster.

But I was pulled from what would have quickly become an all-encompassing tomb of regret and pain and wonder by a small inclusion in the image's background.

In the upper right-hand corner stood a barn, much like any other one might find in a child's drawing or book. The barn was red with the typical white **X** adorning the large doors on its face. But on top of the barn was an outline of something, the remnants left over from some addition to the drawing that had been reconsidered...that had been erased.

I gently took the paper from my wife and held it up to the light. It had been thoroughly erased, but as anyone who has written or drawn anything in pencil before knows, what you erase never goes away completely. In this instance, it was another **X**, one that had originally been perched atop the roof of the barn like a sign.

"This...that has to be it," I said, not even directly to Kimmy, but rather out loud, to get the information out to the world. "She has to be trying to direct us to where she is. They didn't want her to give out that detail so they made her erase it, right?"

"I don't know," Kimmy whispered, her voice shaking. She tried to say something else, but the words got trapped in her throat.

As I stared at the picture, and the barely visible **X** that once decorated the roof of the barn in the corner of the page, Kimmy unfolded the other piece of paper. Another letter:

Helo new Daddy and Mommy,

I hope you know that I am not a bad mean man I just rilly like the pichures and want all of them to look at all the time. I just rilly wanted her to be my frend and now she can live with me and make pichures all the time. I promise I will not hurt her becuse I do not hurt my frends if I did that I would not be a very good frend myself. We would like you to visit to see that she is happyer here then with you. I dont want to tell you rite away because then you will come rite away and I dont want you here before you have had a chanse to calm down. And i wont tell you where we are hehe you have to find us.

What I am saying sir and maam is that she now lives here but if you can find us you can visit but you have to come alone or bring just her mommy. If you bring anyone else or if there are polise I will skin her like a dear and where her face to gut you before you evin get close.

I know you miss her because she is grate so as a jescher of good will i have sent you something BUT YOU CANT GO TO THE POLISE LIKE YOU USALLY DO. I have let you talk to them to much and that is nice of me but not nice of you so you have to stop if you dont stop i will feed katie her own skin and that would not make me a vary good frend DONT MAKE ME DO THAT

III

The letter was, of course, unsigned.

I dropped to the floor and started scattering things around.

"There was a package, like a bag, a small bag," I said. "Here."

I picked it up. It was the type of packaging that was effectively a broken paper bag but with bubble wrap inside. It was no bigger than my hand, sealed once over one end.

I looked at Kimmy again, tears in my eyes, more hesitant than I'd ever been. I knew that whatever this package held would be something I wouldn't want to see, potentially even something I couldn't handle seeing. It suddenly felt as though everything that happened to me, from something as menial as stubbing my toe to something so horrible as finding some grotesque gift from a deranged stalker, could be the thing that finally broke me. I was still hanging on by threads, but any one thing, no matter how minute and seemingly insignificant, could sever those threads and send me crashing down. I thought it was a miracle that it hadn't already happened.

But I slid my finger under the space in the top flap of the bag and saw it poke out the other side - that's how small it was. I tore it open and caught a whiff of a foul odor; it wasn't overpowering or even especially strong, but it was there. I squeezed the sides of the package, opening the top like a mouth, and peered inside.

I stood in place for a moment, hardly hearing Kimmy ask what it was, and before I knew it, my entire body was shaking, almost convulsing. She jumped when all in one motion I dropped the package and screamed a deep, guttural wail, and sent my hand through the wall behind me. I pulled my hand out, scraping it against the splintered slats behind the drywall, ripping the skin on my knuckles away. A second punch next to it left a gouge on top of my hand, and the third tore apart my knuckles even more. My final blow to the structure of our home came from the top of my head as I sent it through the wall next to the three smaller holes, leaving a concave bowl of cracked drywall and chipped sky-blue paint. The final hit seemed to immediately return me to rational thought, and I spun around.

"I'm sorry." The words poured from my mouth before I had a chance to think about them. I had never exploded like that in front of Kimmy before, and I suddenly felt the emptiness that comes with the realization that you've made a huge mistake. But she wasn't afraid of me. If she had any thoughts on my outburst, it was nothing short of complete understanding.

She stood with her hands cupped over her mouth and nose, tears falling from her eyes and traveling down from the tips of her index fingers. Her gaze was directed at the floor, where the small package had fallen and its contents had spilled out.

There on the hardwood floor, one fully out, the other still just barely nestled inside the small bag, were two fingers from the hand of a child.

Fifteen

There wasn't a debate to be had. No weighing of options. No sitting down to strategize.

"We can't show this to Morgan, or—or anyone," I said, my breath moving faster than I was able to intelligibly speak. "If he says he'll...do that to Katie if we bring cops, he'll do it. I have to go, right? I have to get her."

"You have to calm down. You--" Kimmy started, but I cut her off. My eyes tunneled, laser-focusing on the barn in the corner of the page and the remnants of the X that once topped it.

"Calm down? I—this is it. This is our chance."

"How do you know? Because of an erased 'X'? It could have been a mistake. It could be an imprint from another drawing she did on top of this one."

"Well..." my voice started loud, but after a pause, I was all but whispering. "...what else do we have?"

My eyes welled with tears, tears of anger, of frustration, of desperation. Kimmy took my hand and said, "You're right. There is nothing else. We have to try. We have to see if it means anything."

I looked down at her shining brown eyes. "I will. I'll--"

"We will," Kimmy interjected, and I saw the resolve on her face.

"We can't both go. There's Alex--"

"He can go to my parent's."

"--And what if it goes wrong? If it does, at least Alex still has one of us."

"I know she's a daddy's girl to the highest degree, but she's my fucking daughter, too. If you're going, so am I. That's all there is to it. Do not try to--"

"Kimmy." I knew she wouldn't give in. And she was right. It may have been irresponsible for both of us to go, but I had no more of a 'claim' to our daughter's safety than she did. She was equal parts us. "Call your mom. I want to leave tomorrow, so we can get out there by Thursday. I want to go during the day."

Without a response, Kimmy left the room. I stood with the drawing in my hand, eyeing it again, every line, every color. The erased X on top of the roof of the barn had to be Katie's way of telling us where she was. It had to be. Why else would she have drawn it in the first place?

I carefully folded the paper twice and surveyed the destruction of the room before me. As I formulated a plan, I began to clean up the art studio.

I wanted it to be just how Kimmy and Katie had set it up when we moved there so that when we got our daughter back and this nightmare was over, she could get right back to work.

Sixteen

I

Alex was still young, but passed were the times when he was too young to know what was going on. He didn't know the particulars, but he knew something was amiss. He was already still reeling from the sudden and gutting absence of his sister, and learning that his mother and I would be leaving for a few days left him feeling even more abandoned than he already was.

"You're going to be staying with Lola and Grandpa," Kimmy said, kneeling in front of our boy in the foyer of Shawn and Dana Hill's house. "Just for a few days, honey."

"Where are you going? Why can't I come with?" Every word that passed by his trembling lips made it clear that it was all he could do to not break out into a full sob. This was at least the fourth time he'd asked those same questions, but they would be the last he would speak them to us.

"We have to…" Kimmy looked up at me.

We had debated over the merits of telling Alex the truth, that we were going to be attempting to recover Katie and make our family whole again. We didn't want to lie to him, but we ultimately decided that we couldn't take the chance of getting his hopes up and failing.

"This is just a trip for mommy and daddy, bud," I said noncommittally. "But we both love you, and we'll be back soon, okay? We promise."

I knelt down and hugged my son, and he asked, "Will you bring Kakie back?", and it broke the already-shattered pieces of my heart into smaller shards.

"Alexander Joseph Luthor, better known as Lex," I replied, though without the enthusiasm that usually accompanied the references I made of their names. "Katie is thinking about you right now, thinking about how when she gets back she's gonna watch alllll the movies you guys like together. That's all you need to worry about, dude. You just need to be ready for when Kakie gets back because you guys are gonna have some late nights."

I wrapped my arms around our son and squeezed him tight. In truth, I didn't know what was going to happen. I didn't know if we were going to bring Katie back. I didn't know if she was going to come back at all. Hell, I didn't know if me and his mother were going to come back at all. For all I knew, we were orphaning our son the moment we stepped out the door.

"We're going to have fun!" my mother-in-law's accent-heavy voice chimed in, and I wiped the tears from under Alex's eyes as Dana stepped closer to us. "Your mom and dad will be back soon, honey."

Dana hugged her daughter and told her she loved her, and that she would see her soon, and then repeated it almost exactly with me, then stepped beside her grandson.

"We'll be back before you know it, sweetie." Kimmy knelt down to Alex and planted a kiss on his cheek. Our boy nodded and wrapped his arms around his mom. I know that she too was doing her best to not make it feel like the last embrace they would ever share. "Go ahead with Lola."

She brushed her own tears away and watched as Alex wiped his nose on the sleeve of his sweatshirt and walked down the hall next to Dana.

"As your father, I have to try one last time to dissuade you from this." The boom in Shawn Hill's voice was considerably dampened by concern and worry. "But I know it won't work, so I'll just tell you to please, please be careful."

"I know, daddy. We will." Kimmy hugged her dad, and then he turned his attention to me.

"You're walking my little girl into the snake pit," he said, this time much more sternly. "But I know you're doing what you need to do to save yours, and I know you'd prefer to go alone but she won't let you. I know you're in an impossible position, but you both need to be smart. The second you can call the police, you do it."

I simply nodded to acknowledge his advice, and that was good enough for him. Taking a tight grip on my hand and shaking twice, he said, "We'll see you in a few days. All three of you."

Not of my own volition, a thought materialized in my mind, but I snuffed it out before I could speak it.

Or none of us.

II

As a rule, I've always been a very cautious driver. Since getting my reckless driving out of the way in my teenage years, and then developing a perpetual anxiety over years of driving with a revoked license, I rarely speed aside from the appropriate five miles per hour over the limit, I come to a complete stop at stop signs, and I seldom chance yellow lights. Kimmy always says that I drive like a grandma, but in reality, I was just invisible. I was the driver no one noticed, and that was just how I liked it. But that day I forewent my typical law-abiding ways and weaved from lane to lane on I-70, my knuckles white as I gripped the steering wheel. Our first stop after leaving Kimmy's parent's house had been an electronics store, where I bought a radar detector that occasionally beeped and twice served its primary purpose of telling me when to slow down, lest we have our already horrible trip made worse yet.

The drive east through moonlit Colorado might very well have been beautiful, but I didn't notice. My sight was tunneled in an ever-shrinking vignette that started at the edges of my vision and gradually tightened as we got closer to that small town in northern Kansas. This would be my third and last time there.

One way or another, this would be my last time there.

We had left just before 8 P.M. intending to drive through the night, which, according to the app on Kimmy's phone, would bring us to the small town around seven in the morning. We had debated on if we should drive through the day, find a place to sleep that was near enough that we could still get there, and have the whole of the following day to do what we needed to do, but ultimately decided that neither of us would sleep anyway, and the sooner we got there the better.

The soundtrack to our drive was the third season of Archer, but neither myself nor Kimmy was really hearing it, and we certainly weren't laughing. Kimmy sat there with a frightening visage of determination. She knew as well as I did that when we found what we were looking for, we might have to do things, cross lines we never imagined ourselves as having to cross, and I think that despite me being the one who had a decidedly violent past, Kimmy was even more prepared for any eventualities than I was.

We spent much of the first ¾ of the drive with few words exchanged between us. The last time we'd shared a drive that quiet and tense had been during one of our few noteworthy fights, although this was exponentially worse. I think each of us was trying to preemptively rationalize whatever our forthcoming actions might have been, and I think we were both trying to ward off the admission that we were hoping we would get to cross the line that separated rescue from revenge.

As we crossed into Kansas, Kimmy took my hand in hers and my nearly pinpointed vision opened back up considerably. She lowered the volume on Archer and asked what the plan was.

My silence lingered for another few moments. What we would do once we got to our destination area had been the only other thing on my mind. "I honestly don't know. All we're really going on here is a barely visible **X** in a kid's drawing, which I know, I was the one to say that that's all we need, and I really do think it will be. But there's a fuckton of farmland out this way, and there are probably a ton of barns. Regardless, though, we're going to drive until we find ours. We'll ask any and everyone we can. We'll stop at Daisy's…hopefully this time I won't be kidnapped. We'll stop at the motel, everywhere in between and outside, and we'll ask if they know of a barn that has something to do with an 'X'."

She nodded her head, and in my periphery I then saw her look at her feet, accompanied by a sniffle.

"We're going to get her." I squeezed her hand twice. "And she's going to be fine."

I said the words with as much conviction as I could muster, but the image of Katie's little hand less two fingers was embedded in every syllable.

"Ow!" Kimmy quietly but sharply exclaimed, and I realized I hadn't loosened up after the second squeeze, only continued constricting her hand in mine. I let go and apologized, but she reached back and grabbed my hand again, and looked ahead at the flat road rushing under us at ninety-eight miles per hour, and five words passed by her lips as certainly as if she could see the future.

"She's going to be fine."

III

Things became familiar right around the same area as my previous trip, the one in which I'd been abducted and subsequently allowed to leave. And where the trees and fields and landscape at large seemed more foreboding then, they were downright haunted now. Every structure could be the place our daughter was sitting at the whims of a torturous monster with two fewer fingers than she had when we'd last seen her. As we barreled down the two-lane road that would eventually allow a left turn into the parking of Daisy's Diner, I noticed the burnt-out husk of some structure I'm not sure I ever realized had been there in the first place. The grass seemed paler, the air heavier.

This seemed like a place the rest of the world forgot about, and maybe it was.

We rounded the familiar bend and there stood Daisy's Diner, up ahead to the left of the road. The sun was hardly over the eastern horizon and gave the restaurant an almost ethereal glow. I put on the left turn signal and veered into the empty parking lot, pulling into the spot closest to the door. As I put the car in park, a man in jeans and a red flannel shirt exited the eatery with a white styrofoam cup in hand. He nodded once and raised his coffee in salutation as he walked past our car, then walked down the road in the direction from which we'd come.

In all of a second, I peered through the windows into the Diner, able to see where I was sitting with my family when all this began. Inside was the waitress I'd had interactions with before, Roberta, putting a bottle of ketchup on the table at the booth nearest the door. It seemed to me that Roberta was the sole server at Daisy's Diner, as I'd never seen anyone else taking orders or delivering food. It looked as if she regarded our vehicle for a moment, then went back to what she was doing.

Without a second thought, I opened the door and stepped out of the car, but Kimmy called out to me.

"What if they're…" she began as I put my forearms on top of the car and leaned down to look in at her.

"If they're what?"

"It's just…you've been here twice, and both times, bad things have happened. They didn't do anything when you were taken from here, and the cops didn't do anything when the car was broken into. This place doesn't want to help us. This town, this horrible fucking place…" her voice cut out before she could continue.

I crawled into the front seat of the car and ran my hand over Kimmy's long brunette hair. There was some driving force in me that was pushing me to go into the restaurant and force information out of whoever may be inside it, to extract whatever pertinent details I could by breaking, smashing, destroying. Something told me that there was a piece of the puzzle that could be found inside; all I needed to do was spot it. In retrospect, it was an impulse decision to go inside; Kimmy was right - this small town in northern Kansas did not want to help us. On the contrary, this was a place that seemed to want to devour us, to swallow us whole. But right then, I just wanted to ask a person from this area if they knew of any barns with an 'X' on top, and I was suddenly reminded of how thin the reasoning for our returning to this place really was.

"Come with me," I said. "Stand at the door, keep an eye on the car so that fuckface can't sneak up on it again. We'll be in and out in under thirty seconds. This lady just seems like…like if this place was a person, it would be her. We could save ourselves a ton of time if she can just say, 'oh, yeah, there's a barn with an X on it down the road two miles', you know?"

Kimmy took a deep breath, nodded, and got out of the car. We stepped through the first door, and my wife took up her position, perched halfway inside the small vestibule between the restaurant and the outside while I stepped through the door and into Daisy's Diner proper, the DING from above the door giving me the feeling of a long needle puncturing my eardrums.

Roberta was at a table near the back of the restaurant when I stepped onto the frayed carpeting.

"Sit wherever," the waitress called out to me as she walked behind the counter and grabbed a pot of coffee (one cup shy of being full) from the burner, heading towards me. Her tone was brusque, and I tried to tell myself it was due to being early in the morning, but a larger part of me felt it was just the garden-variety negativity of this place pouring out of her.

When she laid eyes on me, there was an instant of recognition, a familiarity that she couldn't place, and her eyes hinted that she was cycling through her memories to try to place me.

"Need to ask you something," I replied with a similar bluntness, cutting right to the chase. Our daughter was somewhere nearby suffering any number of horrors; I didn't have time for pleasantries. She looked at me quizzically. "Do you remember a while back, like...Jesus, like four years ago, a car got broken into in the parking lot?"

Her brow furrowed, but then a wave of realization washed over her face all in a moment and was suppressed in the next as she steeled herself. The fact that this woman was, at best, wildly unobservant, given the fact that I had vanished from her restaurant for an entire day and she hadn't noticed, made it even more surprising when she did indeed recall the incident that had kicked off this entire bloody, traumatic ordeal.

"I do. Police came, all that?"

"Yeah, that's it," I said. "Do you--"

"You were here another time too, year ago or so?" she interrupted me, and at that point, I knew she knew who I was.

"Yeah, yeah, that was me. Sorry about that, by the way. I was having a...bad day."

Roberta didn't answer, just picked up a towel and started absentmindedly wiping down the counter around the coffeemaker.

"Do you remember who was here that night? The one where my car got broken into?"

The waitress scoffed and took a step down to clean an unwiped space on the counter. "Honey, I don't remember what I had for breakfast yesterday."

I hung my head, pinched the bridge of my nose. "Yeah...one last question. Are there any barns around here?"

She scoffed even louder this time. "Did you drive here with your eyes closed? Farms is all there is around here. Farms have barns. Throw a rock in any direction, it'll bounce off three of them. I can tell you where some grass is too, you need me to."

My jaw clenched. I turned my head and saw Kimmy doing the same towards me, then returning her focus to our car and the area around it. A combination of words, both biting and accusatory and still in search of information, crept up the back of my throat, but through sheer force of will, my tongue pushed them back down. I was tempted to ask about a barn with an 'X' on it, but something told me not to.

"Thank you. You've been exactly as helpful as you've ever been," I said, and turned to leave. DING. I nodded to Kimmy to go, and she held the door for me as we left Daisy's Diner for what would be the last time.

"Anything?" she asked once we were in the car, but I hardly heard her. I was too busy watching Roberta through the window as she stood behind the counter looking out at us.

"Huh? Uh, no. No, of course not. That woman is fucking useless."

Roberta peered out at us for nearly thirty seconds before going back to wiping the counter, and as Kimmy and I pulled out of the lot, an old, beat-up Ford Escort pulled into the spot next to ours, and a man and young boy got out, laughing about something. Seeing this father and who I assumed was his son enjoying their morning overwhelmed me with a profound sadness that made me miss both of my children, and I gripped the steering wheel tight as our car idled in the middle of the long two-lane road. Kimmy reached over and put her hand on mine and brought me back from spiraling down into my misery.

"Pull up the map of this shithole," I said as I pulled off to the side of the road just ahead of Daisy's, and she did. The amount of space between any denoted landmarks stood in stark contrast to the maps we usually used in the more metropolitan areas in which we lived. Large gaps sat between the few businesses this town held, and it appeared that all that space was the farmland. In our trips around the country in years past, I distinctly remembered much of the farmland being labeled by the name of the owner's business for which they farmed, but that wasn't the case here. It was just blank.

"We can't just assume that the place we're looking for is in this town, either." Kimmy pointed out. "Like, I assume it's close, but there's no guarantee it's here here."

"Yeah..." I replied, pressing my thumb and index finger to the screen of her phone and pinching, zooming out on the map. "Jesus, look how much farmland there is. Just around this town is what...like four hundred square miles of farms and woods?"

Kimmy looked over at me, and I knew at once what she was thinking.

"Guess we better get to it."

IV

Even though we couldn't assume that the barn we were looking for belonged to a farm in the immediate area around the town, I reasoned it was a safe bet. I pointed out that it made sense that both times I had been here before, the person responsible for our misery had been nearby. I had always assumed that this person had somehow been keeping tabs on us - such was the reason for our convoluted plan to get out of California - but that theory and the idea that they lived nearby weren't mutually exclusive.

As such, we began our search in the farmland immediately surrounding Daisy's, which in turn led to the farmland that surrounded the Whitmore. There were structures on each - various barns and farmhouses and shacks and sheds - but none that had anything like an 'X' on display like it was in the picture.

We drove around for nearly three hours, going up and down both paved and dirt roads between tall stalks of corn and wheat for thirty, forty miles at a time. We would get to a spot where we could see what constructs the land had to offer and put a pin in the map on Kimmy's phone when it didn't feature what we both did and didn't want it to.

And then we took a right turn, and a half mile up the road sat a left turn onto a dirt driveway that was blocked by a single chain hanging across it, with woods on either side of it. I felt a lump form in my throat as I read the rusted sign that hung sideways from the center of the chain:

BiloXy

Agriculture

"Oh my god," Kimmy said, her eyes welling up with tears once again.

A fire in my stomach told me this was it. It had to be. The dirt path was lined on either side by tall, looming trees, going down about a quarter mile before disappearing around a rightward bend a way down. I immediately checked the surrounding area for cameras; the man who had taken our daughter had always seemed exceptionally prepared, always one, two, ten steps ahead. But there were no cameras, at least not as near as I could tell. There were just trees. Rows and rows of trees standing like walls along the dirt road.

"We have to find the house or the barn or whatever buildings this farm uses. I bet there's a big ass 'X' on top of one of them." Kimmy nervously chewed at her thumbnail as I looked over at her. I reached and slid my hand between hers and her mouth and brought it down to the console between us. "Hey. Either she's here or she's not. If she is, we get her back. If she's not, we keep looking until we find the place she is. Everything else in between doesn't matter. We're going to do what we need to do. That's it."

She nodded, then took a deep breath. "Let's go."

I pulled our vehicle to the side of the road and backed down a slight slope between two trees so it was out of sight. We elected to walk, for however long it took. We didn't know if we even had the element of surprise going for us at all, but figured that we should try to preserve it if we did. Even if it were a sliver of a chance for a minuscule advantage, we wanted it.

V

I could feel my heartbeat in my throat and the back of my skull as we got out of the car. The rear door lifted in its almost-silent glide, and when it was open I lifted the false floor of the trunk that was meant to house the spare tire but now contained a collection of knives and pipes and a crowbar. Kimmy and I had debated the merits of getting a gun in the early days of this ordeal all those years ago, but ultimately decided against it. But even despite my abhorrence of them, not having one now felt like I was somehow not utilizing every tool available to get our daughter back to safety. But it didn't matter now. Kimmy and I each took two knives and secured one on our waists, the other on our ankles, then she picked the crowbar, me one of the two metal pipes. I put the false bottom back on without securing it and quietly closed the trunk.

With our weapons in their rightful places on our persons, the pipe and crowbar clutched tightly in our fists, Kimmy and I shared a hug. We embraced one another in silence, but we both knew that it might very well be the last time that happened. One or both of us might not make it out of this place. I pressed my lips to the top of her head and held them there for a moment, and when Kimmy broke the silence between us, it was with two words I hadn't expected.

"No clenching."

I relaxed my jaw, looked down, and saw her looking up at me with a warm smile on her face, one that I returned. Without another word, we turned and began walking through the woods parallel to the dirt road, which sat off to our right about a hundred feet. A cool breeze passed through the trees as the undergrowth crunched lightly beneath our feet. Up above, the sun beat down unfiltered, and the shadows seemed to be darker than they should have been, and I had the same feeling I felt as a child after I'd just seen a horror movie - that something was waiting for me in each and every one of them, wanting to draw me in.

We took the walk slowly; I didn't want to rush and fall victim to any traps our tormenter might have set. As we made our way, the humming of grasshoppers and the chirps of birds seemed to turn the volume down on themselves, and then all at once, the forestry seemed to fall wholly silent. The bend in the dirt road that we could see from the street turned rightward and extended at that angle for a few hundred feet, then veered left, and at that point, the woods transformed into the farmland we'd seen so much of over the previous hours.

We were relatively deep into the trees, so we ventured in closer to the road, and by the time we reached the end of the right curve and the beginning of the left, we couldn't see over the nearly eight-foot-tall ocean of corn stalks. With knives in our hands, we pushed through the stalks, getting deeper into the unknown acres that belonged to BiloXy Agriculture. We moved at a soft angle until we were nearly at the dirt road and then moved directly to it.

And as I pushed through the final row of corn before that pathway, the opposite side of the road's crops ceased in a straight line, and beyond it sat a large field with three structures.

A farmhouse, which even from the distance we were at appeared to be dilapidated. A smaller building next to the farmhouse that looked to be a garage of some kind, with a rusted blue pickup truck sitting on cement blocks in front of it. And a large red barn with white doors and a large rusted X perched atop the slanted roof, stylized in the same way as the one on the sign that blocked off the dirt road that had led us to where, with any luck, we would find our kidnapped daughter.

Seventeen

I

The sea of corn in which we stood stretched further downwards in a perfectly straight line the way we had been heading, running alongside the large field that held the three buildings, eventually meeting a massive crop of wheat that ran behind it and stretched for as far as we could see. The habitable area was almost enclosed, like it was separate from the rest of the world. In my mind, I viewed it as its own level of hell.

I looked at Kimmy, a single tear trailing down her cheek as she surveyed the land before us, her crowbar gripped in her shaking hand. I took a deep breath, telling myself that we were almost there, that this was almost over.

"Let's keep going through the corn, get as close to the house as we can while still being hidden. We can cut over into the wheat, go to the house. It'll be the shortest distance out in the open. There's gotta be a backdoor."

She didn't need to say anything, but I knew Kimmy had the same thought that I did - that this man who had developed such a fixation on our daughter seemed to think of her more as a friend than anything else. The letter he had written her for her birthday, which now seemed like an entire lifetime ago, came to mind:

Dear Katie,

I would like so much to be your frend. I don't have a lot of frends, but youre pichures make me so happy and they are so good! You are a vary vary good artist and to be a friend with someone so tallented would be so fun. I dont think youre mommy and daddy would want us to be frends thow so maybe it could be a fun secrit. I want you to draw me lots and lots and lots and lots of pichures so that I can look at them all the time. I hope we can be frends.

Kimmy and I agreed that there would likely be no deciphering the person who had been terrorizing us. There would be no "figuring him out". The man who had been doing this seemed like a puzzle with half the pieces missing. In one respect, he seemed illiterate, simple-minded, and childlike. But he was also meticulous, vicious, and evidently put a great deal of forethought into his actions against us. We had no idea what horrors he was subjecting Katie to, what he was...doing to her, what he was making her do. But if we went by his letter, he wanted Katie on this farm to do what she did best - art. And if he really wanted our daughter to consider him a "frend", it stood to reason that he would put her in the house.

We moved. We followed my rudimentary plan, still moving slowly, and after a few minutes we were near the point where the corn met the wheat, and I poked my head out to see if I could spot anyone there. I saw no one, just a deterioration of the facade of the house that I hadn't been able to see from a distance. The white paint was faded in some places, completely gone in others, leaving the brown and oftentimes rotted wood underneath it visible. Garbage littered the front yard - soda bottles, empty chip bags, crumpled-up fast food receptacles. A window facing us had been shattered outwards, as evidenced by the shards of glass in the grass below it.

The wheat was much easier to move through, although it was also more visibly disturbed as we contorted our bodies in our best efforts to do so as little as possible. After only another minute, we were standing at the edge of the wheat field, not a step away from the backyard of the farmhouse.

II

A rusted swing set with one leg shorter than the rest stood at an angle, one swing's chains wrapped around the support bar at the top until the seat touched it, the other with one chain snapped, leaving its seat vertical and nearly touching the worn away ground underneath it. A faded green plastic sandbox in the shape of a turtle sat off to the right, only the sand had been overtaken by the overflowing amount of garbage it now held. Off to the right of that was the turtle's shell, which sported a crack that cut through ¾ of it.

More garbage was strewn about the backyard, and my thoughts drifted back to when I lived in the inner city, where the act of throwing your refuse out the window wasn't met with derision, but indifference.

This place was worse. It was an amount of trash that seemed almost deliberate, like whoever lived here had made a conscious choice to eschew typical home waste management.

The rear face of the house was similarly disheveled, with pieces of the siding missing and what appeared to be a wholly unfinished paint job, one that told me the previous color of the house was a soft blue. A window stood near the top of the back of the house, directly above the backdoor, which had been decorated with deep gouges that spelled out "HI MOM", and I felt the bottom of my stomach drop out. I wondered if that message had been there before our torture had started, or if the vicious, hurried scratches were put there recently as a kind of callout to Kimmy. I looked over and saw the same wonder - and fear - in her eyes. Reading this monster's most recent note, the entire subject matter was painful, but that he referred to my wife and me as "Mommy and Daddy" made me sick to my stomach.

Kimmy and I shared a glance and both scurried across the back lawn, carefully avoiding discarded styrofoam cups and crumpled-up bags and plastic wrappers from candy bars. I slinked by the hanging swing while Kimmy went around the swing set entirely, stepping between the turtle and its cracked shell.

When we reached the back of the house and crouched beneath the window next to the door, I held my index finger to my lips and just listened for a moment.

A calm wind…

The rustling of the wheat and the corn and the trees that bordered it all…

The squawk of a distant bird…

But no movement inside the house or anywhere else.

III

The window was coated with a layer of filmy grime both inside and out, making it nearly impossible to see through it to the inside of the house. A small spot in the bottom right corner did allow me to learn that the back door opened to the kitchen, and I told Kimmy as much. We agreed to stay together, opting not to make the same mistakes as the characters in our favorite horror movies. After another deep breath, and while staying as low to the ground as we could, we climbed the two steps up to the back door. When I attempted to turn the doorknob, the door simply pushed open; the tumbler in the knob was broken, and thus the door didn't close properly.

The back door opened directly into a tiny foyer. Directly ahead was a staircase that led down to pure, empty darkness. There had once been a door there, but, as evidenced by the splintered wood around where the hinges used to be, it had been forcefully removed. To our immediate right was the filthiest kitchen I've ever laid eyes on. Dishes were piled up in the sink, caked with unfinished meals that had long since molded and now housed families of maggots and lingering flies. It appeared that someone had attempted to make the tower of ceramic plates and bowls even taller, but their new additions had fallen to the peeling, yellowed, cracked linoleum floor and shattered. Moisture had seeped in behind the bright yellow floral wallpaper that bordered the mess of the kitchen, leaving it peeling in the places it wasn't outright torn off. Off to the other side of the kitchen was an open door leading into a small bathroom that, even from the distance I was at, I could tell had been condemned to a similar state of disrepair.

The smell was horrendous. It stung my nostrils as I took my first step into this house, this house that in any other scenario I would be certain was abandoned, condemned. My eyes watered from the smell and I had to choke back a gag as I turned around and motioned to Kimmy that we would first investigate the basement. I took my phone out of my pocket and shined a light down the stairs, getting a narrow view of the cold cement walls.

To my surprise, the stairs made minimal noise as we descended, even despite feeling as though they might snap in two as I put my weight down on them. I stepped onto the unforgiving concrete floor of the basement and found that it opened up to both sides. I chose to go left and found a collection of metal shelving units that held innumerable mason jars filled with jellies, jams, fruit preserves, vegetables, sugar, salts, peppers, and more. More garbage was scattered around the floor, and the smell made Kimmy gag several times, to the point I thought she might vomit. She composed herself, then added the light from her phone to mine as we stepped to the back of this side of the basement, finding that it wrapped around to the opposite side.

Kimmy was ahead of me at this point and came to a sudden stop as she somehow simultaneously gasped and had all the air extracted from her lungs.

"What?!" I whispered sharply, quickly stepping next to her, and then nearly dropped the pipe I had been clutching as all the air in my lungs joined Kimmy's on its outward journey. I saw what had stopped her in her tracks, and suddenly my world started spinning and I had to put my hand on the back of one of the steps to steady myself.

The walls on the right side of the basement were covered with pictures of all sizes, of all manner of different subjects, in all different mediums. Paintings, markers, crayons, colored pencils, regular pencils, graphite, and charcoal, all in Katie's distinct style. There must have been two hundred pictures taped to the rear wall and the one it connected to on the right side of the basement, all overlapping one another in a huge collage.

"Jesus..." I struggled to make my vocal cords produce the necessary sounds. I stepped up to the wall and held the light up close on a magic marker portrait she'd done of herself, which was captioned in big black letters scrawled over the bottom third of the page, '**BEST FREND**'.

"Katie..." Kimmy said, absently examining a painting of a large tree.

At the front of the basement and far off to the right was a threshold of a different room. I nudged Kimmy and directed her attention toward it, then we stepped carefully in its direction. Kimmy removed the knife on her hip from its sheath, prompting me to do the same. My heartbeat was like a bass drum in my ears, and I was clenching my teeth so hard I thought they might shatter in my mouth. Kimmy had a look of pure determination on her face, but I knew that she was simply filtering her fear through a facade of seeming ready for whatever awaited us around every dark corner.

With my knife at the ready, I quickly rounded the corner and flashed my light inside, then quickly turned around, tears pouring from my eyes, bile rushing up my throat and ejecting from my mouth, hitting the floor with a splat.

"No, no, no, NO, NO," I began pleading, each syllable louder than the one before it until Kimmy rushed up to me and put her hand over my mouth.

She calmly shushed me as I shook violently and nearly crumpled to the floor.

"Oh my god...oh my god...Kimmy, she's—he fuckin'—" I couldn't go on. I pressed my face into my wife's waist, the world crashing down around me.

IV

In the adjoining room was a metal table, the kind you might find in the kitchen of a restaurant. Atop the table was what equaled nearly two whole corpses. There were four legs, four arms with three hands totaling thirteen fingers, two torsos that had the skin folded open like an autopsy, the organs strewn about, and two scalps with brunette hair that was caked together in lumps by the deluge of blood that covered the entire gruesome scene.

"Oh my god...no..." Kimmy whispered to herself, and she stepped away from me, turning towards the macabre collection of children's limbs. The smell stung my nose as I sniffled, and I couldn't bring myself to turn around and see what she was doing. I heard her nearly silent footsteps move into the small area, followed by a rustling like she was moving things around. I buried my face in my hands and cried. It felt like my world had imploded, the pressure of this entire situation finally causing my life to collapse in on itself.

At that moment, I wanted nothing more than a half gram of heroin. Such moments are the ones that remind me how perpetually close I am to relapse and losing everything I've worked for. A close second to my yearning for that gray powder was a visceral need for violence and destruction. I was going to find whoever was on this property - or wait for them to get back if they weren't already here - and beat them almost to death with my bare hands. When I was finished, I would wait for them to come to, and then I would light their house on fire with them inside. Then I would piss on the ashes.

I stood up, my mind a fog of anger and grief and confusion, and just as I was going to take my first step towards my rampage, I heard Kimmy's voice from behind me say something, barely above a whisper, almost as if she was talking to herself.

I turned my head, though I kept my attention on Katie's drawings. I wasn't sure if I had actually heard my wife say anything, or if I was just hoping I had.

"Nick..." her voice was on the verge of tears. "...it's not her."

I spun the rest of the way and saw Kimmy standing in front of the metal table that held the gnarled viscera of the victims of the kidnapper, who was actually, to be more accurate, a murderer. I hurried next to her, needing to confirm for myself that my daughter hadn't been dissected like so many middle school science class subjects. The skin on the bodies looked soft, decaying. The heads - aside from the scalps that had been ripped off - were nowhere to be found.

"How do—how do you know?" I barely managed to ask.

The four arms weren't organized, but they were in the same general area. Kimmy pointed to the hands one at a time and said, "The hands. Look."

I reluctantly moved in closer to the severed appendages. When Katie was five years old, she tripped while playing outside in our driveway. Around the walkway that led to the front door of our home in California was a small river of decorative pebbles, some of which were rather sharp. When Katie stumbled to the ground and broke her fall with her hands, some of the sharper pebbles had dug into the skin of her palm just below her left thumb. The resulting cuts had formed a rudimentary smiley face on that fleshy part of her hand, leaving a scar in the same formation, light enough that you wouldn't notice it if you didn't know it was there. She always said that when she waved to someone, they were getting a smile too.

But the three bloodied hands on the slab were free of such a scar, and an exclamatory gasp escaped my mouth.

It wasn't her.

I pulled Kimmy into me and wrapped my arms around her and squeezed. She let out a few sobbing breaths, then stepped back, steeling herself. I took her lead and ran a hand down my face, then reflexively cracked my neck, suddenly feeling like an action movie cliche. Only then did I realize what this room was.

The cold, dark enclosure stretched back about ¾ of the length of the entire basement, and the rear wall was covered by a white, bloodstained sheet. This was the makeshift film set in which a little girl in a princess dress spent the last few minutes of her life horrified, ultimately butchered by the same murderous animal who had taken our daughter.

Something perhaps obvious then dawned on me: the hand we'd received shortly before the Christmas that seemed to be a thousand years ago was once connected to this body, and that this body had once worn that princess dress.

I shined my light and stepped over toward where that child had given a haunting performance under the direction of the presumed owner of the house. As badly as I wanted to find him and get Katie back, I also wanted to give justice to the girl who brought Princess Penelope to life, to make it so that she hadn't died in vain. I wanted to learn her name, to give the people that she'd been taken from closure. I knew how they felt, the emptiness in their hearts, the waiting, the praying. But my thoughts quickly returned to the present situation. There was still hope that Kimmy and I could be spared the greatest trauma a parent can suffer. All we had to do was find our daughter.

V

We moved silently, avoiding the crunching bags on the basement floor. We ascended the steps and entered the squalid kitchen. Used napkins and paper towels were caked with grime and sat collected in small piles on the floor, the round kitchen table, the counter. Plates and bowls and cups and silverware were encrusted with black and green grime, the leavings of unfinished meals. The smell once again wafted in our faces, carried on the back of a gentle breeze that came from the front of the house.

We stood as still as statues for a moment, listening for...anything. Some kind of movement, a rustling, some idea of where anyone was. The only sound we heard was the soft whisking sound of the wheat flowing back and forth in the wind, and the occasional shuffling tree branches in the distance when the breeze picked up more forcefully. Walking through the kitchen quietly proved to be an arduous task, with all the garbage and discarded food crunching and sliding underfoot. The kitchen opened into a living room, which to its left connected to what was supposed to be a dining area, but in reality was all just one big open-floor garbage can filled with more of the same that we'd found in the backyard and basement.

There were two couches forming a half-square that were stained in some spots and cut open in others, stuffing spilling out like the guts of a smashed pumpkin. A coffee table rested in front of one of the couches and had another fifteen or so pieces of Katie's, all ones we'd never seen, scattered and piled atop it. The light green wallpaper was ripped and shredded, and deep gouges decorated each of the walls we could see, as though someone was thrusting a knife into them and putting all their weight on it to slice through the drywall. An entertainment center opposite the couches held a TV with a smashed screen, and yet another piece of daughter's artwork taped over the damage.

Straight ahead was the front door of the house, and to the left were stairs. With the ground floor void of any people, we went to move upstairs but were stopped in our tracks. The walls from the landing of the stairs and up to the second floor featured the only decorations we'd seen that weren't produced by our daughter's hand - photographs. All the pictures were framed, some with cracked glass. Taking care to avoid the loud refuse that adorned the steps, we examined the hanging photos.

"No fucking way," I muttered under my breath, barely loud enough for Kimmy to hear.

On the landing of the steps was a vertically oriented snapshot of Daisy Diners' premiere server, Roberta, clad in an ill-fitting wedding dress that forced the stressed flesh of her massive breasts out over the top. She was standing in an awkward embrace with whom I assume was her husband, the man who had handed over the keys to rooms 3 and then 5 at the Whitmore Motel. The next two pictures leading upstairs featured that same pair, and in one of them, the man who had walked into Daisy's all those years before and asked whom the blue Hyundai parked out front belonged to stood between them, arms slung out over their shoulders.

The next one featured the Billings, both father and son, in civilian clothing, the flannel and jeans that seemed to be the area's uniform. To the left of the younger Billings, the one who had actually been of some help to me when I'd been abducted from behind the restaurant, was another man, this one in a t-shirt and jeans, gauntly thin with a wide, gummy smile. I had no way of knowing for certain, but I assumed that that man was Dave, the nine-one-one operator.

Two more pictures featured a few people I didn't know accompanying the ones I did, but the final picture that adorned the walls before we reached the top of the stairs was a group photograph featuring Roberta, the man from the motel, both Billings men, a young man I didn't recognize and another that I did, the latter of whom was off to the side of the picture, nearly out of frame. The familiar face belonged to the man who had picked me up as I wandered aimlessly after leaving the TV House in the middle of the woods. The man I didn't recognize was younger by about fifteen years, with a head of greasy, thin brown hair, and was moderately overweight, wearing a dirt-stained wife beater and pants that were held up by a length of orange extension cord. I thought that if this house was turned into a person, it would be him. In the background was another man, but it appeared as if his face had been intentionally scratched out.

All of these pictures made me sick to my stomach. They had to all have known. Each and every one of them. I thought back to the interactions I'd had with each of them, in an instant recalling the odd mannerisms they'd displayed, hints that they were aware of our plight and the person responsible for it. But it didn't matter now. Right now, we just needed to find Katie.

At the top of the stairs was another bathroom, but where the downstairs lavatory was dirty, this one rivaled the depths of the deepest sewers. Piss and shit filled the bowl, completely coating the riser and spilling over onto the floor. As we climbed the stairs, I thought the odor of the house couldn't get any worse, but laying eyes on the second-floor bathroom seemed to permit my senses of smell and taste to add to the foul collection. The rest of the floor was wet, littered with molding clothes and towels.

Down the upstairs hallway were two doors on the left, one closed, the next open, and another on the right at the end of it. A smaller door, likely to a closet, adorned the wall between the bathroom and that last door. I handed my crowbar to Kimmy and retrieved the knife from my waist. I stepped gingerly over a bag that once held paper towels, and directly onto the corner of an empty Oreo package, which produced a crinkling sound that felt loud enough to wake the dead. I froze, but as I stood still, I found myself thinking that this place had to have rats and that such sounds must be common.

When nobody emerged to investigate the noise I'd made, I continued, gingerly turning the doorknob to the first door on the left. I pushed it open and peered inside. Only clean behind the door, the floor was an ocean of trash, so much so that it made the rest of the house look clean by comparison. It was piled ankle-high from wall to wall, even in the closet that was missing its door on the opposite end of the room. A mattress sat on the floor, stained with god knows what, and a single blanket was crumpled up at the bottom of it. In the corner of the room was a sight that brought with it a nearly crippling wave of nausea: several, maybe six or seven, pairs of children's shoes, all filthy and stained with blood.

Kimmy poked her head into the room and saw shoes, but she didn't react. All I could think was that when this was all over, she was going to have to confront all the horrible things she'd seen today - we both would. But there wasn't time for that now.

We shuffled down the hall, where Kimmy took the lead into the next room, finding it similarly filled with garbage. Across the hall was the cleanest room in the house. There was a mattress on an actual bedframe, and that mattress was covered by hastily applied sheets and blankets. A dresser with a non-shattered television sitting at an angle atop it stood next to the door, and minimal garbage peppered the stained carpet. An open window sent yellowed curtains gently billowing.

Just as I was about to remark on the relative cleanliness of this solitary room, we heard the first noise that wasn't from nature or one of us since we'd arrived - careless footsteps trudging through the ocean of trash downstairs. We stood perfectly still, waiting to see if whoever was down there was going to stay there, but they didn't. The footsteps and the smashing and crunching noises made their way through the kitchen and living room, then turned up the stairs.

I immediately gripped my knife and turned around, ready, if not praying, for someone to come upstairs, someone I could vivisect until they told me where Katie was. It would frighten me soon thereafter, and still frightens me, how much I regressed at that moment, but then exponentiated on that propensity for violence. That wasn't me anymore, but at that moment, I wanted nothing more than to brutalize as the children in the basement had been brutalized.

That is, until Kimmy reached up and put a hand on my shoulder. I looked back at her and she mouthed "Window," and pointed to the open space in the wall behind us, just outside of which was a low, angled roof with a chimney that would, with any luck, block anyone else who might be elsewhere on the property from seeing us. We took soft but quick steps across the room, careful to not hit any of the few pieces of garbage. Kimmy went out first and I followed, and we crept out of the line of sight of anyone who might enter the room.

We listened to the person reach upstairs, hawk what sounded to be a mighty ball of phlegm up from his throat and spit it out. He then walked to the second bedroom, rustled around a bit, and then headed back downstairs. After a moment, a man emerged from behind the house and headed straight for the garage, entering through a side door. From our angle, we couldn't see the man's face, but he appeared slightly overweight, and for a split second, half an instant, I thought it appeared that he was wearing a mask.

It was him.

The man who had broken into our car and stolen our daughter's drawings.

The man who had entered our motel room while we slept.

The man who had come into our home and left a gift, who had knocked me out and delivered me to a bizarre enclosure filled with TVs, appeared on them all, and burnt that enclosure down.

The man who had kidnapped our daughter.

VI

My mouth went dry and my hands started shaking, but Kimmy caught me before I tipped too far in the direction of rage and despair. She put her hand around mine and squeezed twice. I took a deep breath and nodded to tell her I was okay.

We crawled back in through the window and made it downstairs quickly. It appeared we still had the element of surprise, and I intended to use it. I was going to kick the door open and press my knife into the man's throat. I was going to force him to tell me where Katie was, one way or the other.

Back outside, we stayed low and hurried to the rear of the garage, which held two windows. We crouched beneath the window closest to the house, and I took a deep breath. I raised slightly, doing my best to see inside, but some sort of metal rack and its contents prevented me from doing so. So we moved down. Another deep breath, and Kimmy and I both lifted ourselves just enough to see inside.

And what we saw was that overweight man, with a hand-colored blue and pink mask, standing at the window, looking right at us.

Eighteen

"HI MOMMY AND DADDY!!!!!!" the man in the mask shrieked in a high, child-like voice, then turned around and began sprinting toward the open door next to the main garage door.

Kimmy took off first, and I followed only a few steps behind. The man barreled toward the barn with the 'X' on it, the right door of which was slightly ajar. We ran after him and watched as he slinked through the space in the door, disappearing into the darkness within. Kimmy came to a stop just short of the door, and just as I was going to rush in through the same space, Kimmy yelled out, "Stop!", and I obeyed. She said to open the doors, thus allowing sunlight to pour in.

I gripped the handle on the front of the door on the right while Kimmy did the same on the door next to it. Just as we began to pull, the sound of quick footsteps rose from silent to imminent, and the doors burst open, the man falling through them. The left door knocked Kimmy to the ground, and I heard her breathe in an audible gasp - the wind had been knocked out of her. As for me, the corner of the large door I had intended to open struck me above my left eye, sending me to the ground with the feeling of blood pouring down the side of my face.

My vision was blurred for a moment, but I saw the man in the mask push himself up from the ground with cackling laughter, and as he began sprinting towards the cornfield on the other side of the barn, he yelled out in a sing-song voice, "YOUUUU'LL NEVER FIIIIND HERRRR", and laughed some more.

Kimmy was up after only a few moments of deep breaths and running after him. Not wanting her to face him alone, I attempted to stand, but the world around me spun and I toppled back to the ground.

"KIMMY!!!!" I screamed out for her. I tried to get up again, failed again. I wiped the blood that was trickling over my eye and scrambled over to the leftmost door of the barn, which had crawled open after pushing Kimmy out of its path, resting against it, trying to get my bearings.

And then a sound.

I don't know if that sound started at that moment or if it had been happening before, but I was too dazed to know it.

It was a sound that I will think of every day for the rest of my life. A sound that will bring me solace in difficult times.

It was a voice marred by tears, quiet but insistent.

It was a voice I thought I would never hear again, and a word I thought I'd never hear that voice speak again.

"Daddy…"

I listened as intently as I could manage through a splitting headache to make sure I wasn't imagining it.

"Daddy…mommy…" followed by sniffles.

I used the wall to steady myself and stepped on weak legs into the barn. It was an open floor with a tall canopy that overlooked the ground level. Various pieces of farming equipment were off to the left, but the right side of the barn was largely empty but for a handful of hay bales. The words caught in my throat as I tried to call out to Katie. I finally managed to say her name, just loud enough to be audible. I heard her again. She was somewhere to the right of the cabin, near the rear wall. I again wiped the blood from my eye and told her to yell, to shout, to scream, to be louder, and to keep being louder so I could find her.

I followed her voice as she called out to me, and as I neared the rear wall of the barn with the 'X' on it, her voice shifted from being in front of me to below me. I dropped to the ground and pushed aside the hay that lay scattered on the wooden floor until I found a handle and padlock laying flush with the floor. It was a trapdoor.

"Katie!! Katie I'm coming! I'm here! I'm—cover your ears, I'm gon —I'm gonna break this lock!".

Without waiting for a response, I used the dull, pointed end of the knife's handle, which was made of harder steel than the rest of it and is known as a "skull cracker". I rained down blows on the lock as if I were stabbing it, thrusting my arm over and over and over again. The metal collided with the lock, weakening it, and after several more smashes, it finally separated. I dropped the knife and used shaking hands to remove the lock. I tossed it aside, then lifted and turned the empty half-circle knob, then threw the door open.

Katie sat up, having been on her side in a space only just large enough to hold her. Her hair was slicked against her face with tears and sweat, but she fell forward and wrapped her arms around me and squeezed me in the tightest hug she'd ever given me. As I broke the hug and put my hands on the side of her face to examine her, a gunshot rang out.

Nineteen

"Kimmy," I said, barely audibly and almost absentmindedly.

My heart sank to my stomach. She didn't have a gun. At the same moment I had gotten my daughter back, so too had I lost the love of my life. And somehow even worse, she would never know that Katie was safe, never be able to experience that flood of relief I felt when the uncertainty gave way to Katie falling into my arms.

I wanted to run out and find Kimmy, to make sure she was safe, but I couldn't lead Katie into even more danger. I rose to my feet and hurried my daughter across the barn. She didn't have shoes on and was wearing the same clothing she'd had on the night she was taken - blue pajama pants and a plain white t-shirt, both of which were considerably dirtier.

Once at the door, I told Katie to stay inside, just at the threshold where I could see her. I took a step outside, fighting the urge to sprint out into the vast expanse of corn on the other side of the barn. Instead, I called out.

"KIMMY!!!!!!" My vocal cords were only just able to produce the sounds, but through sheer will, I managed to scream. I screamed her name again. And again.

Finally, after my fourth time shouting her name, I heard a quiet, "Yeah", void of all emotion.

"Kimmy?!" I took Katie's hand and led her down the face of the barn towards where her mother had followed the man in the mask and scanned the brown and yellow and green wall of crops. I looked for any movement in a stalk of corn, listened for any shuffling.

And then she emerged into visibility, plodding through the stalks a few rows in. Katie and I rushed towards her but came to a standstill when she stepped out of the vegetation onto the cut grass. She walked listlessly, her head hanging.

She hadn't yet seen Katie, and when our daughter said "Mommy", life returned to her and she let out a joyous yelp, dropping her knife to the ground and covering her mouth, then sprinting to Katie and receiving the same enthusiastic hug I had. I wrapped my arms around both of them, but our reunion would need to wait.

"We need to go, now," I said, with no room for argument. I wanted to know what had happened. I wanted to know what Katie had been subjected to, but we didn't know when anyone else would be home. We could reasonably assume that Roberta and the man at the motel could be expected to stay absent, but there were other people in those pictures, people we didn't know, not to mention the Officers Billings.

So we ran. We cut across the property, then through the wheat, then went back onto the dirt road to move quicker than we could have through the corn. Finally, we cut into the woods and made it to our car.

The girls got into the backseat and I behind the wheel, and we sped away from BiloXy Agriculture and the house of horrors that stood upon it. I kept my eyes on the rearview, certain that I would see someone chasing after us. I didn't bother asking Kimmy what had happened yet - she was too busy sobbing, holding Katie in her arms.

We passed Daisy's Diner, and it was at that point I pulled my phone out. I scrolled through my contacts and called Detective Alina Morgan, who answered on the second ring.

"Detective Morgan? It's Nick—Botic. Nick Botic. I need you to do something, okay? Listen to me. I need you to call Jewell County, 'Jewell' with two 'L's. The sheriffs there. Tell them they need to get to Republic County, or just call the sheriffs from Republic, or the fuckin' FBI, I don't know how it works. Tell them there's a farm with—there's bodies. And the cops there, the town's cops, I think they might know about it, so I don't want to just call nine-one-one."

"Where are you?" the detective replied. "What's going on? What happened?"

"Just—just call the fucking cops here, the cops that aren't local. We saw pictures of them hanging up in the house with the people who took Katie."

"People? Wait, you found her? Mr. Botic, you found your daughter?"

I looked in the rearview and thought that Kimmy might never let Katie go again. "Yes. We got her. Tell them they need to go to BiloXy Agriculture. That's the name of the farm...the company, or whatever."

"Okay, Mr. Botic, where are you right now?"

The adrenaline was beginning to wear off, and the effects of having the skin above my left eye split open were setting in. I was suddenly aware that there was still blood leaking over my eye, and it was starting to feel like someone was hammering nails into my brain one swing at a time.

"I'm...ow, fuck...I'm on the freeway, headed towards...I don't know, some town," a sign was coming up quickly on my right. Courtland | 2 Miles. I relayed our present whereabouts and told the detective that we were headed to Jewell County Hospital, a spot Kimmy and I had picked ahead of our trip to go to, whether it was bringing Katie or ourselves or all three of us.

"Okay, get there, and stay there. I'm calling the sheriffs now. Keep your phone on. You'll be getting calls from...from me, from them, from...just keep your phone on, okay?"

"Yeah, I got it. Thank you Det—thank you, Detective Morgan." My headache was beginning to blind me. I blinked my eyes hard.

"Mr. Botic...are you okay?" she asked with genuine concern in her voice.

"I...yeah..." I veered off to the side of the road and came to a stop. I set the phone down on my lap without hanging up and sat back in my seat.

"Nick?" I heard Kimmy's voice behind me, but it sounded distant. I felt her hand on my shoulder. "Hey, hey!"

"You need to drive," I said as I clumsily climbed over the center console, and then everything went black.

Twenty

I

I remember flashes of consciousness as we pulled up to the hospital, being lifted from the car by paramedics and laid on a stretcher, wheeling through the hospital halls. But I finally fully came to a short time thereafter with a monstrous headache on top of a localized pain above my left eye. I was in a hospital bed, dressed in a white and green gown with my boxers on underneath, and an IV in my arm. I blinked my eyes hard, then scanned the room before me. It was empty.

I didn't waste a breath. "KIMMY!!!" I hollered. "KATIE!!!!!" I started to sit up, but just then, a man in Batman scrubs who looked like he'd jumped from the set of a soap opera rushed into my room. A name tag pinned to the left side of his shirt read **Ben**.

"Sir? Sir?" he sounded frantic. "Hey, you're okay. They're okay. Your wife and daughter, they're okay."

I looked past him and saw police in the hallway.

"Where are they?" I asked. "I need to see them."

"I'll go get them," he replied in his attempt at a calming voice. "You just relax, huh? You guys are safe. You're all good. Just sit back. I'll have them in here in just a minute."

I thanked him and laid back, watching the police out in the hallway. The two I could see leaned over to get a better look at me. Nurse Ben said something to the police, who nodded, and then he walked off. A minute went by, and then I saw my wife's beautiful face as she poked her head in. She stepped further in, her hands on Katie's shoulders as she walked just ahead of her.

"Hi Daddy," she said, and tears filled my eyes. "Are you okay?"

"Oh, I'm all good, Kate Mara aka Zoe Barnes from House of Cards. Oof, that was a bad one. Don't be like Zoe Barnes, sweetie," I said, and I could feel my head swimming. Kimmy offered a laugh through her tears.

"Are you okay?" she said, leaning down to kiss me. Even the light pressure on my lips sent a surge of pain through my head.

"Yeah, just the worst headache of my life," I replied. "Are you okay? Is Katie?"

"I'm okay." Kimmy's voice sounded unfamiliar, and I realized that I was hearing it without the tinge of worry that had accompanied it for the past almost four years; it had been replaced by relief. "And Katie is fine. They looked her over, did a couple of tests, did a...a kit."

I immediately knew that she was referring to a rape kit. The idea had plagued me since she'd been taken. I had spent an unhealthy amount of time envisioning the atrocities that she might have been going through, my mind veering off to the darkest depths of human depravity imaginable.

"And everything came back negative," she finished, and I squeezed tears out of my eyes. This had been a horrifying ordeal for Katie, undoubtedly, but at least she was spared being the victim of a vicious pedophile. "She said...honey, tell Daddy what you told the police."

"The big man just made me draw," Katie said as she walked up next to my hospital bed. "And paint and stuff. All day, sometimes all night. Even when I was tired."

I pictured this greasy, sweaty, filthy, overweight man hovering over my frightened daughter, forcing her to draw and paint until her fingers bled and cramped. I imagined his breath as particularly foul, passing through a mouth filled with rotten teeth, through a mask that had marinated in days, weeks, and months of perspiration.

The world seemed to stop spinning; for how long, I can't remember. I was just looking at Katie, at her face that was free of any signs of abuse, her hands which still contained all of her fingers. I thought about what could make a man become so obsessed with something as ultimately trivial as a child's artwork. An adult's obsession with a child was no novel occurrence, but there is typically a sexual component to it, one that was absent here. I looked at my daughter and reached over, laying my palm on her cheek, and asked, "Are you okay?"

Katie nodded and put her arms up, then leaned forward for the kind of awkward hug that happens when one of the huggers is laying down. When she rose, she stepped back over to her mom, who knelt down and kissed her forehead.

"Why don't you sit down here, sweetie?" Kimmy motioned toward a chair on the opposite side of my bed. Sometime between our arrival at the hospital and now, Katie had acquired a yellow legal pad and a handful of pens and permanent markers. Even despite her countless hours spent doing work over the last month and a half, it was still all she wanted to do. If this hadn't soured the idea of being an artist for her, nothing ever would.

II

Kimmy took the chair next to Katie and brought it around, sitting down next to me. She took my hand and planted a kiss on my cheek.

"What happened?" I asked quietly enough that Katie wouldn't hear. "I heard a gunshot. I thought you--"

"I know. I tried to chase him through the cornfield, but it was hard to see. I could hear his steps though, and I was following them, and then they stopped and I heard the gunshot, and it sounded like more running through the corn, but I think it was just birds or animals freaking out or whatever. I know it was stupid, but I went toward the sound of the shot. I like...knew what had just happened. It was off to my left. He had just...shot himself in the face with a shotgun. His head was..." she stared absently at the cover that lay on top of me.

"Jesus." I couldn't think of anything else to say.

A thought crept into my mind, one that I tried to suppress to no avail.

It all seemed too easy.

The man in the mask, which according to Katie she never saw him without, had yelled out that I would never find Katie, and I found her only moments later. She was awake, able to call out to me, hidden only by a poorly obscured trap door and a flimsy padlock.

The man had opportunities to kill all three of us at numerous points in our time on the BiloXy Agriculture property, and he hadn't. He instead had run off into the corn and committed suicide. Killing was very obviously not a new concept to him. There were the dismembered corpses of two children in the basement that confirmed that. Why hadn't he added us to his collection?

But mine was not to wonder. This day was a victory for our family. We had all made it out with minimal damage (physical damage, anyway), and we were safe.

"The cops, I guess the sheriffs or whoever, are going to the farm now," Kimmy continued. "I told them where to look. The field, the basement, the barn, all that. I told them we wouldn't be going back there under any circumstances."

"Good," I replied absentmindedly, still thinking that there was a piece to the puzzle we were missing.

I stared off at nothing at all for a few moments, then snapped myself back and looked over at my wife, who had similarly been entranced in thought. I brought my hand to her face and led it to mine, kissing her, and even through the pain, a kiss had never felt so good.

"It's over," I said. And for the most part, I was right.

Twenty-One

Katie's reunion with her brother could have brought someone back from the worst of depressions. When we walked into Shawn and Dana Hill's home three days after leaving it, Alex ran to his sister so fast that he nearly tackled her. After their hug, he ran back to the living room and returned with a picture he'd drawn. "It's not as good as yours, but I made it for you," he said and handed it to her.

His drawing depicted Katie, sitting on her bed with a sketchpad. I'd never known Alex to care all that much for art, but he knew it was everything to his big sister.

Upon returning home, Kimmy and I met with Detective Morgan, whom we told of our entire ordeal on the BiloXy farm. She told us she would keep us apprised of any developments, and just shy of two weeks after our return, she made good on that promise. While my family and I sat and watched a movie one evening, my phone buzzed. The detective asked if we could come in the following morning, an invitation I quickly accepted.

Kimmy and I entered the police station the next day and were directly escorted to Detective Morgan's office, where she sat behind her pristine desk.

"Please, sit," she gestured to the two chairs opposite her, and we obliged. "So, I'm gonna cut right to it. They have arrested eleven people in connection to your case so far."

Alina Morgan pressed a few keys and clicked the mouse on her laptop a few times, then turned it toward us. There was an array of photos featuring several people my wife and I recognized, and a handful we didn't. The detective explained that they'd found a handful of photo albums in the house, and asked us to point out the people we knew, which resulted in essentially the same group as the pictures on the walls in that horrible home in northern Kansas - Roberta the waitress, the man from the motel, the man who picked me up and drove me to Daisy's after the TV House incident, the elder and younger Officer Billings, and the one who had terrorized us.

"Right. The one from the motel, his name is Joseph Marcel. He and the waitress are married, and this lovely ray of sunshine..." Alina Morgan pointed to the man who had developed his sick fascination with our daughter's drawings. "...is their son. Mr. Marcel here has been working a scam for some time, renting rooms to people, and when they go out to eat or leave the room for whatever reason, he and his son would go in and clean the people out. The guests would call the police, you'd get these two, and they'd throw it to the bottom of the never-ending file.

"Now, I personally think Mr. Marcel could have handled the consequences of the stealing and going into people's rooms, but once they told him he was on the hook for being an accomplice to several murders, kidnapping, et cetera, he started talking."

Kimmy took my hand in hers and we leaned forward as if to illustrate that we were listening intently. The detective continued.

"They lived together in the house where you found Katie. Or, you said you found her in the barn, so they all lived in the house next to the barn where you found her. I've seen pictures...the smell came through them, my goodness. So, their son, Bruce, the one who broke into your car and stalked you all, kidnapped Katie, apparently, he was...I don't know how to put this delicately...he was about seven cans short of a six-pack. Severely intellectually disabled. Which leads me to wonder how he was able to pull off everything he did.

"To make it even...stranger...Bruce and his mother, Roberta, well, according to Joseph, they had themselves quite the relationship. The girl in the video, the one that he..." she trailed off for a moment, not wanting to speak it back out into existence.

"The one he filmed while he stabbed her to death and then sent us the video," Kimmy finished for her, as bluntly as she could have, with almost no emotion behind the words.

The detective looked taken aback. "Right. That little girl, she...was Roberta and Bruce's daughter. As in, Roberta was both mommy and grandma, and Bruce was both daddy and brother."

There was silence while Alina Morgan allowed us to ingest this strange information, and then I broke the silence and asked the first thing that came to mind: "What was her name?"

"As far as I know, she...she didn't have one. That poor girl's life was a nightmare from the day she was born. She--" Detective Morgan's words got caught in her throat as she nearly let emotion overtake the objective part of her that her career demanded. She then shuffled through a few papers and retrieved one in particular. "Anyway. In the basement, they found that little girl's body all...ahem...dismembered...then they found the torso, legs, and an arm of another child down there. But then, a little ways into the cornfield, not far from where Bruce gave up the ghost, they found another—or, well, a total of what should have been another three bodies...not all the...not all the pieces were there..."

"Fuck." I couldn't think of anything else to say.

"Mrs. Botic, I've read your statement. A few times, actually, but..." Alina Morgan weighed her next words carefully. "...you didn't see Bruce pull the trigger and shoot himself, correct?"

Kimmy looked at me, then back at the woman across the desk. "No, I was like...I don't know...twenty steps behind him when he did it. I just went where the noise was, and he was sitting in that little clearing. Minus a face. It was like he had the shotgun just sitting and waiting. I don't know why he didn't use it on us."

Detective Morgan pondered this a moment, then double-clicked three times, bringing three particular pictures from the array forward. She pointed to two figures in the image on the left. "You never saw these two?"

I leaned forward and studied them for a moment. "This one, on the left, I think he might have been in Daisy's when I was there the second time, before I got taken to that place with all the TVs. I don't know for sure, though. Everybody there seems to buy their flannel and jeans from the same place."

"Okay. Marcel is saying they didn't have anything to do with what was going on with you. He said this one--" the detective tapped on one of the men in the picture. "--is Roberta's nephew, and they too had...benefits."

"Seriously? What the fuck." I wasn't as surprised as my words made me out to be.

"Yeah. Their family tree is looking like a telephone pole. And these two?" She pointed to two men in the next picture, who were standing behind Robert and her husband. One wore a NASCAR hat and had on a pair of beat-up jeans with a flannel shirt, the other wore overalls with no shirt underneath and sported a tangled mess of a beard.

"Never seen them," I said.

"Okay, Marcel said this one here and Roberta had a sexual relationship, and that he knew all about what was going on at the farm and with your case." She pointed to the man in the racing hat. "Just thought I'd see if you'd ever seen him. Marcel is pretty much trying to say everyone was afraid of Bruce, and that's why no one spoke up."

Something about the man in the hat struck me as familiar, but I attributed it to the fact that these people, the ones in that small town, the ones who knew of the atrocities being committed against our family and those children, seemed almost interchangeable.

"And what about this one?" Detective Morgan continued and double-clicked on the final picture, making it take up the entirety of her laptop's screen. It was one we'd already seen, the group photo with Roberta, Joseph Marcel, the man who drove me back to Daisy's after my abduction, and the Billings men. There, on the edge of the photo, was the man in the clean white t-shirt with his face scratched out. It was to that man that Detective Morgan pointed and asked in a tone decidedly more grave than the one she'd had up to this point of our meeting, "What about him?"

I studied the man, his figure anyway, for a long moment. Kimmy did the same. His cleanliness compared to the rest of the people in the photos was staggering. It made him stick out like a sore thumb. Eventually, I sat back, defeated. "No idea. Of course, without a face, it's hard to say. Who is he?"

"We're not sure. Everyone we've talked to says they don't know who he is, but given the fact that his face is scratched out like someone after a nasty breakup, that's a little hard to believe." The detective closed her laptop and sat back in her chair. "It's probably nothing. As far as we can tell, you know, at least at this point, is--"

"Were the other kids artists?" Kimmy interrupted. "The kids he murdered. Were they artists too?"

"Not as far as we can tell. We haven't found any other artwork that wasn't your daughter's."

"Then why? Why would a man who murders children, who has kidnapped a child, not murder her? He had every opportunity to. But instead, he sits her down and makes her draw for three months?"

Detective Morgan sighed. "Your guess is as good as mine on that one, Mrs. Botic. I wish I had an answer for you, but I don't. All signs are pointing to this man being just...off the charts unpredictable. I mean, you can attest to that personally. But it's still early in the investigation. Very early. We're going to keep digging, keep working with Kansas, keep talking to this fucked up family, and we will find all the answers. I didn't bring you in today to tell you that we've figured it all out, just to update you. And I will continue to do that."

Kimmy nodded, not wholly satisfied with her answer but understanding that any answer the detective might have had wasn't yet fully formed.

"How is Katie settling in back at home?" Morgan asked.

"Surprisingly well, considering," I said. "She's right back to her artwork, which I don't know how I feel about totally."

The detective laughed. "Well, with this animal out of play, I think you can rest easy. Her work is good, but I don't think you'll be getting any more superfans of his caliber anytime soon."

I offered a half-hearted chuckle; Kimmy sat in furtive silence.

Morgan leaned forward. "Mrs. Botic? You won. Your daughter is safe. If for today—if even for only today, that's all you can hold on to, hold on to it. Whatever else we don't know yet, know that Katie is safe. And every day she's safe and with you is a day you might not have gotten if this would have gone differently."

Kimmy wiped a tear from her eye before it fell. "You're right. Thank you."

We left the police station with as many questions as we had when we entered it. Detective Morgan assured us we would find out all the answers in due time, but I was less than optimistic about that. It bothered me that there were too many unknowns that accounted for integral parts of this story, but I tell myself every day that that's not how real life works. Our conversation with the detective was as close as this movie was going to get to an exposition dump.

And in truth, it didn't matter.

Because Katie was safe.

She was home with us; she was whole, and the man who did it was rotting somewhere in Kansas.

She was home. And that was enough.

Epilogue

I

When I was born, the first words that were ever spoken to me came from my mother.

Every year on my birthday, whether I was still at home in my youth, on the streets doing and selling drugs, in jail, or even up to my most recent birthday, she repeated those words to me.

This small action is something I've adopted into my own parenting. To know the weight behind those words, the truth behind them, is no small thing in my eyes. Those words set the tone for the relationship my mother and I share, and in turn, set the tone for the relationship I share with my children.

II

After we met with Detective Alina Morgan, Kimmy and I picked up lunch for six. Kimmy's parents had spent the previous weeks with us and would stay indefinitely, something that afforded us even more peace of mind than we already had with the way things had concluded. We enjoyed the meal together and spent the day running around outside, and when the sun went down, we played board games.

When the Hills retired to the makeshift guest room we'd set up in the room that otherwise housed the art studio, Kimmy and I got into our bed, joined by Katie and Alex. I could hardly remember the time when I would want them to sleep in their own beds, and couldn't imagine such a desire returning any time soon.

I turned on an episode of The Simpsons, something both Katie and Alex loved, that I was a lifelong fan of and that Kimmy tolerated, happy enough that I wasn't yet allowing them to watch Archer and Big Mouth and Rick & Morty. As Homer, Marge, Bart, Lisa, and Maggie got up to their usual unusual antics, I looked to my left at Katie, whose head was nestled in my inner elbow. Between her and Kimmy was Alex, and I ran a palm over his brown hair.

I looked at my children and my wife, my family, and the first thing that came to mind were the first words ever spoken to me. I too had only spoken those words on the kid's birthdays, but this moment, with all of us together, happy, smiling, laughing, it felt appropriate to break tradition.

I will always love you.
I will always be here for you.
I will always protect you.

End

Acknowledgments

This book would not have been possible without the perpetual support and encouragement of my better half, Kimmy, for whom I must say the following: BAP. No one else will get that, and that's perfectly okay. I love you, Pretty Cat...WE DID IT!!

Thank you to my family, who from all sides have supported my endeavor to write professionally. It is with the encouragement of all of my loved ones that I found the will to continue writing even when the words didn't want to flow.

I would be remiss if I didn't offer my sincere gratitude to the NoSleep community, whose reverence of the original short story prompted me to write this novel.

And from NoSleep, I must thank in particular Felix Blackwell (u/ TheColdPeople), who was instrumental in the construction of this story in its longer form. Your guidance was invaluable over this long process, and I owe you a debt I can never truly repay.

Also from NoSleep, a big, big thank you to Dathan Auerbach (u/ 1000Vultures). Had I not read Penpal, this book would likely not exist. You are a master of our craft, and I can only hope that my words instill the same anxieties that yours do.

Thank you to Matthew M. Bartlett, without your encouragement, this book may never have seen the light of day.

And I must, of course, thank Kevin Smith, the man who unknowingly made me first pick up a pen all those years ago. Without you, there likely is no Nick Botic Horror.

Most of all, thank you, reader. The transition from internet writer posting for free to traditional author charging for my stories is an uphill battle, and the fact that you spent your hard-earned money on this book is a testament to your support of independent authors. Your contribution is making a dream come true, and I thank you for it from the bottom of my cold, black heart.

Author Biography

Nick Botic is an author based in Milwaukee, WI. He has been writing horror for seven years, rising to the top ranks of the 17-million member Reddit community NoSleep.

He lives in a suburb near Milwaukee with his wife Kimmy and their five cats and dog.

He is currently working on a collection of short stories as well as a non-fiction book featuring conversations with modern titans of horror literature including Ramsey Campbell, Laird Barron, John Langan, Paul Tremblay, Matt Cardin, and more.

More from Nick Botic

For 50+ free stories of the terrifying, the supernatural, the paranormal, and the grotesque, please visit nickbotic.com.

Nick also has numerous stories narrated by a variety of voice actors, including the cast of the NoSleep Podcast, MrCreepyPasta, The Dark Somnium, Romnex, and more.